Fishing
the
Jumps

Fishing
the
Jumps

A Novel

Lamar Herrin

UNIVERSITY PRESS OF KENTUCKY

This is a work of fiction. All of the characters, organizations,
and events portrayed in this novel are either products
of the author's imagination or are used fictitiously.

Scholarly publisher for the Commonwealth,
serving Bellarmine University, Berea College, Centre
College of Kentucky, Eastern Kentucky University,
The Filson Historical Society, Georgetown College,
Kentucky Historical Society, Kentucky State University,
Morehead State University, Murray State University,
Northern Kentucky University, Transylvania University,
University of Kentucky, University of Louisville,
and Western Kentucky University.
All rights reserved.

Editorial and Sales Offices: The University Press of Kentucky
663 South Limestone Street, Lexington, Kentucky 40508-4008
www.kentuckypress.com

Library of Congress Cataloging-in-Publication Data

Names: Herrin, Lamar, author.
Title: Fishing the jumps : a novel / Lamar Herrin.
Description: Lexington, Kentucky. : The University Press of Kentucky, [2019]
Identifiers: LCCN 2018042194| ISBN 9780813176826 (hardcover : alk. paper) |
    ISBN 9780813176833 (pdf) | ISBN 9780813176840 (epub)
Classification: LCC PS3558.E754 F57 2019 | DDC 813/.54—dc23 LC record
available at https://lccn.loc.gov/2018042194

This book is printed on acid-free paper meeting
the requirements of the American National Standard
for Permanence in Paper for Printed Library Materials.

Manufactured in the United States of America.

Member of the Association
of University Presses

What falls away is always. And is near.
—Theodore Roethke

I

I HADN'T TOLD THIS STORY in I didn't know how long. The truth was, outside of the family, I couldn't be sure if I had ever told it. So why tell it now? For one thing, I liked and admired and trusted the man I was telling it to, Walter Kidman, a poker partner for the last twenty years, a lawyer in town who took on his share of pro bono lost causes, ten years my junior, which meant he'd just missed the sixties, both the exhilaration and the exhaustion that I had lived through. For another thing, the setting was right, timeless in its way. We were in a lakeside cabin in the foothills of the Adirondacks, a cabin my friend had inherited, which had been built back in the WPA days. At first I'd understood that WPA workers had built it themselves, perhaps that it had even served as a sort of barracks for them, which probably hadn't been the case. Walter was a big admirer of FDR, the nobility of his programs if not of his methods, but it was a modest little cabin, with a fieldstone fireplace, a screen porch, and a compact assortment of rooms, all with an ineradicable mustiness that took you generations back. And surely, maybe even most importantly, it was the lake itself, small enough to see from one end to the other, where motors were prohibited and the transportation of choice was canoes. Out over the water sounds traveled pure. A dog bark, the lakelong caw of a crow. A breeze crisped in the poplar leaves along the banks. One cabin up from Walter's at five o'clock every evening an elderly man sat out on his dock and played his cello in the most meditative of registers, and that sound traveled too.

And we did fish, that afternoon we arrived. Of course, it was the fishing. Walter rigged up two New Deal–era casting rods with tarnished spinners. We tried a few casts, then while Walter paddled, I trailed the spinner along behind us. I thought I'd hung up in weeds until I felt a live tug on the line, an abrupt muscular contraction. The fish never jumped. A bass would have, and then tried to swim under the canoe, while this fish simply resisted until it couldn't anymore. Still, because bass was what I'd mostly caught when I'd fished as a boy, I was thinking bass when the fish became visible alongside the canoe. It was streamlined and long-snouted, with tiny saw-blade teeth. A banded dark-to-yellowing green. The answer came to me even as I asked the question.

What is that?

A little pickerel. You can't eat them, but they're fun to catch.

So it was the quietness, the birdsong, the leaves in the breeze, the trembling reach of the cello we were drifting out beyond, the unruffled water and maybe the way the pickerel looked at me out of the unlidded bead of its eye.

Here, Walter said, let me take him off the hook. You've got to be careful with those teeth.

I watched as Walter took out a small pair of pliers, just as long-snouted, and worked loose the hook. But the fish never stopped looking at me, self-contained and seemingly still in its element. When Walter held it up for me to admire, I nodded, and when Walter held it out to me, I shook my head.

He released it back into the water.

There was a lingering trace of its scent, then the breeze took that away too.

From his end of the canoe Walter was looking at me as he would from across the poker table, as though the bet were mine and sooner or later I'd have to tip my hand.

I didn't mind losing a hand every so often to Walter. He was a firm-principled man whose boyishness was genuine and engaging. Stocky in build, with a round, slightly inflamed face, small active eyes, and curly gray hair. I had always liked that little leap of pleasure in his eyes when he turned over a winning hand.

So, as a contribution of some sort, a chip, say, that I held, I told him, There's another way to fish, you know. It's called "fishing the jumps."

I've heard of that, Walter replied, with his characteristic eagerness. What's that all about?

Pure counterintuitive chaos, I said.

Chaos . . . , he repeated with a questioning turn, as though considering the appropriateness of the word itself, here at the cellist's hour, on this noise-restricted lake. From end to end I didn't see another canoe out on its waters. Most of the cabins were no less humble than Walter's. Small and low-built with patchy screen porches, the screens like luffing sails, no longer taut. Other than the elderly neighbor who came out onto his dock at five every evening to serenade the fish and the birds, the lake seemed turned over to us. We had paddled about halfway down its length. It was surely then, as I shook my head, closed my eyes, and allowed my cousin Howie Whalen to visit me from forty years back, that the story I would tell later that evening took shape in me. Howie Whalen, "Little Howie" Whalen as I'd known him growing up, stood beside the motor in his outboard fishing boat, searching the waters of his boyhood lake for the telltale ripples of a school of minnows being run by a school of bass, all before the surface erupted in a boil as the bass closed in and began to feed. The instant the feeding started, Howie Whalen, still standing, fired his motor and, brandishing his spinning rod outfitted with a silver spoon, speeded into the area of eruption, casting as the boat roared in. He hooked a largemouth on his first cast, and had time to unhook it and throw it onto the floor of the boat, where it flopped, before he cast again into the still frenzied water and hooked his second. I had cast wildly, well beyond the target area, and by the time I could retrieve my lure and cast again, the feeding had stopped. Suddenly we were once again in the center of a becalmed lake and Howie was back beside his motor, scanning the waters for another school of running minnows and another feeding area about to erupt. He resembled Horatio Hornblower in that moment, back there striking his pose. I might have laughed, but didn't. He was the master, a cousin two years my junior, dead now these twenty-odd years.

But it was the quietness, the glassiness of the water you looked out over until at the limit of vision you saw another school of minnows in a patch of sparkling ripples. Then, as the feeding began with the bass lashing their tails, you rushed in to join the commotion. Bass are territorial, Howie used to tell me; if you're horning in on their action, they'll feed that much more aggressively, until they've eaten their fill and the remaining minnows have escaped.

Fishing the jumps.

What will look like chaos to most mortals, I added, but not to this cousin I had.

Some kind of wild man? Walter puzzled. Some nature's child?

I shook my head. I also steadied my nerve. Without warning, I felt my throat began to close. The last time I had seen Howie Whalen, his wife, in a flat and bitter voice, had declared, That man in there is not my husband. Then she'd admitted me to his sickroom.

You fish for the bass when they're feeding in a school of minnows, I told Walter Kidman. The minnows are jumping and the bass are thrashing. Yes, it can get wild. You get in there close. That's really all I can tell you.

But sitting on his screen porch that evening, with that evocative mustiness of rugs and pillows and daybeds and an ash-encrusted fireplace all around us, that smell of generation piled on generation, it all came rushing back. Sipping bourbon on the rocks, and with the bourbon the lingering echo of that cello spreading over the quiet water, a sound that should have corresponded to the solemn beat and flow of your blood as it circulated through your body if your blood weren't, in fact, racing in a crazy rush as though to break free. I told Walter I'd had a family down there, down south, and had once, years ago, decades now, taken a friend with me on what was to have been a fishing trip, which had led to the two of us, this friend, a northerner, a New Englander, and me, being expelled. Expelled? Meaning hustled out of town? Ridden out on a rail? It might be funny in the retelling, I admitted to Walter, and it might even have been funny in an incredulous, drop-jawed sort of way at the time, but those were the sixties, years of such exaggeration that no detail was too insignificant to be politically charged, so even as you shook your head in disbelief it wore you out. A time Walter Kidman had not lived through, but I had.

Walter reached out into the dark to pour me another finger of bourbon. Little Howie Whalen's father, Big Howie, of course, had been a bourbon drinker and so, to keep up with him, had been my aunt Rosalyn. September in the Adirondacks was a world apart from September down south, but the northern coolness was clear, unfreighted, conducive to storytelling, and with no June bugs clashing against the screen or cicadas shrilling on ten frequencies at once, I didn't have a lot of competition.

This is a pretty tall tale, I warned my friend and host.

Aren't they all? Walter said, meaning down there.

Actually, I said, this one starts in Cincinnati, where I was living at the time. On a hillside in a rickety apartment building with jerrybuilt back porches, which should have been condemned, looking over the Ohio River into Kentucky. And the friend I was going to take fishing with me—

The New Englander, Walter interjected.

—yes, Massachusetts, if I recall—had never been south of the Mason-Dixon Line.

This elicited from Walter a skeptical snort.

Except once, I added. His name was Phil Hodge, and on the drive down south he told me that as a paratrooper he had been stationed at Fort Campbell outside of Nashville, and during the Cuban missile crisis—1962, now—he'd been on and off a plane three times waiting to jump into Cuba. He and, I guess, his company or platoon had a specific missile site they were assigned to take out, and the plane's motors never shut off for good until the whole operation had been scrubbed. We'd been that close, he claimed, three times on and three times off the plane, and I had no reason to doubt him.

There was a period of very retrospective silence, reaching back to 1962 when Walter would have been . . . how old? Then Walter broke it, saying, What's that got to do with fishing?

Not much, I said. But it might have something to do with tall tales.

To get Phil Hodge to come along on this trip down into Dixie, I had described for him fish all but jumping into the boat. That is, I'd told him about my cousin Howie Whalen and fishing the jumps. Maybe Phil Hodge thought he had to tell me a story about almost jumping into Cuba to even the score. But I doubt it. He was a pretty serious fellow.

What did he do?

To make a living? The same thing I did at the time. Try to teach some half-literate kids how to write an intelligible English sentence.

Walter gave a sympathetic chuckle. He took a drink. I heard his wicker chair crackle as he shifted weight, assuming, I assumed, a more attentive position. For a moment I couldn't see his face. I could see the wiry outline of the back of his head as he faced out along the dock. It occurred to me while he was turned away that I could beg off, that there was enough to occupy us in this sparsely sonorous night on the edge of the Adirondacks, I didn't have to take it all down into that clamorous

Lamar Herrin

South of my youth, where, given the undertow in family histories, one thing would always lead to another. My friend Phil Hodge, whom I had not seen or heard from in the last forty years, had supplied enough of a story. Three times on and off a plane that had never shut down its motors. I remembered the anxious anticipation in his voice when he'd told me the story, no doubt the disappointment, too, and that hushed air of enormous consequence there were no words for. But, as I then recalled, Phil Hodge had not told me the story on the way south but on the way back, when we were lying out in a tent beside a lake three hundred miles north of the one we'd been barred from, with a stringer full of fish. All those fish, I reasoned to Walter, must have loosened his tongue.

This trip south would be one of the last times I'd see my cousin Howie Whalen before he was diagnosed with a brain tumor and his head had swollen to the size of a lopsided melon. The loss—the family's, the town's—was incalculable. But Phil Hodge, of course, didn't know that. When Phil Hodge met my cousin Howie Whalen, Little Howie was hale and whole and still the master of whatever game came within his sights. Fish the jumps? No one could do it with more winning small-town southern panache. And it was a revealing story I was about to tell Walter Kidman, but so predictable in its way that a social historian could file it away in a footnote. You could start with the great plantations, which had long ago disappeared, but since no small southern town, it seemed, could exist without its patriarch, in each town a textile mill had appeared to take the plantation's place. The textile mills had given rise to apparel plants, which during World War Two had gotten rich by producing, in addition to soldiers' uniforms, an abundance of duck cloth for such necessities as parachutes and pup tents. After the war, those plants quick to reconvert to the production of shirts and pants for ex-soldiers whose wardrobes needed to be replenished had gotten richer. Howie Whalen, Big Howie Whalen, had seen it coming every step of the way. With his florid jowls, his barrel-sized belly, and his quick and fluid little strut, he rescued the town and took his seat behind the driver's wheel in a succession of black Cadillacs. At his side he had my mother's youngest sister, a blue-eyed, black-haired beauty, Aunt Rosalyn, whose every utterance before she could reach the end broke up into laughter, and who made it her business to distribute Whalen largesse to the family at large.

From the perspective of nieces and nephews and cousins by the score,

6

the Whalens led fabulous lives, and growing up I had caught some of their luster. For eighteen years an only child, Little Howie Whalen had everything, including his own private zoo which contained at one time, incredibly, a lion cub, as well as monkeys and llamas and armadillos and iguanas, along with a boa constrictor, and a pair of ponies, of course, followed by horses, which we rode along trails through the pinewoods every time my family visited their town. Little Howie even had his own groom, an ageless hunchback named Johnny, who responded to Little Howie as though he were Big Howie, and whom Little Howie treated with the proper grownup mix of condescension and concern. And, of course, the Whalens had houses, one on the ocean and another on that mountain lake, an hour's drive away. Then, when a second lake was created closer to their town, with a three-state shoreline of twelve hundred miles, they had a house there too, and a whole flotilla of speedboats and houseboats and pontoon boats and Bassmaster fishing boats. They had a cabin cruiser that slept six in case they wanted to cruise those twelve hundred miles. Before my family and I left town after one of our visits, our last stop was always at the plant, where we'd be outfitted with shirts and pants, pajamas and windbreakers, and anything else that caught our eye for the year to come. Aunt Rosalyn would insist. We'd hold out our arms and she'd pile it on. There was no way to say no. Say no, say I can't wear all of this, I can't even carry it out to the car, and she'd laugh. Her laugh was a rich cascading contralto, and it became a sort of current we rode.

Then, after Little Howie turned eighteen, Aunt Rosalyn gave birth to a daughter, Ellen Rose. There was no way to account for it—for years and years they'd tried—except to regard little Ellie as heaven-sent, meant to be the family's crowning jewel.

I'd touched on some of this on the long day's drive down from Cincinnati. The day before we left for the trip, I'd visited the barbershop to get my hair cut and, while I was at it, the beard I wore neatly trimmed. I didn't mention this visit to the barbershop to Phil Hodge, but I did to Walter Kidman. By the time Walter had come of age in the mid-seventies, the lumberjack look was in, and once clean-shaven, crew-cut America-love-it-or-leave-it bullies might wear scraggly beards and hair down to their shoulders.

Walter said, Okay, I get it, the times, the times. But what about the fish?

7

And I said, Sorry to disappoint you, Walter. But this isn't a fish story.

Howie Whalen? Little Howie Whalen?

Not really. Not yet. If it had been, it all might have turned out differently.

And not Phil Hodge?

No.

All right. I'll play along. Let's say I'm half hooked—I could still get off. A splash more?

I allowed him to pour me more bourbon. I took a deep breath, breathing the mustiness of the house down. And to be clear, I said, the WPA workers did or didn't build this cabin?

They were around, Walter said, they were active in the vicinity. Down at the other end of the lake there's a bridge with their names on it. They had to sleep somewhere when they were doing the work.

I'll give you that.

Amazing, he said, shaking his head. They were everywhere. And they built things to last.

Not everywhere. Not so much in the South, I said. At least not as much as up here.

No?

You'll have to look a while down there to find a bridge or a park or a dam or anything with a WPA plaque on it.

Wouldn't that be someone like your uncle's fault?

For the record, Big Howie was no uncle of mine. Rosalyn fell for him, that's all.

Rosalyn had been a Pritchard, one of the Pritchard girls. My last name was McManus, first name Jim, neither little nor big.

Aunt Rosalyn, who never stopped laughing, Walter reminded me.

Oh, she stopped, all right, I said.

And another silence fell. I listened for sounds from cabins up the lake, and didn't hear them. No clatter of after-supper noises, no voices raised or held in check, no music, no cars pulling in or pulling out. No owls in the trees. No loons on the lake although I'd been told there were loons and, once I heard them, I'd never forget their mournful wails. Just the amplified sparseness of insect sounds and the lingering echo of a fish that had splashed no telling when.

Actually, it's a funny story I was going to tell you, I said, if you're willing to take it that way.

If *you* are, Walter corrected me.

You're a northerner, I advised him. Try seeing it through Phil Hodge's eyes.

To begin with, Phil Hodge had never seen kudzu. He'd seen tumbledown shacks and abandoned farm buildings and billboards whose last images had blanched out or peeled off with the years, but he had never seen those odd-angled eyesores rounded out in great transformative swells of spring green. Phil Hodge didn't talk a lot, but until he got used to the kudzu, he couldn't help himself. He could call to mind any number of half-abandoned factory towns up in Massachusetts where they should plant this stuff, even though that far north he knew the kudzu would never survive. I told him he was right, and added that the kudzu was lovely to look at, but unless you trimmed it on a daily basis it would swallow you along with everything else. Plus, it was snaky.

A good number of those half-abandoned towns up north had lost their factories to some of these right-to-work southern towns we were passing through, and then those southern factories had built newer versions of themselves on the outskirts of town. These newer plants were single-story, football-field-sized affairs, so low-slung they reminded me of bunkers. The loading docks were serviced by trucks and not by trains running on spurs of track alongside.

I caught myself trying to re-create my boyhood days in these towns for my friend Phil Hodge, and stopped. I refused to wax nostalgic. Instead I told him about my aunt Rosalyn and her family. Big and Little Howie, and their daughter Ellie, barely four. But I didn't really tell him much about them, either. Remember, we were going fishing. I spent time describing the lake up in the mountains, where I assumed after staying a night with the Whalens we would spend the four days we had left, reliving my boyhood visits and catching fish. Fishing the jumps. That we could do. I had never fished the jumps without Little Howie in the boat, but I could see him so clearly, could remember every move he made—the timing, when to go still, when to roar in—that I convinced myself I could take his place. He was a very handsome man, Little Howie, with blue eyes and black hair like his mother and, utterly unlike his father, something Greek—the high-bridged nose, the sculpted brow and jawline—to the cut of his face. As far as fishing the jumps went, Little Howie's message had been clear: Don't be bashful or proud, be patient, go still, then get there quickly and feed as hungrily as the bass.

9

But this is not a fishing story, Walter reminded me. Am I to understand you never wet a line?

If I answer that question, I said, I may lose any hope for suspense I ever had.

Well, wait a minute! Walter stopped me. For the record, you *did* catch fish. There was that lake on the way back north you said you and Phil Hodge stumbled on. In fact, I think your expression was a "stringer full" of fish.

But not, I said, fishing the jumps.

When you were lying in the tent, Walter went on with his recollection, and this Phil Hodge had you back on the brink of a nuclear war . . .

And you were a boy, Walter. What do you remember about the Cuban missile crisis?

What do I remember? I remember in the house some . . . tension but some excitement, too. It all sounded like a movie my parents had missed the ending of . . . a lot of questioning, second-guessing . . . something like that.

Well, here's what I remember. I thought we were in for it. The Kennedys were young and glamorous and untested. The Bay of Pigs, what we knew of it, had been a disaster. Khrushchev was as wily as they got, then when the time came to pound his shoe on his UN desk, he could do that too. Probably the only reason Phil Hodge was on and off that plane so many times was because nobody in Washington knew what they were doing. I was in college, worrying about some term paper I'd been assigned to write. A bunch of us had crowded around a blurry black-and-white television outside the administration building, and I remember thinking, No sense beginning that paper now. Which was no small consolation, believe me. It was a clear fall day, and I took a deep breath of clear fall air. Meanwhile . . .

Your friend Phil Hodge is getting on and off that plane.

Which I guess was *his* assignment.

We both drank at that moment, and in the motor-free silence that followed I had a recollection of Phil Hodge as we cast little floating-minnow lures called Rapalas in and around the shoreline brush of a lake some three hundred miles north of the one where we would not wet a line. I saw Phil Hodge hook his first fish—a smallmouth, almost three pounds, we would later learn—and turn to me with a look of such profound relief

I could call it wild, maybe even a savage sort of relief, all the more so since Phil Hodge had a New Englander's long-boned face with eyes that, before they revealed any clear-cut emotion, would narrow their line, as his mouth would, and leave you guessing. But with a fiercely fighting three-pound smallmouth on the hook, his eyes had flown open and his mouth had dropped wide, and it was as if he'd become a believer, after all the disbelief he'd been asked to stomach until then.

What you also have to keep in mind, I reminded Walter, is that new lake with its twelve-hundred-mile shoreline that passed very close to the Whalens' town. Built eight to ten years earlier—just the right time span for a first generation of bass to come of age. We would have our choice, Phil Hodge and I. For old times' sake, that lake of my boyhood up in the mountains, and our own boat, our own quarters. But for sheer poundage and thrill count, I said, we might want to fish the lake whose bright red clay banks and cloudy jade waters we'd been driving along for some miles by then.

The Whalens lived in a forest of pines, flowering bushes, and ornamental hardwoods, which the road wound back among. No straight broad avenue with live oaks arching over it, and no columned plantation house waiting to receive you. The Whalen family house was single-storied—I don't even remember a basement—with rooms seemingly added onto rooms at random, and each with its picture window. From wherever a Whalen sat, a car winding in on the drive would be visible. Later, of course, cameras could be mounted at every turn in that drive and intruders identified in a flash, but these were turns among azalea bushes and flowering dogwood trees, and this was that sweet medicinal aroma of pines that relieved me of my political differences and took me straight back to my boyhood, where Aunt Rosalyn would always meet me at the door. I was the oldest of her nephews and nieces, and she was the youngest of my aunts. When she was attending college, she'd lived with my parents for at least one year—a year that I was a toddler—and it was to my parents' house that Howard Whalen had come courting. I had been unwitting witness to it all. Big Howie Whalen—then fit and freshly barbered and in his dashing good looks almost a match for my aunt—in a manner of speaking had to get my consent before he could go off and woo my aunt. He brought me toys. He bucked me up as a champ, I was a helluva fine fella, and I must have consented to his importunities and blessed

11

their union. They had never ceased to exclaim over me as if I was the linchpin to all their good fortune, there from the start. So I could expect Aunt Rosalyn to meet me at the door when I drove up the long winding drive with my Yankee friend in tow.

I had not seen her since her son's wedding, only a couple of years after her daughter Ellen had been born. Aunt Rosalyn was now in her mid-forties. When she opened the door and stood before me for an instant, I had to take hold of myself: tiny folds of flesh had gathered around her eyes; wrinkles fanned out from the corners of her mouth; her hair was showing strands of gray. She seemed just perceptibly to list to one side. I registered the thought that the birth must have been hard. Then Aunt Rosalyn laughed, a more congested laugh than I remembered, and I opened my arms to give her a hug.

Her laugh carried over to mock alarm. What is that? she exclaimed.

For an instant I thought she meant Phil Hodge, whom she knew I was bringing with me. I was about to reply, Just a harmless and well-behaved Yankee who wants to fish. But she was pointing at my face and giving me time to play dumb. I shook my head and smiled.

Better not let Big Howie catch you with those whiskers on your face, she cautioned as she reached out and stroked my cheek. Does Esther know you're growing those things?

Esther was my mother, who had half-mothered her youngest sister, too.

I said, You know, I can't be sure but I don't believe she does. Can't it be our little secret, Rosalyn?

She laughed. Not if Big Howie finds out. Then, as if it had never ceased to be the human comedy, nothing more, nothing less, she laughed again.

I glanced over at Phil Hodge with his freshly shaven cheeks and the clean part in his hair. I had never played poker with Phil Hodge, I told Walter, but, amused or disapproving, he certainly knew how to keep a straight face.

It was then that my littlest cousin Ellie ran in, Ellie who had no memory of me, of course, but who couldn't wait to reach up—I had to bend down—and stroke my beard.

I identified myself as her first and oldest cousin, and her as the prettiest little cousin I had. We were kissing cousins, I concluded, and kissed her on the cheek.

She was indeed pretty and surely a little more adventurous than she allowed her well-behaved self to be. She had large hazel eyes, of a brown so light as to appear golden.

She giggled at the scratchy touch of my beard, or that was the little show she performed. Then she retreated halfway behind her mother, as though inviting me to play ring-around-the-rosy until I caught her. I glanced up at Rosalyn and in that moment found it impossible to accept the fact that my aunt had given birth to that little girl. This was a strange sensation. With Phil Hodge at my side, whom I'd invited down there, I experienced a moment of . . . generational disorientation. Wasn't I the child and Rosalyn not my aunt? I reached out and did something I didn't recall ever doing: I patted my aunt Rosalyn flush against the cheek. I put my mouth to her ear and murmured, You have a beautiful little girl. Then, so close to my ear that her laugh sounded like a husky growl, she whispered back, Jimmy, you better not let Big Howie catch you with those whiskers on your face.

When Big Howie drove in in his latest Cadillac and planted himself in the room, the first thing he said was, Who're you trying to look like, ole Uncle Abe?

And I responded, No, I think I was going more for Robert E. Lee.

For my efforts I got Big Howie's booming laugh and Phil Hodge got his first impression of how Big Howie Whalen could fill up a room with his all's-forgiven bonhomie while off in a corner he calculated his advantage.

And you boys wanna catch some fish.

If you and Little Howie haven't fished them all out, I said.

Little Howie's got all those diapers to change. He hasn't got a minute free for fishing. I'll tell you who *is* the fisherman, though.

Little Howie had married before he finished college. Obeying a summons, I had made a quick trip back from California to be one of his groomsmen—his hunting and fishing and football buddies filled the other spots. His best man, of course, was his father. His bride was his high school sweetheart and maybe the only other person in town whose beauty rivaled his. I'd been not so much dazzled as astonished that a town so small could produce such a pairing. Little Howie had wanted family among his groomsmen, and he'd wanted—as he always had from me—my astonishment. The man who caught fish almost at will was now changing diapers. A natural.

There she stands, Big Howie said, and signaled to his daughter as though cuing her to come onstage. Best fisherman—he corrected himself—best fisher*woman* in the family.

Little Ellie was peeking out from behind her mother now, reluctant, it seemed, to step forth and take her bow. I flashed on her sitting up in one of those Bassmaster swivel seats. Anyone there to witness the feat would give a headshake of incredulity, quickly followed by a humbled nod. Of course she could land a fighting fish practically her own size. She was a Whalen.

The question, I said, is whether we should go up in the mountains or stay down here and try this new lake out. What's your best guess on that? I asked Big Howie.

My best guess? Well, we'll have to see about that, won't we? Now, that would surely depend on . . .

He said this weightily and trailed off as only Big Howie could, waiting to see whether you caught a ride on his train of thought or remained behind, stubbornly stranded, and became an object of charity, which was never without its strings.

And Walter reminded me: If I've got this right, you'd been something like their mascot, their good luck charm, Big Howie Whalen came a-courtin' and you, you little angel, gave your blessing. Am I to understand all that had worn off?

Certainly worn thin, I said, and I remembered Aunt Rosalyn standing submissively off to the side but with a subtly intrigued—call it "gamesome"—smile on her face. And little Ellie standing out beside her now, maybe even more gamesome than her mother, those near-golden eyes of hers expressing an impending delight, while she maintained a soldierly little bearing and waited me out.

And Phil Hodge? Walter said.

Dumbfounded, he'd tell me later when, beholden to nobody, we'd caught all the fish we wanted and begun to savor the last laugh, but not until then.

All because of "it depends," Walter said. Did this Big Howie tell you what it depended on?

Oh, that almost went without saying, although it did take him a while. First we had to go through family stuff. My parents, especially my mother, who for the sport of it occasionally liked to go toe to toe with

Big Howie. My father, who had come off the road and opened a business of his own, which compared to the Cadillac-powered Whalen Apparels barely crept along. My sister, perhaps engaged to the wrong man. My love life or the lack of it, which brought out a wistful sigh or two from my aunt. And so on. Other aunts and uncles and cousins—down there you don't start climbing the family tree unless you venture out onto every limb. Aunt Rosalyn kept worrying that Phil Hodge might be bored by so much trivia, and Phil Hodge, a very measured man, at least until he caught that first smallmouth, assured her he wasn't. We steered away from politics—we tried. If Big Howie had insinuated that everybody north of the Mason-Dixon Line was soft on communism, our ace in the hole would have been that commie missile site that Phil Hodge had been trained to jump onto and take out. Except . . .

Except, Walter said, still alert in spite of the bourbon, you didn't hear that story until you'd gone three hundred miles back north.

True, and it's hard to imagine Phil Hodge volunteering it there at the dinner table.

And your little cousin Ellie? She sat through it all?

She was her father's daughter. If Little Howie had been the town's favorite son, it now had a favorite daughter. I don't want to give you the wrong impression, Walter. Big Howie Whalen was much admired in town. He didn't exactly take the WPA's place, but he helped fix things up. He donated money for parks. The library. Outfitted the town's baseball team. Kept the Little League going. And he kept an eye on race relations, too. In his plant he had blacks working alongside whites— Well, not exactly "alongside." Whites did the design work, the tailoring and the sewing, blacks the pressing and bundling. For the most part, civil rights marchers went somewhere else. He was given civic awards—and he made sure that I as a Yankee convert saw all the news clippings, all the photographs and plaques. I was just hoping he wouldn't pull them out and force them on Phil Hodge. And he didn't. He might have even been a little wary of Phil Hodge. He didn't know just who he had seated at his dinner table. He knew me, or he thought he did. He knew me from a baby on up. And, it seemed, I wanted to take this Yankee friend of mine fishing in one of his lakes—

Twelve hundred miles? Three states? *His* lake? And I assume he only owned his little portion of that one in the mountains.

A sweet little portion—but true enough.

And not all the fish, not all the bass and certainly not all the minnows.

Not even a man like Big Howie Whalen could lay claim to all the fish in the sea—or a mountain lake.

So what did it "depend" on, then?

Naturally, what I decided to do with those whiskers of mine.

Oh, right, right. Of course. How did I forget about the "whiskers"?

Neatly trimmed—

You know, Jim, I'm sitting here trying to picture you with a full beard.

—by a professional barber, I continued. Hair nice and short, too. I'd gone for the haircut—the beard trim was an extra.

I assume you and Phil Hodge took it as a joke. Big Howie Whalen sounds like a man who loves the sound of his own bluster.

Until the next morning we did. A very tiresome joke. But then my aunt Rosalyn appeared in our bedroom, which had been Little Howie's bedroom when he and I were boys, and stood at the end of my bed holding a tray with barbering instruments on it—a silver tray with different-sized scissors and razors and lathering brushes and a lathering bowl—and said, You know, Jimmy, Big Howie is serious, just like I told you he'd be. And for once in her life she didn't laugh.

She didn't plead her husband's case, either. She stood there with that tray in her hands like a maid come to serve us breakfast in bed. She wore a sheepish smile, really a resigned and powerless look on her face, except, of course, a Whalen was never powerless.

So I laughed for her. I raised up on my elbows in bed and looked over at Phil Hodge, also up on an elbow, looking at Rosalyn and then looking at me, and I laughed. The sun was shining through the window, you could hear the birds, this was a room I'd slept in many times before, when a world of plenty awaited Little Howie and me out there, or so it had seemed.

I said, Rosalyn, what a way to wake a man up. Unless I'm still dreaming. Am I dreaming, Rosalyn?

And she said, Big Howie said you terrified little Ellie with that thing.

Really? Terrified her? And what did Ellie say?

Why don't you just cut it off, Jimmy? You'll look a whole lot better, you know you will, and then the two of you can go out and catch all those fish.

Terrified her?

Because if you don't . . .

For the first time she glanced over at Phil Hodge. Her shoulders slumped, and for an instant I thought she was going to drop that tray. She shook her head. Then she sighed, one of those sighs in which you might hear a lifetime, or a single life-changing event along the way.

I should have gotten out of bed and held her. I played the big laughing incredulous card instead and told her not to worry, to leave the tray, I'd take care of it, and we'd get the day off to a fresh start.

Cautiously, as though it held fragile objects and not shaving cream and razors and scissors and a mortar-like lathering bowl, she placed the tray on what had once been her son's boyhood desk, and when she'd left the room I lay back, arms extended, and said, Can you believe it?

Phil Hodge mulled the question.

That was my favorite aunt, I said.

Phil Hodge continued to mull the scene.

And I terrified my little niece. I struck terror in that poor child. Terror! I repeated, marveling at the word.

Finally Phil Hodge said, What *are* you going to do?

This from a man who'd been poised to jump into Castro's Cuba and take out a Soviet missile that could have blown the world to kingdom come.

Which you didn't know yet, Walter was quick, too quick, to remind me. Not until three hundred miles farther back north.

And I was quick to fire back, What would you have done, Walter? But Walter didn't rise to the bait. He quietly clinked the bottle against my glass, then against his own.

Call Big Howie's bluff? I said.

Is that what you told Phil Hodge? Walter asked, and I said no, that I lay there and worked out a whole scenario in my head in which the northern-looking Phil Hodge and I, a brazenly bearded turncoat, reeled in fish after fish in both of Big Howie's lakes, so many fish in so shameless a fashion that the word began to get around, to the point that one of the town's cronies actually felt compelled to step up to the man himself and, speaking not just personally, no, but for countless others as well, to say, Big Howie Whalen, what in Sam Hill is going on with those Yankee kinfolk of yours?

All Phil Hodge would say was, It's your call. Don't worry about me. I'm along for the ride.

But I did worry about him. We'd driven four hundred miles the preceding day. I had made certain promises, amounting to a boast. Come four hundred miles with me and I'll show you a real land of plenty.

Oh, what the hell! I said. I can always grow the damn thing back. We can go up in the mountains, fish all we want, and never have to see Big Howie Whalen's face again.

I roused myself and took the tray with me into the bathroom. Snip it as far down as you can with the scissors, I told myself, then lather up and shave the rest of it off. Here and there a few white hairs had sprouted in the brown, and I wasn't even thirty years old. Shave them off too. But I looked at myself in the mirror, searching for some comic relief, and ended up shaking my head. Big Howie Whalen was a rich man and a bully, and in that moment my sole possession, all I had to my name, was my beard.

I walked back into the bedroom, returning the unused tray of instruments to my cousin's boyhood desk.

I couldn't, I told Phil Hodge. Came close. I made a glum little laugh.

And Phil Hodge said, So where do you think Little Howie Whalen stands in all this?

Wondered that myself, Walter Kidman said from his dark portion of the screen porch, where to counter a cool breeze coming in from the lake he continued to sip his bourbon. In that moment I heard a distant, waterborne wail, a little otherworldly. A loon? I said.

You know, Walter said, I never got where that expression "crazy as a loon" came from.

Lonely, I said.

It'll go under, come up, call out again, and if no other loon answers, it'll pack it up and go home alone.

Some very good advice, I said. Maybe it's time to go to bed.

Give me a little Little Howie Whalen first, Walter replied. How many diapers can a man change?

Little Howie had had two children in quick succession. So two times however many diapers a toddler goes through in a day. And in the near offing he would have a third. Finally, a fourth. Fathering children as fast as he could catch bass, throwing each fish onto the floor of the boat before casting out for more? Whalens on top of Whalens, as if there were no end to the minnows of the world?

We dressed. When Aunt Rosalyn reappeared at the door of our room, I shook my head and handed her back the tray. Couldn't do it, I said, smiling. Man's gotta stand up for something, I went on, trying to raise a laugh. I'm going to call Big Howie's bluff, Rosalyn.

She shook her head. It was as if I'd just robbed her of a lifetime's worth of merriment, such a depleted expression she wore. But she was not on the verge of tears. She wanted to say, You just don't know, you think you do but you don't, at which point I would have said, Well, why have you been leading me on all these years? Why didn't you say a day would come when there'd be an end to the handouts, no more?

And Little Howie? I said. What do you think he'll say when he hears about all this?

Tired, more tired than angry or disappointed or confused—certainly not confused, for the terms of her life had never been clearer—my aunt set the tray of shaving instruments, surgical in their way, back on Little Howie's desk. She said, He's sitting at the breakfast table in the sunroom right now waiting for you. He's dying to see you and meet your friend, too. He'll tell you where the fish are biting and how to catch them.

Suddenly, I felt touched and relieved. I'd been sleeping in Little Howie's boyhood bed, I'd smuggled in an outsider to sleep where I had slept as a boy. It wouldn't be too much to say that momentarily I felt honored. Thank God I had Phil Hodge there to keep things in a sane perspective.

And so, Walter began, and then paused to see if I'd resent anything resembling a takeover. And so you and Phil Hodge sat down at the breakfast table in the sunroom, with some palmettos, maybe, or some deep-notched banana-leafed plants, you took one look at your cousin, he looked at you in your beard, and he might as well have been Big Howie himself sitting there. Little Howie had nothing more to say.

Not exactly, I said.

No?

He was there to talk fishing.

And not to offer a little sympathy? This was the sixties, remember, with that famous generation gap, your generation and Little Howie's versus his father's. Some advice? Here's how to please Big Howie and do an end run?

No, the part he was there to play was to make it even harder to give up all those fish.

Walter gave it a moment's thought. He'd been right, we'd heard the loon call a second time and then no more. Either the loon had gone under and stayed there or it had gone home.

My cousin, who was being groomed to take over the plant, and would be a great success at it, welcomed Phil Hodge, gave me a grin, never appeared to see my beard past what the grin had registered, never even blinked, showed no sleep-deprived, diaper-changing wear and tear, remained the handsomest and healthiest man in town, and just as his town might come to be thought of as a prototype for other towns down there, so Little Howie Whalen himself might come to be regarded as the South's exemplary young man, with or without a shotgun, rifle, fishing rod, or football in his hand.

He didn't even mention the beard, his father, the ultimatum, none of that?

In the near dark of the screen porch I shook my head.

Nothing more personal? Walter persisted. Nothing that might have made you want to go up to him and say, Damn, Howie, look at yourself! You look great! Sorry it's been so long.

It wasn't that simple, I said. I had Phil Hodge to think about.

Phil Hodge had a front row seat. I can't imagine Phil Hodge complaining.

We had just driven four hundred exhausting miles.

And Phil Hodge had all that kudzu to bask in.

Kudzu gets old fast. It browns out and looks like sludge mud after a flood.

So, let me get this right, Walter said. You sat there and had breakfast with your cousin and not once did you mention the beard and the ultimatum or any of that?

Only at the end. Up to then Little Howie probably thought it was too trivial to waste words on.

So fast forward, Walter said, and I said at the end I did tell Little Howie what was going on, but I didn't call him Little Howie, not with Phil Hodge sitting there. I said, You know all of this is kind of beside the point, because if I don't cut off these whiskers of mine, Big Howie's not going to let us fish in his lakes. I meant to say, use his boats and his boathouses and his tackle, and sleep in his beds, all of that, but Little Howie knew what I meant.

If I've been hearing you correctly, Walter interjected, what you really meant was relive your boyhood memories and through Phil Hodge pass them on north.

I suppose so, although it never seemed as . . . contrived as that.

Or as childish? Hold on to something you should have let go long before? And this friend of your childhood—this cousin of plenty—what did he do?

Little Howie? He just chuckled and shook his head.

He didn't take any of it seriously? Those were the sixties, the riots, the civil rights marches, the Vietnam War.

The reason Howie didn't mention the beard was probably because he considered it as good as gone. Why not indulge Big Howie? Every time you did, Big Howie became a bigger and bigger joke and slipped that much farther back into the past.

He didn't say that?

No, for Little Howie that beard didn't amount to any more than a frown. Don't trouble yourself. Change it to a smile and go out and catch fish. You could see why he made such a good businessman.

Did he?

Before it was over he was doing business in Europe and Japan, and he opened plants in the Caribbean.

Outsourcing?

True, but expanding in his own town, too. He created a line of custom-made clothing that became his pride. He'd begun to take orders from all over the world.

And all this for not saying no to his father . . .

I should have said to Walter, No, for learning how to play his father like a fish. For knowing when to give him line and let him wallop the water and make a big splash and when to reel him in closer to the current day.

I said instead, It's much more complicated than that. Big and Little Howie were stages along the way. There was something like a script—

But the long and the short of it was that Little Howie cut the line and let you sink.

If you want to see it that way, I said. And then Little Howie got up and walked off into a spring morning when half the world was in flower, and Phil Hodge and I sat there in the sunroom and watched his car wind up the drive. You hate to see someone like that disappear into a spring morning when you've got to stay inside.

With a mess on your hands.

It was as if Big Howie and Aunt Rosalyn and even little Ellie were waiting in the wings. I can only guess they'd held off so that Little Howie could work his magic before they stepped in. Back at the breakfast table Phil Hodge had said, So that was the master of the jumps, and I'd said, Among many other things. You know, Phil Hodge went on, he could have given you a hand with his father. He could have vouched for you. Could have said, In spite of his beard, our cousin Jim is no commie infiltrator, no drug-taking free-love advocate, no violator of everything that moves. No hippie hell-raiser, no Vietcong sympathizer . . .

Phil Hodge said all that? He's barely uttered a word.

He has a story to tell, I said. Maybe he was just warming up.

That, Walter didn't tire of reminding me, was later, after all those fish got his juices flowing.

So it was.

Did you ever ask Phil Hodge straight out, Do you want to stay here and fight it out or do you want to go back?

No, not exactly in those terms.

So, he's got to be getting tired of this . . . what? "Predictable" was one of your words, Jim, which may be putting it mildly.

I saw where I'd gone wrong. Two Yankees, I'd invited Walter Kidman to view things through Phil Hodge's eyes and, as right-minded as I viewed him to be, Walter was a much more disputatious man than the laconic Phil Hodge. The story was not done—not by a long shot. But the loon had gone home and Walter's interest was wearing thin. Or the bourbon had ceased to do its job.

And neither Walter Kidman nor Phil Hodge was family. Certain family stories never got old.

So, picking up the pace, I told Walter that no sooner had Little Howie's car—not a black Cadillac, which for all I knew might have been out of production by then—disappeared up the drive than Big Howie, Aunt Rosalyn, and little Ellie, whom I'd terrified—or was it traumatized?—walked into the sunroom. Big Howie sat down across from me, took a quick look at the beard and shook his head. Quickly I shook mine. Can't do it, Big Howie, I said. It wouldn't take much, Jimmy, Big Howie replied. I wouldn't know how to start, I claimed. What if I went uptown to the barbershop and had them do it there? Big Howie shook his head again.

No, we don't want that. A professional, I insisted, who knows what he's doing. I looked Big Howie in the small, flesh-embedded eye. I had to remember that, on his own terms, no one had been more generous. Don't they have experience uptown cutting off beards? I asked before answering myself, No, I don't guess so, hard to see how they would. Maybe, I tried a different tack, we should head on south and look for another lake. Big Howie sat back and smiled. Wouldn't recommend that either.

Turn around and head back north?

Probably a better bet.

Even though the fish are bigger down here?

Even though.

We sat and looked across the table at each other. This was not an unfamiliar face-off, only more consequential, and I hoped Phil Hodge was taking note. I looked at Aunt Rosalyn, who many years ago had taken her vow and with a heavy heart was now standing by her man. Little Ellie was on guard but very alert, and later, I knew, I would want to know just how much of this she remembered. Terrified? Traumatized? I drew a deep breath and entertained the thought that this was the moment when the branch of the family tree I occupied was about to crack. Then I played a hole card, which until that moment I hadn't realized I'd been holding.

A hole card? Walter said. It sounds to me like you were playing with a stacked deck.

I think I'll call Esther, I announced to the table at large, and see what she has to say about all this.

I heard Aunt Rosalyn draw a breath but not release it. Big Howie seemed to set his jaw and harden his jowls. Ellie took a cautious step forward.

I said to my littlest cousin by far, My mother, your aunt Esther, has always been a little bossy, but we still love her. I turned to my youngest aunt. Don't we, Rosalyn? She'd hate to be left out of something like this.

To his credit, Big Howie barely hesitated before setting a phone on the breakfast table, lifting the receiver, checking for a dial tone, then moving it across the table to me.

Walter said, That's a poker play if I ever heard of one. I see a man calling your bluff. And I see a man moving his chips to the center of the table. All in.

Big Howie, I said, was never "all in."

A black Cadillac held in reserve?

My mother, who could have gotten mad at me for failing to inform her I was making a trip south, held her fire until she had Big Howie on the phone. It wasn't hard to imagine her face. Its outstanding feature was her widely set blue eyes. So widely set that whichever way you feinted in an argument with her, you couldn't escape the feeling you'd been outflanked.

Big Howie's only point, which he didn't tire of repeating, was that, sorry, Esther, they just didn't do that the sort of thing in his town. Flank him and outflank him again, Big Howie was a fortress unto himself.

I repeat, Walter said: It's a bluff.

My mother asked to speak again to me. Jim, why in the world did you wear that thing over there? What are you growing a beard for in the first place? I thought you had better sense.

I told her it was very neatly trimmed. I asked her if she wanted to speak to Phil Hodge to get an impartial outsider's opinion. My mother didn't know who Phil Hodge was, and I couldn't tell her he'd been a paratrooper ready to jump into Castro's Cuba because I didn't know that yet. She asked to speak to her youngest sister.

Three-quarters, say, of Aunt Rosalyn's expression was resigned. The remaining quarter was sporting, but there were times when Rosalyn did not feel entirely at ease marshaling all that Whalen wealth and prestige, so that her laugh, instead of rising from the mainspring of her being, could come out muddy and forced.

Finally I asked for the phone back. My mother said, I can't understand why you'd want to stay there anyway. Then she asked if her sister and brother-in-law had been drinking, and I reminded her that they had given that up back before Ellie was born. By that time, my mother scoffed, they'd already drunk enough for a lifetime. They might still be drunk. She said, Why don't you just come here? I asked if she'd forgotten I had this friend with me, and she said, Why don't both of you come? I asked her if she could supply some spinning rods, some lures, some good strong line, a bass boat, an abundance of minnows, largemouth bass with mouths so large they could consume—and she cut me off. You need to get out of there, Jimmy. I wouldn't stay another minute with that blowhard brother-in-law of mine. Remind my spoiled little sister I tried to talk her out of marrying him, and please tell your friend that not everyone in the family is like that. And cut off your beard. That may be the only thing Big Howie's been right about in years.

I hung up the phone and pushed it back across the breakfast table toward Big Howie. I nodded for the high quality of his gamesmanship. Smiling, I said, Your sister-in-law said you were wrong about everything and have been ever since you married her kid sister, but you were right about one thing: I should cut off my beard.

Big Howie didn't let a flicker of satisfaction cross his face. He asked his wife to bring me that tray of shaving utensils again.

I asked little Ellie if she wanted to stroke my beard one last time, the way kissing cousins are known to do.

She giggled and half hid behind her mother. Big Howie didn't lose his composure, although I sensed that Phil Hodge thought some sort of confrontation was imminent. Phil Hodge had moved up beside me to let Big Howie know he had an ex-paratrooper to deal with now, one who had some fighting spirit left in him, Castro having escaped him with a beard considerably shaggier than mine—

Except. Walter didn't have to say it, and he did me the courtesy of stopping short.

Duly noted, I said.

Walter sighed, deeply.

Noted again.

I continued. Phil Hodge un-bristled, and Big Howie let my very unseemly invitation to little Ellie pass. Big Howie announced he was off to the plant to join his son. If I ever got around to doing the necessary barbering, Phil Hodge and I could find him in his office where, in addition to getting the fishing plans straight, he'd be pleased to load us down with shirts and pants for the year ahead. He would be in his element and, our arms loaded with free merchandise, we would be in ours.

I asked him for a map of the area.

Aunt Rosalyn knew where the maps were kept, and Big Howie, offering no objection, didn't even have to raise a finger or tilt his head.

With the map spread out on the table, little Ellie crowded in close, and her father didn't motion his daughter away. I leaned in, too. Big Howie, freshly barbered with an aftershave lotion as sharp as smelling salts, placed the tip of an index finger over his hometown. The finger was fat and the fingernail half swallowed. But the nail was neatly trimmed. He said, We are right here, and then I added my fingertip to his and traced a tentative route south, where thin little squiggles of blue indicated that other streams had been dammed where other bass and minnows might have gathered to feed and be fed on. Big Howie waited until my finger had come to a stop, near a town called Barston, before moving his larger finger back north and dragging mine with it in the undertow. We went right by the lake with the twelve-hundred-mile shoreline and emerged in a state that certain politicians and their pollsters might classify as swing. And, indeed, there was a sizable squiggle there, bloated in the midsection. Big Howie thumped it with his fingertip three times. He'd heard some fellows had been catching fish up there, he said.

The road north was the road we'd come south on. I looked at my aunt Rosalyn, who'd gone missing behind an expression of she'd-told-me-so subservience, and when was I going to learn? Reverting to small talk, she asked, What in the world is Esther up to now, Jimmy? We really didn't get a chance to exchange a word.

I shook my head. You know Esther, I said. All politics is local, and she's in it up to her neck.

Not running for office, is she?

My mother was the most up-front behind-the-scenes power I knew—but local, at most countywide. She knew where her interests lay. Contrary to what she would now profess, she had once seen to it that her kid sister was thrown into Howie Whalen's arms, even though she might have risked her own son's welfare in the process. In effect, bartering her son for future Whalen wealth and prestige.

What? What's that? Say that again, Walter said.

Another story, I said, but back before I can be trusted to give you a reliable account.

Let's hear it. You, the precious little boy, a cupid whether you knew it or not, in exchange for a Big Howie Whalen?

Don't you want to hear how this story ends first?

I assume it already has. Big Howie goes off to the plant although it's Little Howie who is pretty much running the show. Aunt Rosalyn sits out under her cloud until the sun comes out. Little Ellie doesn't forget, not entirely. When she's a grown woman, she'll stroke a man's beard and remember yours and the time you stood toe to toe with her father, whom she will not have ceased to adore. And you and Phil Hodge will get the last laugh. A three-pound smallmouth—pound for pound the best freshwater fighting fish in the world, or so I've been told.

We drove north, out of Whalen country and into another state, a nice scenic two-lane road back then. The kudzu was still a sight to behold. And thanks to the kudzu, anything not fit to be seen wasn't. We came to the crest of a hill. Down below lay a valley, which the road dipped in and out of. A police cruiser was parked down there. We had an excellent view. We watched as the patrolman slowed down the two cars preceding ours, waving both through. Us he stopped. A state highway patrolman— Which state, you ask? Did it matter? The sunglasses, the broad-brimmed hat, the square jaw, the thin-lipped mouth, the freshly shaved beard. The all-season weatheredness. With due deliberation the patrolman noted my beard and maybe Phil Hodge's Yankee leanness of countenance. Where you boys from? We told him. Where you off to? Going back home. Plan to stop on the way, maybe do a little fishing? We said, Now, there's an idea. The patrolman smiled and held it for a moment longer than you'd expect him to, just in case he decided to take it back. We smiled, too. Then he waved us through without inviting us—Y'hear—to come back, but an irreproachable pro nonetheless. We weren't halfway up the hill when we saw him pull a U-turn and drive his cruiser back the other way, up his half of the valley and out of sight. To make his report.

You think so?

No doubt.

A state away? How many miles?

Doesn't matter. Big Howie Whalen carried his weight.

Walter emitted a groaning, throat-clearing sound, as if a load had momentarily been lifted from his shoulders before being lowered back onto them. We were tired and it was getting late. The bourbon was half gone. Walter made an attempt to rise, only to fall back in a crackling of wicker. The crackling seemed to wake him up.

You know, Jim, he said, when all is said and done, that's pretty much a shaggy dog story.

Befitting a beard, I said.

Neatly trimmed. You must have seen it all coming, and you must have seen the ending too.

If we did, I allowed, we didn't foresee that stringerful of fish. I mean, we were casting up into some heavy brush and, that I remember, we never got hung. The bass tried to get back up in there after we'd hooked them, of course, but not one of them made it. One of those days.

Did you ever let Big Howie know?

Now that you mention it, I don't think we told anybody.

I laughed under my breath. Settled back myself. Held out my glass, which Walter met with a precise clink, a perfectly struck note, which the night carried through to the end. I thought of that neighbor's cello as it had lingered. Then of the bass we'd caught on that extraordinary day years after Phil Hodge had not jumped into Cuba. Muscle memory, the ratcheting reel, the bass dragging out line, but slowly, slowly giving way. Pull up. Lower the rod tip as you reel in. Pull up again. No thrashing, no minnows jumping. The bass might jump, flashing that forest green stripe they wore from gills to tail, but the bass were coming home. We didn't lose a one.

My muscle memory. And Phil Hodge's, wherever he might be. Not Walter Kidman's, of course.

I said, Walter, I want to make it up to you—and I truly did, even though a small voice in my head advised me to call it a night—forcing you to sit through a shaggy dog story like that.

A short-haired dog story?

Well, as a matter of fact, that's *exactly* what I want to tell you. How did you guess? A short-haired dog story.

Maybe when you were just a toddler, fresh out of diapers, but maybe not, and Big Howie—

Who was not so big then.

—came courting.

But you'll have to cut me some slack. This goes way back, and I'm feeling my way.

And your mother was willing to do some fishing herself, and you, you little angel, were the bait.

No, Rosalyn was the bait, and the short-haired dog's name was Bing. Named for Bing Crosby, my mother's favorite crooner, mellow-toned, pretty bland-faced when you came to think of it, and the dog Bing was a Boston bulldog, with black and white markings, pointed ears held to a quiver, and milky black eyes that bugged. A belligerent expression on its face. There was a family photograph. Bing's face seemed to emerge from a muff my mother carried or some sort of fur she wore. My mother was beautiful and, in spite of the photograph's patina of age, radiant, her hair as long and soft and naturally waved as Bing's was fiercely short. At that time Rosalyn was an exceptionally pretty, sparkling young woman, her suitor Howie Whalen equally attractive in a slicked-down, collegiate way. My father was long and lean, more spare-boned but not unhandsome himself. It was spring. My parents had bought some land, which had been expropriated by the state and was about to be converted into yet another lake. But there was time left for a stroll through woodland before it all went under. A path through the pines with that pine duff underfoot. I was . . . three, make it three and a half, but no more. And out of diapers. There was no doubt about that. A three-year-old toddling through woodlands with his diaper full of shit and the story makes no sense.

A story that had been told and denied many times, told and recast to suit the teller and the times. It was spring. It was the South. There were two pairs of lovers, one young and untested and caught up in a delirium of flirtation, the second not yet old but saddled with cares and anxious for a time and space of their own, and there was a boy and a dog. The path was soft. The day was warm, the breeze scented with pine. There was a freshly awakened chorus of birdsong and insect buzz. Overhead, between pine boughs, a hawk rode currents of air.

The mother and father, the sister and the suitor, the boy and the dog all strike out together. But with turns in the path and modest ups and downs, before long a certain spacing occurs. Rosalyn Pritchard and her suitor Howard Whalen come to a turn where they pick up their pace. Or, sister Esther and her husband Frank, with covert glances and knowing nods, slow their pace and deliberately fall back. Spring, and not just the smell of pine but, drifting in and out on a random breeze, jasmine and wisteria. Blackberry brambles back off the path, surely some banks of honeysuckle, too. The young lovers stride out ahead, the tested lovers, the proven lovers, gradually fall back. Spring. It is not the season for surveillance. Allow the flirtatious Rosalyn and that wooing machine named Howard Whalen to have their fun. Meanwhile the tested lovers, the proven lovers, can sample a bit of the season for themselves. They too stop to share a kiss. But the path is soft and the flower scents are sweet and that scent of pine is like a fresh sanctioning spirit overflowing the land, and the proven lovers may, in spite of themselves, fall to their knees, as the kid sister and her persistent beau have surely done themselves, many turns farther along.

At some midpoint on the path the boy toddles along after the dog. The dog Bing is as finely muscled as a skinned rabbit and makes projectile-like rushes at everything that moves along the path. The boy calls after him, "Bean! Bean!" and hurries to keep up.

It is then, with an unseasonable deep-in-summer dry-seed sound, that the snake strikes. A growling, lashing, hissing battle ensues. The little boy scoots back on the path, giving his dog Bean and the snake room. A smell like the thinnest of gray shadows falls over him. He hears a gnashing growl deep in his dog's throat, a sound deeper and longer-lasting than a dog that small should be able to make. This goes on and on. Then, as if by mutual consent, the dog and the snake pause in their struggle before the growling and the lashing start up again, but fitful now and in slow enough motion for the boy to see that the dog has the snake clamped in his jaws and that the snake has its thick, scaly body, the color of old putty and winter leaves, looped around his dog's lower half. The snake's eye looks sleepy. There is a pearling of blood on Bing's black hair, and the boy knows the snake's fangs have been in his dog's neck.

Only later, when the snake is still and the small dog is stretched out beside it, does the boy realize how large the snake in its dead weight is, and only then does that the full foul smell of the snake reach him, the under-porch, inner-earth odor of a cave, dry and damp, leaving him little air to breathe. His dog Bean sends him strange glittery glances. He begins a light, insufficient pant. Even at three, or three and a half, the boy knows he has witnessed a heroic deed.

It is at that point that his parents come strolling up the path to find him and Bing, and that his mother gives a choking scream, followed by a full-throated one that reaches his aunt Rosalyn and her beau Howard Whalen farther down the path and brings them to their feet. The boy's father picks his son up and goes over every inch of his flesh, searching for the twin punctures and the pearling blood. He slows himself down, checking and double-checking, before announcing to his wife, who is panting herself now, No, nothing, not a trace, nothing! Rosalyn appears on the scene, accompanied by her Howard Whalen, prepared to go to battle himself, welcoming the screams as a chance to show his pre–Big Howie Whalen worth. Rosalyn gasps and runs to her sister. Howard Whalen, finding nothing to pit himself against, moves up beside his future brother-in-law and his son, the little blue-eyed and golden-haired boy, with his mother's curls yet to be shorn, who has been their cupid up to now. How? Why? When? But with the small dog dying before them and the enormous snake stretched out along the ground, no one needs to ask a thing. Where were they when the snake struck and the dog leaped to the boy's defense, intercepting, as the story would quickly have it, its mortal enemy in midair? Where were the boy's parents and the boy's aunt and the man who would woo her and win her hand? Forging ahead, or at a more than leisurely pace bringing up the rear. The path soft, the breeze sweetly laden with scents, the day long. Playing their parts, forming a family, circling their wagons around something like a primal secret, which, surely, each family must have. A short-haired dog story that the undergrowth would take under, or the kudzu would soon overflow—

Walter, silent until then, interrupted me. Didn't you say that land was due to be flooded?

I did, I said, and it was. At least, I think it was. This was not a story certain family members wanted to dwell on.

Why not? The net result is largemouth bass instead of rattlesnakes.

Don't play dumb, I said.

All right. Answer this. You were there, but just out of diapers, three, at the most three and a half, you said. If you don't remember it, who told you?

Now I played dumb, although the truth was I didn't remember who'd told me. Except for me, all the participants were dead, starting with the dog Bing, and what was left behind was the story itself, like some founder's myth enshrouded in the mists of time—or waves of kudzu, which were snaky, everybody knew that.

Walter's next question caught me by surprise. Did you ever tell Elaine this story of when you were a little boy?

Elaine Sinclair had been my second wife. Walter and his wife Molly had introduced us. Elaine and I had remained close and still saw each other, frequently with Walter and Molly, but since the divorce we'd lived in our own private residences.

No, I said. I don't think so. Why?

No reason.

Anyway, I remind you we were leaving the women at home this weekend.

You're right. My mistake, Walter said. We were.

But, no, I repeated in a tone even I could hear as strangely hushed, vaguely amazed, I don't think I've told this story to anybody but you for a long, long time.

Walter rose in a last crackling of wicker. He made the effort. He stretched. He yawned—it was all a bit of a show, as if he hadn't heard what

I had in the hush of my voice, or had not detected the pull of the story's undertow and wondered where it might carry us from there.

Then, as he was about to pass by me on the way inside, he paused and appeared to entertain a recollection. A primal secret, he repeated thoughtfully, followed by, Something each family must have. Those were your words, weren't they, Jim?

He knew they were. It was squarely in his nature, this need to pin it all down.

It's always seemed, he went on, that in storytelling primal secrets can get a sort of poetic pass. Whereas in a prosaic court of law . . .

What are you getting at, Walter?

Something "fishy" about your chronology there, Jim, he advised. According to the calendar most of us go by, the Howie Whalen you and Phil Hodge drove four hundred miles to see, this bassmaster cousin of yours two years your junior, should have been toddling through those soon-to-be-flooded woods with you. In which case, Big Howie and Rosalyn would have been man and wife, and Little Howie's diaper probably *would* have been full of shit. Lovers up the path and lovers down the path, but if it's sweet smells you're after, you'd better double up on the honeysuckle and the jasmine and the wisteria . . .

Straight talk, Walter, I said.

But he chose to be cryptic. A primal tale for a primal secret, he said. And a poetic liberty, courtesy of the court. But one helluva short-haired dog story, Jim.

Then, stifling a yawn, he announced, I'm going to take your flirtatious Rosalyn and her "wooing machine" of a husband to bed with me, for something, he implied, as incidental as a little bedside reading. If you don't mind.

His hand fell on my shoulder as he passed beside me, lightly, but the effect was to hold me down. Did I mind turning Big Howie and Rosalyn, Little Howie and little Ellie, whose life had been a disaster for the last twenty years, over to Walter Kidman? As mischievous as he might enjoy being, I trusted Walter, he was a good friend and a good lawyer—and, in matters of confidentiality, a good lawyer was the next best thing to a priest—but in fishing the jumps there comes a moment when an insatiable hunger rises up in you and everything turns wild. Hard to imagine that now, sitting before a lake as quiet as this one, with the fish bedded down and the loons gone home and the ghosts of WPA workers asleep in their beds.

II

THE NEXT MORNING WALTER wanted more. He'd slept on it, he said, and as far as he was concerned, Big Howie Whalen was over and done with. Hadn't he seen him and his black Cadillacs before? And his strut? And his barrel-sized belly? And, sad to say, maybe his wife Rosalyn was done with, too—I myself had made that clear, hadn't I? Rosalyn had taken her vow and, in honoring it, become who she was. But Little Howie Whalen, who looked forward and looked back and was really performing a sort of straddling act, as, Walter supposed, most young men of his generation had had to do, North or South, sixties or not, nothing particularly remarkable about that, he realized, but still, to have made a success of it and then to have had his life cut short . . .

I held Walter off.

I'd woken up before he had, not at all hung over but with a pleasant sort of vacuum in my head, and taken the canoe out before the sun began to beat down. I'd paddled out to the center of the lake, then floated. To see how long I could nurse that little clearing in my head along. A hawk or buzzard tacked overhead for a while, a frog or two croaked, a pickup passed on the lakeside road with something quietly rattling in its bed, and then, from down the lake, I heard the voice of a child. A boy's voice, excited, asking for somebody to come out and look at something he'd found. Something from the natural world, I assumed, that the night before when the boy had gone to bed had not been there. Finally, though, a boy who'd begun to whine when nobody came out to share his discovery. It occurred to me I could paddle down the lake and get him to show me whatever it was. But the effort it would take to reach a whining child put me off. I lay back and closed my eyes again and, as the sun rose higher, sculled the canoe closer to the shore and the shade of the tree line, until the sun found me there too.

Walter had prepared us a full breakfast. He'd awoken with a big appetite, I with less of one. I nibbled on the sausage and the pancakes sweetened with maple syrup from a farmer's market up the road and kept that empty spot in my head unoccupied as long as I could. There was a town nearby called Easley's Falls that Walter thought I might find a curious, quaint remnant, so at midday we drove over there and had lunch in the bar of all that was left open of an old hotel, which looked across the main street in town to what had been a first-class trout stream back before acid rain reduced the fish population in almost all the Adirondack lakes and streams. The Highland House, this ex-hotel was called, and the man who waited on us, in answer to a comment Walter made about a possible revival of the town, responded that that pendulum had better swing back fast, because they were counting the days around there. A man with no identifying marks—no tattoos, no scars, no earrings or piercings or any adornments of any memorable kind—and with what looked to be an irreversible pallor to his face. Walter had a clear memory of a fine chili served in this hotel down through the years, and when our orders arrived he found no evidence of a falling off there. As Easley's Falls and the Highland Hotel had gone into decline, Walter might even go so far as to say that the chili had become that much more aggressive, as if throwing up a last defense.

After lunch we stepped back out onto Main Street, where by my count there were five antique dealers within a single block. They looked closed but, Walter assured me, all you had to do was pound on the door and someone would come out from in back. There were still bargains to be had. These stores had been picked over in the more prosperous years, then abandoned to their own devices, and through some strange biogenesis had managed to keep their floor space crowded and their shelves stocked. Walter mentioned a dumbwaiter table his wife had discovered in one of them—he spoke her name, Molly—then pantomimed a slap on the face and begged me to pardon him again. Through the clouded show window we were standing before, I saw a mule collar leaning up against a copper tub. I might have gone in and bought the mule collar as something to be hung around the neck of the last person to speak the name of his wife or his ex, the dubious prize you took home with you, but in that moment I realized that north of the Mason-Dixon Line I couldn't remember even seeing a mule. These were southern animals, hardworking and unprocreating dead ends, so that when they were gone, the mule collars were all that was left.

The WPA had not touched this curious and quaint town. Or perhaps they had built it in its entirety and here it still stood.

Except for a small hexagonal clay-colored brick building. That Andrew Carnegie had had built to house the town's library. It stood out by itself, as resolutely closed as a missile silo from the Cold War.

Did I want to look around some more? And there were a couple of other towns nearby.

I had a memory of Walter's neighbor, the cellist, out at the end of his dock, playing not a lament, as I recalled it now, but a sort of salute to the evening. I told Walter that I was not averse to looking around at other towns, but by five I wanted to be seated there when his neighbor struck his first chord.

Walter laughed knowingly, as if I was not the first guest of his to be seduced by that sound. The cellist's name, he informed me, was Byron Wainwright. Nothing very mysterious about his story. Had sold insurance all his working life, Walter believed. A widower or probably divorced. Children or somebody that age had visited, with children of their own, but then the visits had stopped. At first his music-making had been entertaining—perhaps, given Wainwright's lonely circumstances, "endearing" was the right word—but finally it had gotten to be something that in a small way you came to dread, that same sawing back and forth every evening promptly at five. Walter said, I would say go up and tell him how much you like it, but encouragement may be the last thing he needs.

I clarified my position. I didn't exactly say I liked it. I said I wanted to be there when he struck that first chord, then maybe the second and third. Everybody needs to have a chord struck for them to get an evening under way. Don't you agree, Walter?

Walter cocked his head in a studied frown, an expression I'd seen him make at the poker table when he had every reason to believe he was being tempted into a call, or being cajoled into folding a winning hand. But by five we were sitting in a pair of Adirondack chairs on a little terrace built above Walter's dock, bourbon back in hand, waiting for the music to begin. I calculated the distance at some hundred feet up from Byron Wainwright's dock, which would locate us at a hard angle back over Wainwright's left shoulder were Walter's neighbor to sit out at the dock's end. And there were some lakeside bushes that partially obscured us. We were in no real danger of being observed observing him. I glanced at my watch and gave Wainwright a grace period of five minutes, or conceded that I might have been five minutes fast. But it was only when I stopped counting and closed my eyes that, coming out of that motor-free lakeside noise of bird chirp and insect buzz and of tiny waves lapping the shore, I heard, like a gathering breath, the first chord being bowed, and then the second, like the sound of that breath being expelled, and the evening was under way.

I told Walter Kidman that I had made it cross-country to Los Angeles before Howie Whalen, Little Howie Whalen, summoned me back. Why LA? The lure of permanent summer? The showbiz capital of the world? A combination of the exotic and of mainstream America as it had poured in? An unreal world for those of us who hadn't settled on a reality yet? I didn't know, but I could tell Walter one thing, which might sound like the most hackneyed thing going: where I was brought up, if you hung around town after you graduated from high school, not to speak of college, you were committing a vaguely shameful act. Implicitly, you were confessing to something, a lack of manly fiber, initiative, or to a willingness to plow ground that somebody else had cleared, to take refuge from the seasons in somebody else's shadow. If you never left town, already you could find a marker in the cemetery bearing your name with only the death date left blank. The continent had been settled, the West had been won, but if you were at all sensitive to that sort of thing, some ancestral something still pulled in your blood. So you packed up and set out for somewhere out there.

Even though Howie Whalen had stayed put, Walter reminded me.

That was Howie Whalen and that was the Deep South. The Deep South couldn't afford any loss of manpower. The Deep South was still in a defensive mode. The young men might have felt like cowards if they left, sneaking out of the fort at night, that sort of thing. And anyway, Howie Whalen couldn't leave if he wanted to. It all depended on him.

As long as the lakes didn't get fished out.

I listened to Byron Wainwright play his cello for a while—still getting under way, a stumbling, searching sort of serenade—then said, We've left the fishing behind, Walter. I was twenty-three. I had answered an ad and taken a job with an independent film producer, a Frenchman I thought was mostly made up and couldn't really believe in, but who had money and was looking for scripts. Then he had a script about the outbreak of the Korean War, about a South Korean soldier and a GI and a Korean girl caught in between, and was looking for the actor to play the GI, an unknown he could launch. At a sort of skeptical remove, I got caught up in the search. Apparently the Frenchman had known a GI during World War Two back in France, somebody from the heartland, but rangy like a Texan or a long corn stalk, who might or might not have survived the war, but who served as a prototype for the actor he had in mind. And he had money, this Frenchman, he claimed to have come from a titled family back on the Continent, and he had assembled a modest little team. There was a girl I took up with, a team member, short-haired, short and slim-hipped, with an androgynous air and a will-o'-the-wisp way of turning up here and there. We both had office duties and gofer tasks to perform, but I knew, whether my employer did or not, that you couldn't count on her from one day to the next. She was like a spirit-waif of the business. She may have been the only girl I knew out there who had no interest in getting in front of the cameras. The Frenchman picked up on something in her, though. If anyone was going to find him his heartland man, she was. The rest of us went through the motions, brought in sheets of photo-graphs, composites, eight-by-eleven glossies, newspaper photographs and clippings we'd happened on. We arranged a few interviews—I wouldn't call them auditions—but nothing clicked. I admired to the point of incre-dulity the Frenchman's patience. World wars had been fought where he came from, civilizations had risen and fallen, and here he was in Holly-wood, California, precisely on Sunset Boulevard, waiting for us to bring him his man. At times he could make it seem like a joke—a sort of bur-lesque of a life's goal—then look at you with sad and soulful eyes and all but plead, as if his life was in your hands. Which was another sort of theater that maybe only my friend, my sometimes girlfriend and his employee, understood—

Did she have a name, this spirit waif? Walter interrupted, which in the pause that followed allowed Byron Wainwright's cello to climb from a mostly gloomy brooding toward a less encumbered, more aspiring sound, if you were willing to overlook the crudely bowed notes and the instrument's general deterioration.

I'm sure she did, I said.

Which you are withholding for dramatic effect?

No, because I keep thinking her name was Ellie, and I wonder if that could be true.

Why not? It's not that unusual a name, and you were a continent apart.

Not for long. It was about then that Howie called me and asked me to come back and be in that wedding of his. He had barely turned twenty-one. He would marry his high school sweetheart. Since junior high they had hardly been out of each other's sight, if you forgot about the times Howie had been off fishing and hunting and playing football with those town buddies of his. Or the times he'd been off with me when as a boy I'd been brought to town. You see what I'm getting at, don't you, Walter?

I see how you've set it up.

It's how it was, I said. The continent was drifting, tilting toward LA. Titled Frenchmen were showing up looking for heartland war buddies or someone to play them. There was a mix of identities on display out there—

Including two Ellies.

The Cuban missile scare had come and gone, but it would be another two to three years before I'd appear in their town sporting a full beard. The key now is to try to imagine what it was like to leave behind a world where almost everybody was looking over his shoulder to be sure a camera from some production team was tracking every step he took, and return to one where people performed their roles as though by birthright, and not according to some crazy script.

Did you ever really read that script?

An American GI at the outbreak of the Korean War training his South Korean counterpart, only to fall in love with the South Korean's girl and then to nobly give her up— No, I never read it, Walter. I knew of its existence only as bait. It was a wonderful contrivance. The New World, the Old World, and an Older World yet. What actor, what wannabe, wouldn't—

Rise to the bait? You're fishing again.

You've got to remember what was still going on back then. Do you think John Wayne, Gary Cooper, Burt Lancaster, all that crowd were trained at Juilliard? They were discovered. Working the oil fields or performing circus tricks. At one time the Frenchman hinted that he'd had some keepsake from his American to return to his family somewhere out on the Great Plains, which could mean anywhere from Texas to the Dakotas. Even that he'd gone there and spent time, futile months and years, looking for—what? The right homestead? I never really believed him, although he might have believed himself. Europeans love all the Great Plains myths. They picture themselves escaped from their Old World binds, wandering around in all that space. He wanted you to believe his American had died as a hero liberating France, but he also wanted you to hold on to the possibility that his American had survived and returned to his Great Plains and that that keepsake, whatever it was, a medal of some sort, or something whittled, say, out of mesquite, would serve as a kind of homing device and they'd link up. I know he was late in getting to Hollywood, so he must have spent a lot of time out there on the Plains. If the whole thing wasn't made up. But by the time I joined his little team, actors *were* being trained at Juilliard or in acting schools out there. There were still plenty of young hopefuls parking cars and striking poses for producers, or driving down the Strip in convertibles with a windblown look sprayed into their hair, but things were about to change in a big way, the Frenchman knew it, and—

Give me a name, Jim. Not just a Frenchman. You're forcing me to picture Maurice Chevalier strolling down the Champs-Élysées.

Charles Millesaints, I said. His name was Millesaints. Does that sound aristocratic enough for you?

De Millesaints?

Short, forget your lithe, worldly Old World aristocrat, but short, burly, ruddy and pebbly in his complexion, as if he had been wandering around the Great Plains for years and the elements had taken their toll.

But he wouldn't give up.

Not while I knew him. But you're missing the point, Walter.

Which is?

All that sad and silly flux out there, sad because it was so silly, versus—

What you came back to when your cousin summoned you, to represent the family, to perform the role you'd had written in since birth, in exchange for all the handouts and all the fish you'd caught, to be a groomsman of his.

All it took was an airplane ride and I was standing in a small-town church whose distinctive smell probably still came from those hymnals fitted in the back of each pew, in spite of all the flowers, the perfume and cologne, and Big Howie—

—the best man—

—was standing beside his son, both in dark suits with white carnations in their lapels, and Little Howie was looking up the aisle, waiting for the bridesmaids to work their way down before his bride appeared. I saw Little Howie in profile, which, as they say, was nothing less than Greek, and when his wife-to-be appeared—

What could it hurt, before you go any further, to give her a name too?

—when Laura Kingston appeared on the arm of her father, when "Here Comes the Bride" sounded and there she came and I put the two of them together, Laura Kingston and Howard Whalen, Laurie and Howie, and they stood side by side, that was when I almost broke out laughing at the colossal silliness of that world I'd left in LA. That Saturday afternoon in a First Christian Church in a small town in the South, there was more beauty on display—real beauty, Walter, unfabricated beauty, beauty as natural as the buds to the trees—than had ever paraded up and down Sunset Strip or through all the soundstages in Hollywood. When my cousin and his wife-to-be took their vows, you could hear all the parts fitting together, you could hear the deeply satisfying sound of a whole being formed. A simple ceremony, a single take. No cut-and-print except what you printed and kept in your mind.

But I could tell Walter wasn't getting it. He thought as a young man I had been dazzled and, having worked for the brief time I had out in Hollywood, had come to my cousin's wedding primed, when in fact the opposite was the case. I hadn't been out in LA for more than eight months and already I was jaded. My tolerance for young, good-looking hopefuls preening in and out of the public eye had hit rock bottom. You could see through everybody out there, and what you saw was—nothing. A dull and glamorous sort of sameness. Why had the Frenchman come looking for his American in the midst of all that? Because he had a script, and because his American had grown to such enormous proportions in his mind's eye that he would only fit on the silver screen.

Although we never talked about it in just those terms, I sensed that my Hollywood Ellie knew all that and only by keeping in motion did she manage to take a certain delight. Imagine her delight when, as later happened, she'd lit on the Frenchman's American, that Plainsman of the mysterious keepsake and very few words, and turned him over to her boss. Imagine it before it turned to disgust. But Ellie didn't really register disgust. Maybe later when she had the proper scales to weigh her delight in and saw that it came to nothing. If, for instance, she'd been standing at my side, playing her part as the groomsman's spirit waif, and had seen my cousin marry his bride, and seen the way the town gathered on the street below, and the way the church doors opened and Howie and his wife, Big Howie and my aunt, and the other little Ellie, a toddler still, stepped outside, and cameras were not rolling and klieg lights were not blazing and there was no director there to call, Cut and print, none of that. A certain family in a small town, the right people on the right day. I said to myself, Damn, now there's a good-looking couple, that's what it's all about. Let's see how long they can make it last.

Walter would have to have been there. Those towns had a way of calling everything in around them. Rumor had it there was a big sophisticated world out there, but if something claimed your attention—genuinely claimed your attention—a town like the one the Whalens lived in became a stage sufficient unto itself. To be off in the wings was to be off in nowhere. Howie Whalen was not much taller than average, a shade under six feet, the shoulders not noticeably broad, the hair black and the eyes blue, a way of standing, squarely but lightly planted, with no need to run, really, since the world came to him, no need to move at all. But when he did, he was as supplely knit as some animal slipping through brush. If you studied his face, you kept waiting for the blue eyes under black brows to turn cold, but they never did. Unlike his mother, he wasn't a big laugher, but the eyes shed light, a calming and even a companionable light, so that not only family members but also his workers, when he came to take control of the plant, could be said to bask in him, to take what he offered since it was, or always seemed to be, more than enough.

As an only child he'd been spoiled, of course. He'd gone through all that had been laid at his feet so quickly he was always ready for more, but even then you got the impression he was simply biding his time. When his sister was born, it was not competition he felt but relief. He was said to have matured. For the record, he was no longer spoiled. He needed

41

none of it, things moved in and out of his hands freely enough; except for the real trophy-sized ones, he released the fish he caught; and game, even game that he killed in what must have been a moment of supreme intimacy, you could also say he'd released. He was accompanied by spirit deer, spirit bear, spirit long-horned sheep. Unlike his father, he did not have to wrest a business out of nothing and then hound it along; he could grow into it, and worker by worker, plant by plant, country by country, he could expand. It was a natural process, he was nature's child, and nature always had her favorites.

His wife, Laura Kingston, now a Whalen, actually did have skin the softness and hue of a magnolia blossom, and eyes with shifting planes of rich brown light like a buckeye. Hair a lustrous chestnut brown, lips so lovely you couldn't imagine them uttering an imprecation. In her smiles she held something back, and her laughs were never at full strength, there was always something left, something it was easy to suppose just for him. At full height she reached to his ear, and when she whispered an intimacy to him, you wanted—at times badly—a code of some sort that would allow you to read to the exact degree the crease in his smile. She was well-mannered; she was trained—self-trained; she struck, perhaps not as commandingly as he did, that balance between a small town and a large world. There was some mental instability in her family, but an aunt of Howie's was also out on that limb. This was the South, womanhood in the South, and there would always be casualties. To all appearances she was very happy, but she was always on alert. She kept waiting for her prince of a husband to fail her, and he never did. Not until the end. Consequently, she lived a blissfully provisional life.

There on the church stairs, as Howie and Laurie Whalen stood in full view of the town, you could see all this, and you could sense what it meant. Surely, there were those who begrudged Little Howie his privileges and extraordinary good fortune, but they were vastly outnumbered by those who basked in the day's well-being, as if every single one of them had been invited to the wedding feast. There was a feast, of course, where the family at large would assemble—my mother, father, and sister among them—and where the family would close ranks around our standard-bearers, where, whether we thought of it that way or not, we paid obeisance to the two people who were so obviously deserving of it, but that was not the moment that counted. That was a stroke of fortune, call it the crowning reach of the family tree, the latest and grandest instance of Whalen largesse, as if we'd all stopped by the plant and instead of common cotton Rosalyn had piled cashmere into our arms. But the real moment, the moment that counted, came when Howie and Laurie stood on the church stairs and were joined by Big Howie, Rosalyn, and their little daughter, and the townsfolk did not break into applause, but there was a murmur of such deep approbation that it was impossible to imagine anyone left out. I was reminded of when the earth trembles, when the earth becomes a vast unifying tremor but stops short of becoming a quake. As if the earth, in its own measured way, were leading the applause.

Which sounds, Walter said, positively medieval, but I assume you already know that.

Look at it this way, Walter, I said. The town made its peace with Big Howie Whalen. He cruised around in his black Cadillacs, expected and got their applause, and gave them jobs and the necessary perks. Paternalism pure and simple, but the town put up with Big Howie because he got things done and because they knew they had Little Howie waiting in the wings. This was the day Little Howie and his bride stepped out onstage. A changing of the guard.

And this Little Howie they worshipped—

I didn't say they worshipped him.

—they murmured their universal approval of, then—

And his beautiful bride.

—was the same Little Howie who let his father run you, his bearded first cousin, out of town?

Little Howie saw the humor in it at once. How foolishly both Big Howie and I had dug in. It's taken me all this while.

Walter, whom I'd seen work in court and whose style was so deliberate it could drive young assistant district attorneys wild, let out a guffaw, and it was only then that his neighbor Byron Wainwright became aware that he had an audience. He was bowing away in that moment in a mounting crescendo, and a guffaw wasn't what he wanted to hear. Walter stepped out to wave an apology down to him and with the bourbon bottle motioned Wainwright to come up and join us, but the damage had already been done. Wainwright picked up his cello (but left his stool) and walked back up his dock. It was getting dark, but enough light was left so that I could make out an old, stiff-backed man, long-jawed and bony-browed, plowing ahead like a figurehead on a ship.

Sorry about that, I said. And Walter replied not to worry, that Wainwright would be back the next day at five o'clock sharp.

And anyway, he reminded me, it was time to eat.

Walter fried pork chops and browned some potatoes and I tossed a salad, but neither of us was hungry. The chili, we agreed. The evening paled out again along the lake, then the darkness in its cloak of coolness seemed to rise from the lake's depths. We stood on Walter's dock, looking out over the water and noting at the far end some other dock's light, an evening star sort of effect, tempting us to set out and guaranteeing safe passage. Finally Walter said, as if musing to himself, What's the point of listening to the rest? Little Howie exceeded all expectations, the town prospered, the town loved him, his wife did, his children did, and then—what was it he had—?

A brain tumor.

A brain tumor did the rest.

No point, I said. No point at all.

The funeral was held in the same church they were married in. With some exceptions—and my father was one of them—the same people came. But there was a whole international contingent, too. There was a deputation from the Dominican Republic, where the Whalens had opened a couple of plants. There were Italians. Brits. A Japanese gentleman. It was not easy for me to understand how Little Howie had endeared himself to all these foreigners, other than through some extraordinary combination of personal characteristics and astute but unaggressive business savvy. He did business and it was as if he'd given them a gift. As if he were showing them a path. Even as a little boy he liked to follow the sinuous paths the deer made in the woods below their house. You could trust the deer, he'd tell me, and never get lost. But those paths were narrow. You had to learn how to slip along them through the brambles, or the thorns would tear you up. His sons, he had two—

Wait! Walter stopped me. Didn't it ever occur to you that this was the man your Frenchman was looking for, not a Plainsman but a southerner dash hunter dash fisherman dash absolute natural in everything he did, including business? And with a Greek profile in the bargain. And a beautiful wife. Sure, it did.

I didn't deny it, although it had not occurred to me. Howie Whalen was ours. He may have had his admirers the world over, but if he wasn't in his town or on his lakes or in his woods, I couldn't visualize him. Not passing through airports and landing in foreign lands. Not strolling down foreign avenues. Only once did I visit him in one of his plants—his home plant—when he'd taken my measurements, with his own tape measure gone over my body, my neck, my waist, my extremities, to make me a suit of clothes, but I didn't want to tell Walter about that. Maybe later. A suit I had worn to Howie's funeral and not again. I preferred to leave Walter with the image I'd started with. Howie fishing the jumps, with an unflagging and unerring exuberance casting into that upheaval, then standing calmly above it all, eyes on the distance, waiting for it to erupt again.

His sons, I repeated, never set foot on those deer paths. His first was bookish, unathletic, almost gnomish when you compared him to his parents, a quiet and gentle boy but hard to account for. His second son was the fourth of his children, and he looked like Howie—in the eyes at least, the black brows, and the full mouth, with a pout you could only hope he'd grow out of—but there wasn't enough time, Howie fell ill and there wasn't time for the boy—

Name? Walter said.

—for little Joey, I said, to measure himself against his father, to out-fish and out-hunt him and out-win the town's approval.

And go out and marry a girl as pretty as his mama, too, I bet.

I don't know, I've lost contact. I don't know what's happened to any of them. There were two girls in there, too. They each inherited a million dollars when their father died and probably went off and spent it as fast as they could. Laurie . . .

Yes? Walter said when I hesitated.

She remarried, or that's what I heard. There may have been some prescription drug problem, some addiction of that sort, but . . . I don't know . . .

I peered up the lake at that distant dock light. A cool breeze had now begun to blow. Keep that light in sight and I wouldn't lose them. Blink it away, I told myself, and they'd be gone. Maybe I *had* drunk too much and the storytelling had taken on a life of its own. Maybe I could prolong the blink and get rid of everything south of that line those two intrepid surveyors had plotted out where a road, eventually a turnpike, would run.

Even in a continent this vast, a single infinitesimal line like that could make all the difference, become in effect a fault line along which a country would break apart.

After the wedding, the next time I saw Howie and Laurie was up at the lake in the mountains where already they had their own house, which they called their fishing cabin. It sat back up off the road, not on the water. There was a semi-steep drive. I was to call for Howie up there at some very early hour and out we'd go, not to fish the jumps, since that was best toward midday when the water had warmed and the minnows rose, but up in the incoming stream mouths as fresh food washed down. I took my time walking up the drive even though I only had a day in the mountains, with no idea now, thinking back on it, of where I had come from and where I was to go. I was on that drive, then on the side porch and quietly knocking on the screen door. They'd left the main door open to let in the breeze. I knocked twice and then, not wanting to knock a third time, I peered through the screen mesh to see what I could. I had not been in this cabin. I did not know the bed stood on an oblique line of sight to that door. I saw my cousin roll out of bed and lift a hand in my direction to signal he was on his way. I turned and gazed down the dirt drive to the glitter of lakewater across the road beyond the trees. I heard my cousin pull on his pants, buckle his belt, scuff around for his sneakers until he'd put them on too. He visited the bathroom and then came out. The lakewater had not ceased to glitter as he searched for something in a kitchen cabinet and then in the fridge. After he closed both doors and began to move in my direction, I had one last chance before he joined me to peer in through the screen door again, and I seized it. Past the veil of that black mesh, I was able to make out Laurie Whalen as she lifted her head off the pillow, with her dark hair tousled over half of her face. She said something indistinct to her husband as he passed by. Howie may have mumbled something back. But before he could join me, Laurie had raised her head a notch higher, turned it in a slightly unnatural position toward the screen door, so that her hair fell more freely, and looked at me as I looked at her. I saw the dark shine of her eye, part of her chin, and a crescent of her cheek. That deeply shaded magnolia glimmer of her skin. I believe she said, Luck. She certainly said something before she sleepily spoke my name and her head fell back into the pillow. But all through the morning as we fished, her hair kept getting in the way, and the cicada screech back in the marshy bottomland where a stream entered the lake kept me from hearing her voice and the exact intonation she had given to my name. Howie pointed out where a sycamore limb had fallen across the stream and told me to cast just beyond it, letting the lure go still before twitching it in a crippled minnow effect. The bass, when it struck, left behind a radiant crescent of spray. The secret, of course, would be to coax it, not horse it, over that fallen limb and not get hung. It was tedious and strenuous and finally exhausting, but I reeled it up beside the boat, then reached down and grasped the lower lip, where it was possible to all but paralyze a bass, and held it up for Howie and his wife—the glimpse I'd caught of her—to admire. I would never see her again with her head half raised from a pillow, her hair falling freely across her cheek, and that would also be the last fish I'd catch with her husband looking over my shoulder. He was married now, had begun a family, and as a remarkably young man was taking over at the plant. It was possible I never went fishing with Howie Whalen again.

A sad story, however you look at it, Walter observed, standing beside me, out at the end of his dock.

Yes, a sad story and one that had worn me out. It left a weight on your shoulders, and under that weight it sometimes required a special effort to continue to believe that there was anything extraordinary about the Whalens—that in any given town down there a comparable tale couldn't be told. For what family, surely some of them losers, didn't have a fabulous story to cling to, and what fabulous branch of an otherwise unillustrious tree was ever exempted from death? A sad story. It might indeed make you believe in some kind of curse, I said. Big Howie made a fortune from the perils and excesses of the times, Rosalyn laughed it all off, Little Howie, as gifted as they got in those towns, was really a performance artist, who through some wholesome sleight of hand made believers wherever he went. And Ellie . . .

Yes?

Ellie is still with us. She's had a life.

Unterrified? Untraumatized?

No, I wouldn't say that.

We paused at that point. Darkest night had fallen, but that distant dock light remained lit. Walter and I had come up here to step away from our lives for a long weekend—not that our lives were hemming us in.

Lamar Herrin

After a period of some ill-advised advances and some tactical retreats, our lives had settled, and although our ages and professions were not the same, the way we'd come to terms with our lives and made our peace might have been. This was the way it was going to be. Who could have foretold it? This was the town, these were the people, this was the professional path you found yourself wandering down. Time to stop wandering and make it yours.

The curse, I told Walter, was probably as simple as a law of physics. Powerful families, when they came apart, came apart powerfully. They were sailing along, they hit a reef, they cracked up and created their own whirlpool going down. Power was relative, of course. Whirlpools came in all sizes. Some you could stand close to and get a spectator's thrill. Others you'd better not.

Howie Whalen had done all he'd had to to deserve a funeral like the one he got. For all his success, he remained bound to his town. He'd carried his boyhood friends with him—with their crudity and their loyalty and their blind spots as adults. He spoke in the town's own unlordly drawl. Certain evenings he sat on a bench in the town's square and chewed the town's fat. He lingered outside the post office to chew the fat there too. In church he laid one arm along the back of a pew and in turn gave each of his sons a father's conspiratorial wink, as his school buddies grown into fathers undoubtedly gave theirs. That man up there sure can preach, he'd whisper, but hang on, buddy, we'll be out of here soon. You'll be back playing, and I'll be too. At home, on matters of etiquette and good taste he'd defer to his wife, and on the niceties of social intercourse, but the town as he knew it best was mostly out of doors, and out there he was the town's townie.

So when Howie offered himself to his workers as a substitute for any union they might want to join, they came to him freely, and if it wasn't a sensitive personal matter, he'd walk them out of his office into the open, where they could be joined by others, and where business, money matters, job grievances could become a social occasion and a way to talk things through. And Howie did this not because it had become a successful tactic in heading off trouble before it started, but because he took a genuine pleasure in his workers' company, they were who he was, townspeople of his, and surrounded by them he felt himself grow, a pleasurable sensation, to grow and grow (unlike his father, whose growth was all flesh) until his well-being seemingly knew no bounds.

48

Yet he was still Howie, still Little Howie, however important an international figure he might become. I visited him on occasion, not often, but I kept in touch with his mother, my aunt, and his sister, grown into a teenage Ellie, and I watched his father drive around town as if he'd never ceased to be the ultimate authority, had never gone unconsulted for long. There goes that man again in his black Cadillac, and in deference other motorists might hug the curb. How Big Howie managed to fit his ever enlarging belly under the steering wheel was anyone's guess. He put in token time in the office, the founder and now emeritus of the whole enterprise, and when Howie went on his business trips, his father went to the plant and in effect represented his son. When his son came back, Big Howie devoted his time to his daughter, this gift he'd received out of the blue to grace his retirement, whom he taught to shoot quail and pheasants on the wing, to cast and to hook a fish, salt or freshwater, and if it didn't dwarf her, to clean it on the spot. And to drive a speedboat with the wind whipping her hair; soon thereafter, a Cadillac. Big Howie, no longer as mobile as he'd been, basically sat back and marveled at his daughter, and Ellie, no longer little, approaching womanhood but still within reach of her father's shadow, must have kept telling herself, I'll indulge him for a while longer, the rest of this season, say, but not the next. I'll become my own woman then. He'll see.

Little Howie always called his father Big Howie, regardless of the occasion, in his presence or in the third person. Ellie called him Daddy, with a sweetness and a sadness that let you know, regardless of how hard her father might try to play the clown for laughs, or to give an out-of-bounds shock, he could do no wrong. She was her daddy's pet, and Big Howie was a fair facsimile of his old self. Rosalyn—

And that question you wanted to ask her? Walter broke in.

Ask Rosalyn?

No, Ellie. Remember? If she'd remembered stroking your beard?

The truth is, I forgot about it. Later . . .

Later?

Later I'd learn she hadn't.

How much later?

Much later. It depends, Walter, if I can keep this up.

I drew a deep breath. We were back in our chairs, steep-slanted, so steep that once you got into them it took an effort to get out, with bourbon on the armrests and sweaters over our shoulders. The moon would

be late to rise. There was dock light on the water and a fugitive flash
when something broke the surface farther out. We'd yet to hear a loon.
I did hear that boy again, whose discovery in the morning had attracted
no corroborating witness, and whose whine now had a loon-like moan to
it, perhaps, until somebody, a man, abruptly shut him up. I drew another
deep breath.

Walter, I said, section 807 of the U.S. Tariff Code. Does that mean
anything to you?

Walter was a criminal attorney, not a civil one, and couldn't be
expected to know his way around these tariff codes. Except that years ago
section 807 had created quite a stir, since it was the provision that made
outsourcing or offshoring profitable for American firms. In effect, section 807 stated that for imported goods made abroad of U.S. components,
duty would be charged, upon reentry into the United States, only on the
foreign value added. That "value added" corresponded to what it cost to
assemble those components into something as recognizable and salable
as a shirt or a pair of pants. Foreign "value added" also depended on the
value of the currency in question against the value of the dollar, and since
certain countries were willing to devalue their currencies to attract U.S.
investment, "foreign value added" frequently meant next to nothing, what
you'd toss into a beggar's can. You calculated your import duties off that,
and they were incalculably small. Your cost was essentially limited to the
price of the material at home, the negligible wages you paid the foreign
workers, and the shipping of the finished product to retailers, which was
why outsourcing and offshoring had become code words for corporate
disloyalty and greed. Towns in the United States whose jobs were lost to
outsourcing were being blown off the map. When Big Howie, with his
distrust of all things foreign, got wind of what the son was proposing to
do, he was slow to come round, but once he understood that the only way
to continue to compete was to ride 807 as hard as they could, he said, All
right, no reason to go any further than those *maquiladoras* right across the
border in Mexico. They'd be quick and close and the Mexican govern-
ment had just devalued the peso.

Is it coming back to you now, Walter? I said.

Walter turned and faced me. He cocked his head at a disbelieving
angle. This is not the picture you've been painting for me, he said. I would
have guessed that before he outsourced, Howie Whalen would have gone
down with the ship. Little Howie Whalen.

Howie Whalen was not fond of sinking ships or fishing boats or sinking vessels of any sort. His overriding intention all along was to save the town.

And to get rich.

Richer, I said.

Go on, Walter said.

He was a townie, I reminded Walter, maybe the ultimate townie, so it only stands to reason he'd go in search of a town.

Not the *maquiladoras*?

That was what Big Howie would have done, expedient to a fault. But from the very beginning Little Howie had in mind some Latino equivalent of the town he lived in. He had a vision, and it probably had Juan matching up with John, Carlos with Charlie, Anita with Annie, that sort of thing, so the first thing he did was to take a crash course in Spanish, and do a little reading on the side to see how badly the Spaniards and the *norteamericanos* had abused their privileges in these countries up to then. I know he made trips to Central America, Costa Rica I believe I heard, but a number of American firms had already crowded in there. He ended up in the Dominican Republic. Maybe he jetted into Punta Cana and began to go back in time from there. A town on the northeast coast. Bella something. Maybe he just strolled into it and with a fruitful, Johnny Appleseed sort of intuition dropped a seed to see if it would grow, and it did. He arranged a deal to everybody's advantage. If Howie Whalen had a businessman's credo, it was that money ungrudgingly made bred more of its kind. It was like fertilizing a garden well at the start. Thereafter, it bore the best of fruit. Howie paid his workers considerably more than any other outsourcer who had come through there, and he flew back frequently as the machinery was shipped in to be assembled and the bales of cloth, cut to the company's specifications, were unloaded to be sewn into shirts and pants. He met Juan and Carlos and Anita. Of course, with his beginner's Spanish coming out on that drawl and with his singular good looks, you can imagine. They lined up to work for him, and they worked well. I don't want to paint too rosy a picture, Walter, Howie was an American, after all, and the dictator Trujillo—you'll remember him, the one your FDR was referring to when he famously boasted he was a son of a bitch but our son of a bitch—

And it took one to know one, I've never disputed that.

Yeah, well, for a lot of people Trujillo and the *yanquis* went hand in hand, my hand in your pocket, yours just a little bit in mine. But that's not what I wanted to tell you. This town business, Walter. This townie's banner my cousin proudly flew. I came back through his town to see my aunt and, in effect, to renew acquaintance with Ellie, now that she'd become engaged, but it was during that trip that I visited Howie and Laurie out in their new house—a mansion-sized place with a sort of French Provincial façade—built over that twelve-hundred-mile lake Phil Hodge and I had not fished. Howie and I did not talk fishing or much about family either, even though his children were in and out. I sat down to dinner with them. After having given birth four times, Laurie Whalen had gained a few pounds and a certain measuredness in her movements and a certain tolerance for turmoil, but she had also gained a glow in her face and a depth in the shifting planes of her eyes it was hard not to linger on. Her beauty had settled, become more accomplished; her children might mildly misbehave, especially Joey, the youngest, but she'd learned how to wait them out, and while she waited it was as if she was conducting her own private tally and allowing you to see how masterfully it had all worked out. When she looked at her husband, basically what she was saying was that there were no words.

Eventually the children asked to be excused. Howie had something he wanted to tell me, not man-to-man talk, but something that had its roots in the family, perhaps, or reached back to our childhoods. Laurie accompanied us out to their deck, looking down on a finger of the lake and a boathouse so large it might have housed their family a second time over. She took my hand and reached up to kiss me on the cheek. Her hair, perhaps a bit muted but still lustrous, brushed against the side of my face. It was orange blossoms, not magnolia blossoms, I'd swear I smelled. Don't let him talk your ear off, she whispered, which was a strange thing to say, since Howie was more of a listener than a talker, and then, having listened, a talker with just the right words.

Howie'd had a vision, it turned out, down in that town where he'd been setting up his plant, a vision of a routine occurrence, so routine, in fact, it happened every Sunday evening, and in all the towns down there. In an age when "courtship" might be considered an archaic word, he'd happened on a Sunday evening paseo. I was to picture the town's main square, its *plaza mayor*. At its center a bandstand or a fountain, or a heroic statue of some sort, at its margins small trimmed trees, dense with shiny leaves, and large gaudy flowers that would be giving off a heady scent if the spicy meat and fruit smells coming from the food vendors in the surrounding streets were not so strong. There would be music, perhaps from the bandstand itself, or from speakers mounted on the trees, or music accumulating in the evening air from a thousand different sources, and the beat would be festive. Then I was to picture the young women of the town promenading around that bandstand or fountain or statue in one direction while the boys and young men would be strutting and careening around in the other. And there would be yet a third circle for the married couples and especially for the mothers of the young women so that they could observe their daughters and note which of the young men allowed their lustful eyes to linger longer than they should. And then there would be benches off to the side, or steps or low walls to sit on, where visitors such as Howie Whalen might admire the whole spectacle and come away with a sense that they had seen the town spiraling in to a point, the town in its entirety, generation after generation, wheels within wheels, with nothing left over.

One evening Howie Whalen had observed such a paseo in the town where he'd come to locate his plant, and he invited me to believe he'd gone into something of a trance. It was the brightness of it all, the color, the lively salsa step to the music, it was the sense that it had all been choreographed like this since time began, that some things never changed because they were eternally fresh, and then it was those circles of townspeople rotating in opposite directions, closing on that hypnotic point. Howie smelled sizzling flesh and a gaudy gush of flowers, fruit rinds, cheap perfume, and the day's dust. He had never been much of a drinker—not with Big Howie's example before him—and except for a few immersions in collegiate kegs of beer, intoxication had never been a part of his life, but he quickly became drunk on it all then. The girls circled with their arms linked. Some of the boys linked theirs or threw their arms around each other's shoulders. The older couples or groups of women were linked too, just more sedately. There was nowhere for an outsider to break in.

A church, with a stucco colonial façade and a statue of the Virgin in her niche over the door, rose on the far side of the plaza. My cousin told me that he considered going in there to pray. For what? To whom? To the *Virgen de la Esperanza*, the Virgin of Hope, he said. There was something essential, fundamental, about that vision he'd experienced in the town where he'd come to do business, and he didn't want to lose it. Then my cousin looked at me, lowered his head, and invited me to join him—at his own expense—in a laugh, which I did.

But if my cousin was a townie, I told Walter, he was a townie all the way through, and after having experienced such a sight, how could he be anything other than a *jefe fabuloso*, an offshore boss to die for. He could laugh at himself, but that didn't mean he didn't believe it. And I could see that he'd been moved. Someone had to keep those wheels turning—whether in the Caribbean or in his own small southern town—if people were going to get along and work toward a common goal. Then he laughed again, but this time I heard the pleasure in the laugh, something of his mother's windfall sense of abundance. In time it would all come streaming down.

Walter broke in to say, That wheel, those wheels, could have been mill wheels, you know. You'd better have a lot of water sluicing through to keep them turning.

Or everyone working in unison. No one not pulling his weight.

And back home?

They cut the pieces to company specs for the workers down there to sew.

And you're telling me no one got laid off?

On the contrary, I'm telling you that business got so profitable that the workers in Howie's town never had it so good. That Howie Whalen's town became a sort of hub. That for a few years there, tourists might come through to exclaim, Ah, here's the charming little town where it all started. That Whalen Apparels workers began to build houses on the lake, much smaller than the Whalens themselves were used to, granted . . .

I saw that it had become sport for Walter, but who could blame him after having sat through a family saga like this? He said, So, in effect, the original workers became little offshore bosses themselves. John meet Juan. Charlie meet Carlos. That sort of thing. Or they became stockholders. Little Howie Incorporated . . .

Walter?

Yes, Jim.

When you fish the jumps, there comes a moment when the fish are crazy to be caught. If you don't catch them, they'll catch you. Until you run out of minnows.

If I understand you correctly, Walter responded, as deliberately as if he were appearing before a judge and connecting the necessary dots, you're saying there comes a moment when, if you're smart, you'll look for a way to stay sane.

Exactly. Which, if we're talking fishing, I said, means finding a lake like this one. The Whalen fortune came from readymades, which means a lake big enough for any boat you want to run out on it, but if you wanted to restrict it to canoes and a few little pickerel, you're talking customized clothing, one shirt, topcoat, sport coat, and suit of clothes at a time.

And that's what your cousin did? He opened a customized clothing plant?

In addition to his plant overseas, the first, then a second, that is exactly what he did, and Big Howie just shook his head.

Don't tell me Little Howie grew a beard, too! Don't tell me that!

I gave Walter his laugh.

The next to the last time I saw my cousin Howie Whalen, I said, was at that plant he'd built for his line of customized clothes. It was a small plant, a sort of freestanding adjunct to the main one, with an overhead rail system and rows of specialized machines. I walked in on him, I thought, unawares. The building was air-conditioned. The smell was of one vast unspooling bolt of cloth, sweetened by oil. Out of a multipitched hum of numerous machines came bursts of stitching, and I found my cousin standing beside one of his workers seated at her machine with a sheet of paper in his hand. He looked around at me and grinned. Of course he knew I was in town. The grin said as much. He introduced the worker as Doris, then passed me the paper he held, where I could read all the peculiar little specs a man named Roger Gold desired in his suit of clothes and, in this particular row of machines, specifically in his pants. The number and placement of belt loops, the desired depth of the coin pocket, the unusually large cut to the calves. Howie told his worker Doris to take a break, then sat down at her machine himself and showed me how to cut the hip pockets of Roger Gold's pants and stitch them before sending them via the overhead rail system on to the next station, where a buttonhole would be cut and, depending on the spec, either a flap or a tab attached. The material was a pale gray wool, and Roger Gold, I was informed, as though he might be a neighbor of mine, came from no less a place than New York City. Howie was allowing me to believe that if he wanted to show off he could singlehandedly, machine by machine, sew Roger Gold's entire suit. But Howie was not a showoff, and he would never supplant his workers like that. It was the pleasure he took that he wanted me to see, plus the performance of his latest machine and, step by step, the impeccable results. I remember saying that it was a little spooky, the way he could get inside another man's skin like that, and I remember exactly what Howie replied. It does give you a kind of rush. When Roger Gold reaches in his pocket to get a quarter, he'll find it in a coin pocket—and Howie glanced again at the spec paper I still held—exactly four inches deep. Not everyone knows that about the man. Then my cousin laughed, a sweet and sly insider's chuckle that was the very sound of kinship itself. He said, Give me your measurements, Jim, and tell me how far down you want to reach, and I'll make a suit for you.

I'd been used to having clothes—readymades—piled into my arms since I'd been a boy. The worker Doris came back, and Howie led me into his fitting room, where he produced a tape measure soft as a strip of chamois, and as skillfully as though he were feeding out fishing line in the quietest of coves, he took the measurements I shared with all other members of my species. Then he asked for my own specs, the little peculiarities that would distinguish me, say, from Roger Gold. I looked at Howie. I let my eyes linger on the blue of his longer, I suppose, than I'd looked at him before. I told him to surprise me, to make me the suit of clothes he thought I'd like or that I deserved or that best suited me.

Before he let me go, we passed by one of the cutting rooms with its long tables of design paper stretched over fabric, where the parts of a man—legs, hips, chest, shoulders, arms—were sketched out in bright blue ink ready to be cut. One of the men doing the cutting had been there since Big Howie Whalen ran the original plant. He had a kindly face, reddened cheeks, eyes moist like hanging hazel pools, and a mouth slow to lift into a smile. Howie introduced us and waited while we shook hands. Then he told his perhaps oldest and most venerable worker to take a good look at me, because they were going to make me a suit of clothes that would last me the rest of my life.

He made an impression on you, didn't he? Walter said.

Who, Howie? Of course, he always had.

No, no, the plant's oldest worker, the one with the hanging hazel pools for eyes. The one who cut the cloth to get it started.

The suit, I told Walter, arrived a month later in the mail. It was made of a smoky blue worsted, unlike the bright aqua blue outlining the body parts there on the cutting table. I stood before a full-length mirror and didn't have to view myself from every available angle to know that I'd never had a suit like this, and surely never would again. It fit so well I might not have been aware I had it on. It was as if I had stepped into an enveloping element, and when I went in search of those little individual-izing peculiarities, I found none. There was no coin pocket, neither a tab nor a flap on my hip pocket. The belt loops were proportionately spaced. The jacket lapels opened on a flawlessly flared, clean geometrical angle, and the padding in the shoulders was so subtle as to be imperceptible. It was a tailoring masterpiece, so close to perfection it almost seemed abstract, and as an abstraction I knew it would serve me wherever I finally chose to live. I took it off as if I were removing a sacramental garment and hung it in the closet, off by itself at the end.

I didn't see my cousin again until he had exhausted every possible hope of curing his brain tumor—which included a clinic in Switzerland and treatment of some sort in Japan—and word had gone out to the family at large. And over the years I'd indeed been at large, locating and relocat-ing in this enormous country of ours, staying clear of my hometown with the same silly foreboding I'd felt as a very young man. My mother still lived there. After my father died, I visited her more often than I had, but she was a strong woman who had her alliances and didn't need a crutch of a son to lean on. And my sister and her family had remained close by. I drifted. Married for two years a woman far more anxious than I to dis-entangle herself from her family, and when that ended I found myself between a great river and a great mountain range, trapped in all that space. Of course, I thought of the Frenchman for whom I'd once worked, and his perhaps real, perhaps not, peregrinations out on the Great Plains. It wasn't quite the age of Google, so short of a significant effort I didn't know how I could find out if he'd ever made that movie of his. I thought of Ellie, Hollywood Ellie, elusive at the very core of her being, and there were days and weeks when I contemplated tracking her down. She would know what had happened to the Frenchman and his movie, and even if she didn't, the mere act of cornering her would represent an accomplish-ment I could begin to build on. She'd be my trophy. I'd snag her out of the air. In the wake of a busted marriage and in all that hemispheric space,

I'd lie in wait, and while I did, it was only natural that I'd wonder about the other Ellie, now a wife and a mother, and my cousin Ellie would give me my cousin Howie, and no sooner would Howie enter my mind than I'd see him taking on the role of ringmaster in one of those small, outsourced Latin American towns, wheels of the young, the middle-aged, and the elderly turning on themselves, festively promenading, making of their own centripetal pull a cause for celebration. I would gaze off into all that Great Plains space, with nothing to circle and nowhere to cohere, and say, of course, of course.

And that was when word reached me at large and I quickly made my way back to the Whalens' hometown.

My first shock came not in seeing Howie, but Laurie. I stood before their house, their lakeside mansion, and she looked like a cleaning lady who'd gotten off her knees to come to the door. She wore a dark skirt with cloudy smears like detergent stains. A dull mustard-colored sweater. Her lips were dry, and the area under her eyes so washed out that the eyes themselves had a ghostly kind of calm. There was real anger, real bitterness in her voice, but the eyes invited you to stare through them.

Laurie, I said, how are you?

Me? You didn't come all this way to see me.

Both of you, I protested.

It's not Howie, Jim.

I leaned in to kiss her. She stiffened and her cheek went cold. It was yesterday's perfume, or the day before's.

What do the doctors say? I asked.

She responded with a growling, vituperative laugh down in her throat.

It's okay, Laurie, I tried to soothe her.

No, it's not, Jim, she responded.

Will he know me?

Of course he'll know you. You just won't know him.

She pointed down a long dark hall where they'd set up a room for him and a nurse was in charge. It was when I'd started down that hall that Laurie stated, as though for the record, flatly and bitterly plain, That man in there is not my husband.

I paused in my narrative, as I had paused walking down that hall. And Walter intervened. He repeated what Laurie had said. Had he heard correctly? If Howie Whalen wasn't her husband, then who was he? He was sick and dying and now she was disowning him? What could she possibly have meant?

I said, I think in her despair she still meant that there were no words.

And since there weren't, Walter took up my train of thought, she could in effect turn him over to you? Trusting that you could supply the words?

I took a long pull off my bourbon. I'd need to rectify something for Walter. At this late hour of the second evening, I'd need not to change but to adjust my course, which would represent a change, no disguising it, and which Walter, a lawyer alert to the slightest variation in any witness's testimony, would recognize at once.

There's something you need to know, I said. I was fascinated by my cousin, and from a certain distance I much admired him. A huge success story, both in that town and as he took the town with him out into the world. But I was not close to him.

And Walter surprised me by professing not to be surprised. I understand, he said, he was a childhood pal.

No, not really, I said. Not even that. As a child he sat on a source of fabulous wealth, and he could do things other less favored children couldn't do, but I'm not even sure I liked him, and half the time I didn't believe him myself. He was handsome, he'd married a beautiful woman, but in many ways he was a joke who kept having all this business success so finally I had to conclude the joke was on me. And they loved him in the town.

But you didn't? Walter said.

I don't know. Maybe I did. I suppose I wanted to, if only for Rosalyn's sake.

And perhaps it was more for Rosalyn's sake than Laurie's or Howie's or my own that I continued walking to the end of that hall, gave a courtesy knock on the door to alert them I was coming, and stepped into the room as the nurse finished wiping some pablum-like substance off the side of Howie's mouth, in her haste leaving a small smear. Then the nurse left the two of us alone. My cousin sat on a sofa. He had a grotesquely swollen head and an expression in his eyes of some animal wildness drugged into docility. He greeted me with a ponderous grin, which was like a boat capsizing along the line of his mouth. His real grin, his natural grin, had been one of his greatest assets. It had disarmed businessmen all over the world.

My mouth must have fallen open, because he said, as though to reassure me, God has been good to me, Jim.

I said, Howie, I wish there was something I could do.

It's in God's hands now, he said. Then he added in a voice that was a weight-bearing crawl, It's a good deal.

His brows were shaggy, protuberant. He tried to wink.

That man in there is not my husband.

I tried—and failed—to keep Laurie Whalen's bitterness out of my voice. Howie, I said, God got the best of the deal by far.

The sinking grin and the anesthetized eyes—it was like looking through bars at some lethargic animal in a zoo. God's a better businessman, he managed to quip.

Don't give up yet, Howie, I pleaded in a near-whisper. It was very quiet in the house.

His smile was an uncoordinated bunching of muscles over the lower half of his face. I've seen too many doctors, he said. There's not a cure left. He sat in a kind of bearish slump, which he tried to rouse himself out of. Time comes to talk to the preacher and face it. When you do that and add it all up—

I cut him off, surprising myself. It doesn't "add up." Howie, Laurie's not "facing it."

That stopped him. That took that groggy sublimity out of his tone and his heavy-browed eyes. I understood then why it was so quiet. He was off down a long hall, being attended to by a nurse, a mansion's length away from the woman who refused to recognize him as her husband. He needed that distance. Without it, Laurie might burst in at any moment and demand from him a confession. And what would he have to confess? That he'd married her under false pretenses? That when the town turned out to see them wed, that when I flew in from LA to usher guests up the aisle, it would end like this, in disfiguring death halfway down life's path, with money everywhere she looked, millions of it, currency from around the world, pesos, francs, yen, pounds, and none of it worth any more than a Confederate dollar.

Talk to her, Jim. She's lost her faith. Make her see . . . the large picture.

I smiled. I shook my head. I placed a hand on one of his, wasted, inert, but not at rest. I had seen that hand catching fish and I had seen it stitching a hip pocket. With masterful sleight of hand, Howie had run a tape measure up and around and over my entire body.

Reverend Crawly, he went on, won't have any luck with her now. She doesn't want to see his face.

I'm not sure she wanted to see mine.

Just talk to her.

What am I supposed to tell her, Howie?

A heavy swaying of the head. He was shaking it. You're family, he said.

I don't deny it.

Tell her it all adds up. Tell her to have faith.

Faith in what?

He made me wait. A beat, a second, a third. Then he uttered out of a cavernous quiet, Faith in God.

The same God who did this to you?

He didn't answer my question. The figure who sat before me, hulking there, both smaller and larger than I remembered him being, might have belonged to another species entirely, even though the smile he gave me in that moment had a brightness about it, and a warmth, perhaps even a blessedness, once you got past the deformities of the flesh.

I gave in to him. The tears came and I bowed my head. I told my cousin Howard Whalen I would talk to his wife and that I'd be back to tell him what she said. I hugged his sloping shoulders and peptalked him into holding on. I called him Little Howie, delayed just a moment until I was sure he'd heard me and perhaps brought to mind the children we'd been, then I turned and walked out the door.

And down that long hall, Walter said. Let me guess. You didn't see him again, did you?

No, I said.

Or his wife.

Not until the funeral.

Did you try?

I didn't go through the house looking. I did step into their living room. It looked as if it had never been lived in. The long glimmering drapes were closed and the tabletops free of dust. The cream-colored carpet looked pristine. The smell was of some mildly deodorizing wax. I could have stood there and waited for Laurie and the children to appear. Instead, I left.

And failed to keep your promise.

And spared Laurie Whalen that empty plea to keep the faith.

You know, Jim, Walter said in that first brightening of the darkness that a late moon brings, I hate to judge her at this distance and after all these years, but your Laurie Whalen did not behave well.

Not "my" Laurie Whalen, I said.

The only one I know.

She was devastated, what can I say?

And the children were not really children by that time.

Only Joey, the youngest. Maybe twelve then, thirteen.

Did they even see their father? That man in there their mother no longer claimed as her husband. Just how long was that hall?

Long, I said, and dark, with doors down its length, all of them closed.

He had a brain tumor, for Christ's sake! Walter erupted. It's sad, it happens, tumors can leave you deformed, and all those attempts to burn it out of him—

For those of us who'd known him before, I broke in, with no real hope of making myself understood, it was as though he were under attack by some higher power. As though the chain of being had been reversed and he were evolving backwards.

Still, "That man in there is not my husband" is harsh. Could she have been referring to some sort of last-minute conversion, that he was transformed and deformed in that way?

Walter, it's late.

I know it is. Don't leave him unburied, don't leave his widow and children stranded like that.

Not to speak of the town.

Or the town.

But I've already told you. It wasn't only family or the town. It's just possible one man's death might take a whole family down with it, a family might grieve and go into an irreversible decline, but in Howie's case a certain portion of the world gathered to see him off. Closed casket, of course. No one had to risk losing their memory of the man.

You're forgetting Aunt Rosalyn and Big Howie.

No, I'm not.

Well . . .

It *is* late, Walter.

It killed Big Howie, didn't it?

Not at once.

Walter picked it up. Big Howie had to go back to take his son's place in the plant, but this time his son wasn't off on a business trip, or taking a break to hunt long-horned sheep in the Rockies. The Rockies?

What difference does it make? I said. The Canadian Rockies. I don't know.

Or fish for marlins on the high seas.

We never talked about that.

I'm trying to imagine the father becoming the son, that father and that son. I'm trying to imagine Big Howie Whalen, with all that girth and all that swagger, anywhere other than in their small town. Trying to drive his big black Cadillac, for instance, through the crowds of those promenading townsfolk down there in Bella Whatever-it-was.

You don't have to imagine. It never happened.

Or even Big Howie Whalen back at the plant. After the workers had had a long, sweet dose of the son. Straying over into customized clothes. One pocket, one belt loop at a time. Roger Gold. Who the hell was Roger Gold? And what was Whalen Apparels's oldest employee doing over there anyway? The one with the hanging hazel pools for eyes . . .

On a lake this small, surrounded by towering spruce, a crescent moon like the one we had rising could cast little light, and that not for long. Walter Kidman was not looking at me but straight out at the water, peering into its luminous darkness as intently as Howie Whalen might have when he sought that filigreeing of ripples that told him the minnows were on the run and the bass were about to feed. For the thirty, forty seconds, for the minute the feeding lasted, there would be a lavish brocade of foam flashing in the moon before the moon passed over and the bass went deep. But this was a pickerel lake and Walter was hunting fool's gold.

I put a stop to it. I put it on the clock. The day before he died, I told Walter, Big Howie had a premonition. He called on Reverend Crawly in the church and described to him a general weakening all over his body, which he likened to a battery running down, but also to a not entirely unwelcome physical diminishment, a certain lightness on his feet and in his head, as if he were abandoning the outposts of his body and pulling in around the smaller-sized man he'd once been. Why hadn't he gone straight to the hospital, a concerned Reverend Crawly wanted to know, and Big Howie told him because what he was describing felt more like a blessing than an affliction, more in a preacher's line of work than an

MD's. Perhaps even a sign. We must become as children again. How small do you have to be to pass through the eye of a needle and into heaven? Yes, there were signs, and, yes, a lightening of the physical load we carry through this darkened world might be interpreted as a sign of the spirit rising, still, Reverend Crawly would later tell Rosalyn, he had urged her husband to check into the hospital to ease his way to the moment they both knew was coming, and after receiving the good reverend's blessing, Big Howie assured him he would. He'd lost a son, a terrible blow, a son who had exceeded the founding father's dreams for himself in every possible way, but Big Howie had reasons to live, a daughter he'd been given with whom he'd reprised his son's upbringing and two little daughters of hers. If he pictured himself as a mountain, he had an apron of kinfolk spilling down on all sides. He had reasons to stand broad and stand tall. But it was such a blessed relief to pull in, to go small, that regardless of whether the lightness was in his flesh or only in his head, he couldn't bring himself to sound the alarm.

The day after he'd seen the reverend, he put in a couple of hours at the plant, still the businessman, still money-minded enough that if you'd given him irresistible odds he'd make it through the week, the month, and the year ahead, he'd have known to decline the bet—he'd become that light on his feet, that close to walking on air. Arriving home for lunch, he fell on the walk leading up to the kitchen door, and rather than try to get up and continue on, he managed to roll over so that he was looking up through the limbs of trees to where birds, the lightest-boned creatures alive, flitted from branch to branch. His trees, his birds, his sky, his dome of heaven shining through the branches. That was where his wife found him, the dome of his still enormous belly earthbound like the rest of him, and with far fewer mourners in attendance they buried him beside his son. Curiously, though, members of the black community turned out in numbers they hadn't for the son, as if only now did they know for a certainty that with the progenitor's death the Whalen chapter in the town's history was done. They could pay their tribute and turn a page.

Turn a page? Walter wouldn't let it go. By my count you've still got four younger Whalens left. And then there's Ellie.

It's late, I reminded him.

I know it is. And we're getting older by the minute. A touch more?

A touch.

Walter poured, then reminded me, We got a late start. You wanted to hear my unsociable neighbor play that first chord on his cello, remember, before you started it again.

I won't make that mistake a second time.

So there *is* more. We're not done. It doesn't end with Big and Little Howie Whalen lying side by side as the world files by.

I didn't say anything. Curiously, I thought of my ex-wife with whom Walter and his wife had paired me up. Or maybe not so curiously since, once we'd divorced, Elaine had taken on the role of wise friend in my life, a counselor of sorts, and I the role in hers of someone who divulges what might bring pleasure or relief or modest intrigue but spares her all the rest. Had I told her the story of the Whalens, both the long-haired and short-haired versions? Walter, a smart cross-examiner, had wanted to know. No, maybe snatches here and there, anecdotes, if the family were a mosaic, then a chip or two to represent the Whalens, Rosalyn's laugh, the aunt of mine named Rosalyn who laughed up the world's riches, very modest riches by the world's standards, but in the eyes of a boy . . .

No, it doesn't end there, I told Walter. How could it? A second funeral so soon after the first. The family at large now with two big holes in it, pouring back into town. My mother was still alive. Only Rosalyn and my mother would get the joke, which no one uttered, I'm sure, and which wasn't a joke at all but a terrible play on words. Two deaths, one so soon after the other. The Whalen family was . . .

Snakebit? Walter said.

If I could, Walter, I'd ask for that story to be struck from the record.

Too late now. And, Walter reminded me, there's more.

I nodded. My widowed mother, I went on, could look after herself, fiercely if she had to. But not Rosalyn. I held my aunt. There was nothing I could say. And when she laughed, which was really the only way she knew to expel breath, nothing came out. There was still money to burn. And grandchildren. Eventually Howie's children would each take their share of the money and run, at least three of them did. For a time Laurie assumed her husband's place at the plant, dressed in a pin-stripe suit common enough on Wall Street but pretty much unprecedented down there. Soon competitors would spring up, both in town and in towns close by, and Laurie would be hard pressed. Apparently she married somebody, but it ended before it began. She left and came back, it's an old story. She claimed that before she'd sell the house she and Howie had had built, she'd tear it down, which was what she did, and then sold the land as five lakefront lots. Her elder son, Alan, lived with her for a while and it's possible nursed her through a bout with drugs. She put on weight, went through a period of accelerated aging, and then tried to tuck and facelift it all away. I can't imagine it worked. I didn't see her again. When I had a chance to, I declined.

Really? Declined, you say?

Declined. I didn't bite, Walter. I had Rosalyn to worry about, and Rosalyn had Ellie.

To worry about or to bring some comfort to her old age? And two granddaughters, you said.

Both blonde, both pretty. Two little sisters who got along, very polite little girls, who took care of each other and never fought, not that I saw, and when they visited their grandmother took turns in trying to lift her spirits and keep them lifted so that Rosalyn wouldn't see . . .

You're asking me to guess?

I'm asking you to go to bed.

But if that's what you were asking, I'd guess the little girls banded together and behaved the way they did because all they saw around them was grief and mourning and parents who fought. I'd guess that Ellie had married someone who professed to adore her the way her father did but who had his own agenda. Or she'd married someone who quickly diminished in stature once he'd fathered the two girls, a man who couldn't fish and couldn't hunt, had never stood on the line of scrimmage and taken his licks, and who couldn't even defend himself from his wife's attacks, if that was what she chose to do, so she simply seethed, and the little girls went off and tried to make their grandmother happy, the way little boys might go off and build a clubhouse, a little fortress to hide in and defend . . .

Ellie married a young lawyer fresh out of school, I said. He went to work for the plant, handling their legal affairs and keeping an eye on the books. Thin and fit, a runner type. Modest achievable ambitions, but he wouldn't be cheated. I didn't dislike him. Even when it was rumored he'd scooped off more than his share, I didn't hold it against him. When Little Howie died, then Big Howie did, Ellie's husband was smart enough to know that together the two deaths would form a black hole in the family. So he pocketed what he thought was due him, perhaps a little more, and stepped free. Ellie took to drink and got sucked in. Rosalyn, not knowing where else to turn, called on me, and down I went. What more can I say, Walter? She called, and just like a child I went to see what she would now pile in my arms. That's it. Nothing else. Moon's down. Goodnight.

III

My grandmother—my mother's mother—had been a flirt. Before she died she sat me down and told me her life's story, by which she meant her love life's story. So there would be some record. So someone could smile, nod approvingly, and finally applaud. I was to write it all down, and I assured her I would. There was even a way I could quantify her success. Did I know what a Kodak party was? My grandmother had been a Gibson girl, that had been her style of dress, with long flowing skirts, ruffled blouses, a cameo brooch at her throat, and a pompadour wave in her luxuriant auburn hair. Back then, she said, the Kodak company had begun to manufacture their Brownie cameras, and they made so many of them, they could afford to sell them cheap, so cheap, in fact, that a young man of ordinary means could afford to buy one and invite a young lady of his choice out for an afternoon of picture taking in the country. An afternoon because that was when the light was right—remember, there were no flashbulbs back then—and out in the country because that was where the most scenic pictures could be taken. My grandmother, whose Christian name was Grace, chose a snapshot from a stack she kept in what looked like a jewelry box and handed it to me. A slender, tall, and very attractive young woman hung out by one arm from a windmill and allowed the wind to blow her skirt, blouse, and upswept hair. Behind her stretched the countryside. Grace, the young woman swinging out from the windmill, had been on a Kodak party, and here was the proof. In the picture her mouth was open, as though she was savoring the breeze, and with her free hand she was waving, presumably to her date, the picture taker, to indicate what a fine time she was having. The Kodak party ended when the roll of film had been shot and the light had faded. At that point it was customary for the young man to present the Brownie camera to the young woman, as a memento of the occasion, but it was equally customary for the young man to keep the roll of film. When he'd had it developed, he could use the snapshots as bait for a second date, which, depending on the young woman's curiosity and her vanity, she could accept or not. My grandmother told me she collected Brownie cameras back then and invited me to imagine her bedroom at home and her dorm room at school crowded with black boxes. Add them up and I could give a number to it all.

She thought of those cameras the night she met my grandfather, a preacher twenty years her senior that she and a girlfriend had gone to hear. He was something of a celebrity. He helped organize First Christian Churches, and he traveled a three-state area of the South preaching inaugural sermons. That night—it was a Saturday night and his was the only show in town—he was preaching a sermon from Saint Paul on the sanctifying power of marriage: "For the unbelieving husband is sanctified by the wife, the unbelieving wife is sanctified by the husband: else were your children unclean; but now they are holy." The girlfriend Grace had come with kept tittering under her breath, He's looking at you! Oooh, he's looking straight at you! Grace, in her Gibson Girl attire and with her hair thrown up in a bouffant wave, tried to hush her friend, and she tried letting her eyes stray to the stained glass windows, where the early evening light lit up a depiction of Joseph and his coat of many colors, but the preacher with his eyes as black as onyx kept calling her back. Grace claimed she realized then what it was she liked about the picture taking. It was that moment when her admirer had to lower his eyes if he was going to locate her in the viewfinder; it was the sensation of being admired and admired, then left alone on that stage of one. Those Kodak cameras that she had hoarded were taking their revenge. Her flirtatious girlhood was about to come to an end.

The scene at the church door, when the preacher took her slender hand in his broad, Bible-gripping one and said what he had to say, was anticlimactic. He said, loud enough for the girlfriend to hear, and certain prominent citizens of the town as well: Young lady, I am going to marry you. With so many witnesses present, if he hadn't married her it might have been construed as a breach of promise. But Grace believed all had been determined the first time she'd strolled out into the country-side, climbed up a windmill, and then swung out so that the sun and the breeze could catch her blouse and hair and light up her smile. Click. And he really was the most handsome man in the world.

Would I remember all that?

Because of their age difference I was the only grandchild my grand-father would live to see. He would, I was told, wave me off quickly, afraid that too prolonged an exposure to his cadaverous state might mark me for life. I had no memory of him, cadaverous or otherwise, so I took my grandmother at her word. He'd been the most handsome man in the world.

My grandmother gave him four daughters, collectively known as the Pritchard girls. My mother was the first. Esther, a biblical name that my grandmother was led to believe meant "morning star," and a beautiful morning star at that. My grandmother didn't have it in her to be a disci-plinarian, and my grandfather was frequently away preaching those inau-gural sermons, so it fell to my mother to be my grandfather's proxy at home. To her kid sisters she preached the straight and narrow—but with a provocative wink and mischievous grin. Ruth, the exiled, the faithful, was the next-born. She had a sweet, unmarred voice and, along with a girlfriend, sang love songs on the radio. When the war came she mar-ried a sailor, and when the war was over her sailor husband took a job with an oil company that had him transferred over the map for most of his working life. His wife, never a troublemaker, utterly compliant, faith-fully followed. The third of the Pritchard girls, Lily, a flower of a girl, was a preacher's daughter in reverse and made enough trouble for all her sisters combined. She joined the WACs and served as part of the mail detail in the reconquered Philippines, surely sorting letters to some sol-diers no longer among the living. Demobilized in San Diego, she took a year to get back East, a year's worth of vacation days she claimed she'd saved up, and arrived home raw-boned and with a booming laugh. Lily kept the current flowing in the Pritchard family, and the fourth daugh-ter, after which Grace, known to all by then as Mama Grace, told her husband she had tried to give him that son he wanted, tried and tried, and was finally forced to admit defeat, was my aunt Rosalyn, a rose that faithfully bloomed each year and never stopped giving off the most win-

Lamar Herrin

ning of scents. Born laughing, but unlike Lily's laugh, which could knock
you down, or Ruth's laugh, which was like a mild breeze, or my mother
Esther's laugh, which sized up a scene as she happily prepared to take it
on, Rosalyn's laugh rose out of the goodness of her nature, pure and simple, self-replenishing and available to all—until it wasn't anymore. Until
it stopped and everything around her turned grim.

There were many photographs, countless if you included the snapshots, but there were formal family photographs, too, and in them my
grandfather sat erect in a high-backed chair, with a lean, aquiline face,
a full head of still black hair and, yes, very dark eyes. My grandmother
stood, matronly and a bit dazed, at his shoulder. She seemed stranger to
me than the grandfather I had no memory of. Her daughters were artfully positioned around her. None of them was smiling. These would be
happy—happily engaged—women, but they all looked as if they had their
minds elsewhere and were standing sentinel duty until the photographer
dismissed them.

Scroll formal family photographs back through your head and there
comes a moment when something needs to be done. You can't just stand
there as stricken-seeming as the subjects of the photographs themselves.
You can't call out, "And action," as a film director might, for the actors
are all dead. Take a stack of those photographs in your hands and, riffling
through, you might bring them to a flickering sort of life, nothing more.
If screen porches weren't a thing of the past and taletellers so far flung,
you might gather in the evenings on screen porches and tell old tales
until the figures rose before you. Or to be up to date you could transfer
all the family photographs onto some sort of smart phone—an irreversible transfer, a click away from cyberspace—and then to outsmart it you
could throw that phone into the deepest lake you could find, or the one
closest at hand. You could sit there and watch it sink, wait for the bass or
the pickerel to rise. Listen for the farewell wail of the loon.

I held Walter off as long as I could, and when I couldn't any longer I
played dumb.

So what did she want? Walter said.

I'm sorry?

What did your aunt Rosalyn call you down there to do?

You'll have to forgive me, Walter.

For what, Jim? A memory lapse? A failure of nerve?

It was going to be a fishing story.

In which you never wet a line.

You're right. Not in the lake where it counted.

We could take the canoe out on this one.

We could.

Catch a pickerel or two. Or I could go get the bottle.

I've had enough bourbon to last me for a year. Anyway, I thought we finished it.

A second bottle.

And after the second there'd be a third? You weren't planning to ply me with liquor?

Walter gave out a thumping laugh, to add to the other weekend sounds we heard from over the water. Up the lake things were stirring. Voices, dog barks, sawing, hammering, digging sounds, motor-free sounds of manual labor, doors opened to be closed, a child, a grandchild out in the water, snatches of recorded music turned up to be turned down, not yet a live cellist next door. People pulling in and pulling out in their cars, loading and unloading, and down at our end of the lake Walter and I sat there in front of what WPA workers had or had not wrought. I let out breath as quietly as though we were hunters lying in wait. Then I laughed, humbly, as though acknowledging the everlasting absence of game.

My aunt, I said, the youngest, was going to be the first to die.

You mean Rosalyn, don't you?

Youngest of the Pritchard girls. Yes.

And your favorite.

I loved them all. I was *fond* of them all. If we had world enough and time, I would tell you all their stories, but . . . yes, Rosalyn.

And you said she called you down there to ask a favor. She "called on you" I believe were your exact words.

You have a keen memory, Walter.

In my profession . . .

Well, you also have your lapses. Sometimes at the poker table the camaraderie gets the best of you, you know. I probably shouldn't tell you this, but things can get a bit too chummy for your own good.

So you pay a bit for the chumminess, that's all right. Like tipping the dealer a chip from your winnings. The poker table's not a court of law. So it wasn't just to say goodbye.

Goodbye? You mean because of her illness? No, no, she wouldn't talk about that. She knew what was eating away at her—I assume she did. I had only seen her once since the week Big Howie fell over dead outside their kitchen door, it had been . . .

You're counting the years?

Yes, six or seven. But my mother kept me informed. The business was unraveling. Those offshore plants had become independent businesses of their own, which is the way it was supposed to work and the way Howie—Little Howie—had set it all up. The offshore plants serve a sort of apprenticeship to the imperial power, then when they've learned the trade and the imperial power begins to weaken, they're equipped to strike out on their own. But in the Whalens' hometown it was . . . messy. It all fragmented, little plants, niche apparel, exercise outfits, unisex stuff, children's clothes. The meat and potato days were done. Head-to-foot clothing, twenty-four hours a day, that was over.

And the money?

No, there was money.

And houses, lake houses, seaside houses, boathouses, bass boats and speedboats and cabin cruisers and . . . black Cadillacs?

There was money and there was property, Walter. Little Howie had known what was coming, and so had Big Howie. Rosalyn was the soul of generosity, but she was no fool. The Whalen fortune was not enlarging, but it was enormous enough already. Little Howie had put aside his millions for Laurie and their children, and Rosalyn had made sure her granddaughters, Ellie's daughters, would be set for life the day they turned eighteen. That wasn't the problem.

Money wasn't?

Well, it's always a problem, especially if you've got so much you don't know what to do with it.

I wouldn't know.

If at the end it's a load you can't get out from under, not entirely, so just when you want to shuck it all off and rise up like Big Howie, you stumble and fall down. Maybe the curse comes then.

An embarrassment of riches?

Or an affliction.

You haven't mentioned Ellie, have you?

No, not yet.

Only that her marriage had fallen apart and she'd taken to drink.

"Taken to drink" has such an old-fashioned ring to it, doesn't it, Walter? Almost comforting, as if you were snuggling up to a bottle. As if you'd "taken a shine" to it.

I'll say this once, Walter said, even though I think I've said it before. In spite of me prodding you maybe a little more than I should—after all, cross-examination is part of my trade too—don't talk about this if you don't want to.

I paused. I said to myself: That's a friend willing to let you off the hook. That's what friends do. Then I let out a breath I hadn't been aware I was holding. If I don't talk about it, I said, what else are we going to do? Go canoeing, go swimming, go fishing, or go sightseeing? Go find some more WPA artifacts? Start with that little bridge down at the end of the lake?

No, Walter said, rising above my tone, which was a mix of sarcasm and entreaty, I'd drive us over to Lake George. The Sagamore? Have you seen it? Magnificent! A great crescent-shaped affair, every window with a lake view, right out of *The Great Gatsby*. You haven't seen it, have you?

Safe to say, not a WPA project. Or maybe that's where the workers bunked while they built this sweet little place.

Unlikely. I wouldn't be surprised if FDR and Eleanor stayed there, though.

Making a youthful effort, Walter hoisted himself up out of his chair. We could have lunch there, mahogany fixtures, sterling silver, Prince Albert china, white tablecloths under the chandeliers.

Back before we were born, you say?

Back before Eleanor was born—and almost before FDR.

And how's their chili?

Jim, maybe we should play some gin rummy. It wouldn't hurt you to win a hand or two.

Sit down, Walter, I said.

It took him a moment. He turned away from me and looked out over the water. I wondered how long this piece of property had been in his family. Had he himself been a boy here, and in bringing me here for this long secluded weekend did he risk giving something of that boyhood up? I didn't know about Walter. I didn't know if he'd dived off that dock, splashed in this lake, hooted and hollered and made so much noise his father had to come out and shake some sense into him. If he'd scared off the fish or if he'd paddled out there and silently lured them back into the fold. He hadn't said. He'd taken a little pickerel off the hook for me, but I had done all the talking and he had patiently, more than patiently, eagerly and even complicitously, heard me out.

Get away for a long weekend, he'd said. Do a little fishing and drinking and card playing, in the quietest and most secluded place on the map. My ex-wife Elaine had smiled as if the notion—a couple of guys, a cabin in the Adirondacks, drinking and card playing at all of that—was inspired. You two should, she said, as if she knew something I didn't, which she undoubtedly did, many things. We didn't end our marriage, not really, we ended our cohabitation. We each needed periods to look inside, take stock and discover what was worth passing on, and then we made dates. We made love, too, not without passion but in a certain commemorative spirit, you could say with a commemorative passion, but which could come with a real hunger attached. You can commemorate the past more passionately than you'd lived it. It seemed contradictory, but in our case it was true, and I think we got the divorce just to get the state out of the way, with all its side issues and annoying impositions. Then at last things stood out clearly. Divorced, and an unobstructed avenue opened between us.

Elaine and I had met in Walter and Molly's backyard, on their patio, where we'd been invited to supper, and after supper, with a conversational current sufficiently alive, our hosts had disappeared into the house with dirty dishes and not come back out, as if Elaine and I were prize livestock, somewhat past its prime, who'd needed a little prodding, a little pep talk, before we'd been left penned to breed. It was so obvious it was touching, and it's tempting to say to please our friends we'd paired up on the spot. At least we'd both understood that that was what the evening was designed to accomplish. Just before we divorced, we'd had Walter and Molly over to dinner and broken the news of what we were going to do. Unpenned, but eternally grateful, we insisted, to our friends. I was still grateful. I loved Elaine. I depended on her. She scared me a little, the access she had to me, that we had to each other. And, surely, we must have reasoned without speaking the words that access like that could not be available on a twenty-four-hour basis. To save it, to assure it, we would have to portion it out in moderate doses and make it last. Something like that must have gone through our minds. The joy of seeing her and then the joy of knowing that that joy was renewable, that it was a joy that might even be outdone, improved upon, as long as we did not do it to death. Something like that.

Had I told Elaine my short-haired dog story? Walter had wanted to know. Well, why hadn't I? But he had not persisted. And who's to say the story was not apocryphal? Why wasn't there a snapshot of the dead dog, the dead snake, and the miraculously spared little boy? Had no one had a Brownie camera during an outing in the country like that? Two pairs of lovers and no Brownie camera?

Sit down, Walter, I said.

When I drove up that drive to the Whalen house, I told him, with no Howies left, with little Ellie grown up and gone, and with my aunt wasting away, it would be hard to express the desolation of the scene, even though if you had been with me you might have been charmed. It was a summer day, with the heat in the pines, the sort of still, scented heat that makes you believe summer will never end. In the patches of sunlight, pine needles lay orange on the ground, which was a reddish clay with glinting specks of mica, and the birdsong at that midday hour was a subdued, multi-throated warbling overshot by the long strident caw of jays. The immediate area around the house had always been kept kudzu-free by a succession of gardeners, and that was still the case. Rosalyn did not meet me at the door. A black woman named May did, who had been with the family for years and was the daughter of the man named Johnny who had been the groom for Little Howie's ponies and horses, back when there'd only been a prince and no princess. It was May who told me, You sure are welcome, you sure are, then showed me to the sunroom, air-conditioned now, where Phil Hodge and I had once sat with Little Howie, and where Big Howie had later spread out a map to show us where the fish were biting and where we could and could not go. At that same table and under overarching plants that had grown as the family had diminished, Rosalyn sat waiting for me. From her vantage point she would have seen me driving up and surely would have known the desolation I had felt. Favorite nephews and favorite aunts had a special bond. She did not get up. She said, Jimmy, Jimmy, and emptied out what was left of her laughter, as I leaned in to kiss her cheek, which was drawn but not yet slack. She was ill, but not incapacitated. She could have gotten up and met me at the door. But she pulled me in, all the way in. This had been a fishing family, and since she was all that was left of it, there would be a tradition to uphold—

Ellie was left, don't forget her, Walter reminded me. And according to her father, she was catching fish right out of the cradle.

I haven't forgotten Ellie, I said. I mean of the family before then. Before Ellie.

Before you were run out of town for terrifying her with your beard, you mean.

Or traumatizing her, I said.

One or both, Walter said, otherwise you wouldn't have been down there then, would you? You wouldn't have been "called on."

That point is very well taken, I told Walter, who was once again engaged. But not so that he couldn't have been lured away. Had some up-the-lake neighbors paddled down to socialize, Walter would have socialized. He had a capacity, a remarkable capacity, which meant in a court of law he could make a good show of defending anybody.

You could see it all in Rosalyn's eyes, I said. They had always been a bright blue, a translucent, northern lake blue. I assume there were cataracts that needed to be removed and she saw no point in it. The blue was gray now. More accurately, her eyes were a tarnished steel color, and the longer you looked into them, the more you realized they were fixed on one entrenched idea.

Reading the expressions in eyes doesn't always get you closer to the truth, Walter reminded me. But you already know that, Jim.

Maybe not in court, I said, but what happened in that sunroom is essential if this story is going to make sense, and that look in her eyes was part of it. Shall I go on?

Shall I bring the bottle out? Walter said, in part to lighten the tone, but he meant it.

Not yet, I said.

I hadn't seen Ellie since she divorced her husband. Scott was his name. They'd had their fights, but no more than a lot of other couples I'd known with two young kids to care for and egos to trim, and they'd been blessedly free of money worries, except the worry of what to do with so much. Ellie had gotten tall. Height in the family would harken back to Mama Grace and her preacher husband James Pritchard, the grandfather I'd been named for, but Ellie was so late coming to the last of the Pritchard girls that that particular lineage might have seemed more legendary than real. Tall and, unlike her grandmother, thin. She'd passed through a stage when if her chin had not been quite so prominent she would have been considered lovely. The broad and unlined forehead, the high cheekbones, the high and elegantly bridged nose. And then the eyes, in the right light a rich mix of amber and honey and maybe even a tigerish yellow, golden eyes, or greenish eyes with a certain golden cast, large and almond-shaped and, as they used to say, tempting to dwell in for a while.

Walter chuckled. If I could read his thoughts, he was asking himself when was the last time any man could be said to dwell in a woman's eyes and not be laughed out of town. And if he could read mine, he might have understood he was being asked to believe there were still a few places, little retrograde pockets down south, for instance, where that sort of thing went on.

The Pritchard girls were all known for their beauty—even Lily, as rough-cut as she might have appeared to be—and Ellie was one of them. Her chin, though, was weathered-looking enough that I could imagine her out in a fishing boat with her father or in a cornfield on a cold morning waiting for the dogs to flush out pheasant and quail. Big Howie, whose own chin was puffy, boyish and cleft, had left his mark on his daughter there. She'd been a daddy's girl for a period of her life and taken it on the chin.

Walter's chuckle betrayed a certain impatience, I thought.

The thing about Ellie, I told Walter, is that she was a shade away from being a lot things. A shade less hungry for whatever it was she imagined she didn't have and I could even see her as a nun. Those eyes with that golden light looking heavenward or cast down.

Which would make her a big daddy's girl, Walter took his liberty. The biggest daddy of all. More to the point, what drink had Ellie taken to? Bourbon? Had her daddy left his mark on her there?

As I recall it was scotch and not bourbon. And maybe in the summer, like the rest of us, gin and tonics. But . . .

But?

That hard drinking that wasted her away and left her crawling for her life only came later, if you'll permit me to go on. Should I go on?

It's your call, Jim.

Up over the armrests of our Adirondack chairs we sat looking at each other for a moment. Walter had astute eyes, never idle, the brows unruly little arcs of wiry gray hair like the hair on his head. He was on alert, always on alert, but rarely on attack, and then the injustice had to be grave, an insult to one of the few things that all humans should want to hold dear. I had nothing but good things to say about Walter Kidman. Go with him, Elaine had advised. I felt a surge of something rising up in me, some strong mix of feelings made one. I felt sorry for, of all things, this little lake, on which canoers had begun to paddle as though on an early evening stroll. I remembered that look in the eye of the pickerel I'd caught as Walter removed the hook. It said you're out of place. It said we don't fish the jumps up here. A moment's wildness is no excuse. That's not who we are.

I nodded to Walter and continued, It was that look in my aunt's eye, and it was the look that was no longer there. The laughing look I'd known her by was gone, and what had replaced it was as hard as old steel. She said, Jimmy, I have something I want you to do, it's a favor, and the lilt that had gone out of her voice as much as said she would never again be piling things so abundantly in my arms. She needed a man's favor now, from a family's firstborn. I won't say Ellie has fallen in love, she went on. I don't believe she has. But I will say that she has fallen under the spell of this man she works with . . . And I, of course, knew nothing about Ellie working, since my mother had not informed me about that, which was a curious lapse because news of anything that Ellie Whalen publicly did in her small town, such as taking a job, would have spread along the family hotline and quickly reached my mother, even though she lived a state away.

Rosalyn continued, I need you to find out what you can about him, what his intentions are, and Ellie's, and then—

I stopped her. Ellie's working? I said. She's taken a job? Doing what, Rosalyn?

It's not really a job, Jimmy. It's more volunteer work through the church.

She hasn't fallen under the spell of a preacher, has she, Rosalyn? and I couldn't suppress a smile. History's not repeating itself in that way, is it?

She knew immediately what I was referring to, and she chose not to return the smile. That told me everything, that my aunt Rosalyn would disregard the sweetness of an old story surfacing two generations removed to lovingly tie another knot in the family history.

It's an organization, she said, it's run through the church, it's for poor

children, so they'll have something to do, some place to get away to, some
. . . activity, you know . . . She was struggling, she wasn't seeing it clearly.

So it's a charity, I said. Ellie and this man are working together for
a church-sponsored charity, maybe something reaching out to orphans,
and this man—

I'd stepped in, and she reacted to my tone. Her favorite nephew, I
must have sounded to her like some solicitous do-gooder willing to take
the time to lead a feeble old lady through the mists in her mind.

The mists quickly cleared. She was a Whalen, after all.

He's twice her age, Jimmy, she said. Divorced with four children, still
living with their father but pretty much grown. He hasn't been in town
long. No profession anyone knows about. I suppose his profession is charity, and I suppose he believes charity begins at home.

Have you seen him? I asked my aunt.

I have, she said, with that old steel heavy in her eyes, something
implacable there. He looks like a toad.

Rosalyn said that? Walter said.

She did.

You know the image I have of her? I'm lying there where your friend
Phil Hodge lay, and you did too as a boy, and she's standing at the end of
the bed with that tray of shaving instruments in her arms. She has this
confused look on her face, caught in crosscurrents. It's sad and it's sweet.
And she called him a toad?

She did, I said.

Her mind's made up, then, Walter said. She doesn't need you to
enlighten her. She needs you as an enforcer. Or is she hinting that the
toad's a prince in disguise and with one kiss from Ellie—

No, she wasn't hinting that. She was all but stating that the man was
a fortune hunter, and if she was hinting anything, it was that Ellie had
fallen under the spell of a father substitute, but I don't think so. I don't
think that even subconsciously Rosalyn thought that Ellie looked at this
man and saw Big Howie. She would never have called Big Howie a toad.

Mister Toad has a name?

Leland.

Leland . . . ?

Oldham.

Oldham? Old ham? Sure? You're sure Rosalyn didn't make that one up?

No, he was real, all right, and there were four young Oldhams need-ing to be fed and clothed and sent out into the world. What Rosalyn didn't know, I told Walter, was where the children's mother had gotten to, and neither, it seemed, did anyone in town. If Leland Oldham's stock in trade was giving disadvantaged children a break, it only stood to reason he'd start with his own.

A toad, I repeated to Rosalyn. Then I asked her, Does he have any other distinguishing characteristic, in case I see him around town?

I don't want you to see him, Jimmy, Rosalyn immediately made clear. I want you to go see Ellie. But not at home, I want you to take her out somewhere for lunch—

And I will, I assured my aunt, but just in case. Then it occurred to me and I stopped, not sure what if anything would be stirred up, to lighten or darken her mood, by evoking old times. For instance, I said to my aunt Rosalyn, is Leland Oldham clean-shaven?

The laugh she gave me then, Walter, said it all.

So you asked her that, in her weakened condition, and she laughed it off, water long gone under the bridge?

It was this pale, fond, sad, grateful little laugh, as if she didn't expect to have another one and at least could be grateful for that.

Poor Rosalyn. I can't get her out of my mind holding that tray, stand-ing there—*stranded* there—at the foot of your bed.

She said, Jimmy, I've forgotten what you call it, that little tuft of hair at the end of the chin.

A goatee, Rosalyn?

That's it. He has this little goatee, mostly gray hairs, the silliest little thing. Not like that beard you used to have. That was a man's beard. My father had one like that.

I've seen dozens of photographs of my grandfather James Pritchard, I assured Walter, and he was clean-shaven in every one of them.

You think she was losing it, then?

No, I think Leland Oldham had a scraggly little goatee, which she despised. I think she revered her father and she still loved me, and to save some space in her mind she put the two of us together as a way of say-ing sorry for when Big Howie had run Phil Hodge and me out of town. And in that saved space I think she knew exactly what her options were and what she wanted me to do. And she even knew the legal term for it— remember, this was some time ago, in a little town down south.

Let me guess, Walter said.

Go right ahead.

The term Rosalyn was thinking of was "prenuptial," and if you couldn't talk Ellie out of falling under the matrimonial spell of this man, you were to talk her into preserving her share of the family fortune.

Which was enormous, a pipeline coming directly from her father. You're good, Walter. With or without hindsight.

Like I told you, I feel for Rosalyn. Anyone living in Big Howie's shadow all that time, who lived to pile things into other people's arms . . .

She did not believe her daughter was in love with this toad of a man. The Pritchard girls, beautiful women all, did not fall in love with toads. But she knew her daughter was vulnerable, perhaps not that she had begun to drink as much as she had—which would be a drop compared to what she would eventually consume—but vulnerable and divorced and perhaps assuaging the pain and loss just a bit through drink, the taste for which, after all, also ran in the family. And would I get her away and talk to her and demystify her and, if she insisted on marrying the man, who was more my age, not hers, would I get her to sign what Rosalyn had, yes, come to understand was a prenuptial agreement that would protect her inheritance from Leland Oldham and his four children, with ambitions of their own, and allow her, Ellie's mother and my favorite aunt, to die in peace?

She did not say this last, she did not plead to be left to die in peace, but it was the backdrop for everything she did say. She had taken her reading of Mr. Oldham and knew him to be unscrupulous, a demon of a man with or without the goatee, and knew with a fatalistic foreboding that he would strip her daughter of everything and allow her to die a pauper. Rosalyn could provide for Ellie's two daughters in such a way that Mr. Oldham could not get at it, or so she thought, but her own daughter was trophy game, and if I could not stop the marriage, I could stop a hemorrhaging of riches, which Rosalyn was convinced would be tantamount to a hemorrhaging of her daughter's lifeblood. I had been spared by the heroic intervention of a Boston bulldog named Bing, and would I, the firstborn to the first of the Pritchard girls, repay the debt and save the life of little Ellie, the last-born to the last of those girls?

I drew a long breath and slowly let it out.

Walter said, She didn't say that part about Bing and the rattlesnake, did she? There's no final accounting for that story, is there, no firsthand authentication, I mean?

I drew another breath. Closed and opened my eyes and let them drift over the water. Such a peaceful afternoon on this lovely little lake, with the neighbors setting out in their canoes for what amounted to their early evening walk, their promenade, their paseo, and it came back to me, Little Howie watching those festive wheels turning within wheels in his little Latin American town. Bella something. He would soon step into a church and offer his thanks to the virgin overseeing it all.

I said to Walter, What she said was for me to stop it, however I could. Stop it with no questions asked. And then I added, I think you can bring that bottle out now.

Ha! Walter cheered and, ten years my junior, shot out of his chair with a youthful bound. We were drinking Jim Beam, with the Beam men from the eighteenth century on pictured on the label. It was a steady stream of Beam blood, father to son, winding up with one nephew. But Walter took his time coming back with the bottle and glasses. Perhaps he'd visited the bathroom, or up in the seclusion of the cabin had received a call, or, conceivably, had made one, in violation of an agreement we only tacitly had, and while he was gone I watched the canoe tied to his dock rocking invitingly on other canoers' small waves. One couple paddled close enough to realize it was a stranger sitting in one of Walter Kidman's chairs, and their greetings were restricted to nods. Still, I might have paddled out. There weren't that many canoes on the lake, but I could have found a way to get lost among them, and the story I had to tell could have sunk to a whisper and been borne away on the first call of a loon. Or a loon might have dived with it and left it deep down below before coming up to call again. The lakes up here, unlike the man-made ones down south, which had flooded farms and crossroad towns, cemeteries, church steeples and windmills, were mostly glacially formed, tolerable for pickerel but less so for bass, cold and probably too deep for loons to dive to the bottom. But if things did make it down there, they stayed. Last, nonswimming members of the Ice Age might still lie down there while canoes, with a sort of civil inconsequence, passed high overhead. Ice Age malefactors might. Ice Age opportunists out to deprive orphaned young women of their fortunes might lie at those icy depths. I was about to push up, I was gathering the strength to go canoeing, when Walter returned offering apologies. Nature, not his wife, had indeed called.

He poured our drinks, one on his armrest, one on mine, and we clinked

glasses. The toast had been, simply, *Salud.* But the clink of the glasses carried well in this unsultry air and, in what I took to be an unprecedented
occurrence, Walter's next-door neighbor, the cellist, Byron Wainwright,
in that moment stepped around the bushes blocking Walter's dock from
his and appeared before us.

He'd come to offer his apologies. He'd been rude the evening before,
we'd caught him, he claimed, at what he called a delicate moment during
his recital, and cued by the clinking of our glasses had come to ask if he
could join us in that drink now.

He said, his words, I didn't mean to be a crank, it was just that damned
Bach.

He had a long face, a long neck, and folds beneath his eyes. He wore
very baggy pants—I couldn't be sure they weren't pajamas—and he stood
in such a flat-footed way, it was a mystery how he'd sneaked up on us. The
truth was, without his cello he looked bereft.

In spite of his touted neighborliness, Walter seemed taken entirely
by surprise, and I stepped in to tell Byron Wainwright that I'd enjoyed
his serenade and had begun to wonder why all lakes didn't come accompanied by the sound of a cello, it was such—the word I chose was "evening"—it was such an evening-sounding sound.

Byron Wainwright might have flinched, but without a bow in his
hand all his movements seemed jittery and abrupt. I might have quali-
fied what I'd said, I might have added morning and afternoon to evening,
hence a twenty-four-hour sound, but Wainwright played at five p.m. for a
reason, and it was Walter who rose out of the chair he'd just settled back
into and invited his neighbor to occupy it while he went up to the cabin
for another glass, more ice, and one of the wicker chairs from the screen
porch.

I had not meant to suggest that Byron Wainwright had entered the
evening of his life, but I had no idea how sensitive this man was, or how
cranky he could be, and when Walter's neighbor didn't move to occupy
the vacated chair, I had to resist an urge to rise and stand beside him until
Walter returned. Wainwright, I felt sure, had ignored the invitation to sit
in Walter's chair because once down into its slanting trough he'd have to
wonder if, unassisted, he could ever get out. Entering the evening of your
life, you did not sit in Adirondack chairs, even though the Adirondacks
was where you happened to be. Or in its foothills. You did not go begging

your neighbor or your neighbor's guest to help you get upright again. You sat on your stool and played your cello, and when the time came to rise, you used your instrument, if necessary, to pole yourself up. And when your cello had suffered enough abuse, you married again, a younger woman, and humbled yourself before her. Or before your children, you learned how to sweet-talk them. Grandchildren. Here, have a piece of candy. Help the old man up and I'll play you a pretty tune.

I found myself staring holes into Bryon Wainwright, just beneath his bony, dewlapped chin. Our eyes didn't meet, but he surely felt the force of my stare with no way to know that once someone like Leland Oldham had gotten into my mind, it was impossible to get him out, although no toad of a man could be said to have a bony chin. Toads were chinless. They made croaking sounds, they didn't play a cello every evening at five. They lived in filth, in bogs, not overlooking crystal clear lakes. They ate flies, they ate bugs, overate and enlarged.

Before Walter could return, Byron Wainwright, without excusing himself, had disappeared back behind his bushes. But Byron Wainwright was not the toad. He was a lonely, ill-adapted man who was visited by penitent impulses he couldn't sustain, who worked it all out through his instrument and gave his neighbors in the canoeing stage of their lives something to look forward to each evening. And I told Walter, when he did return with another glass and ice and a crackling wicker chair under his arm, that Byron Wainwright had left as mysteriously as he'd appeared and to my regret I'd done nothing to stop him. As his proxy I had let Walter down, and I expected him to show some disappointment. But, with the wicker chair still under his arm and Wainwright's glass in his free hand, he instructed me to bring the bottle and the other glasses and get up to the cabin fast before the music began and Ellie and this Oldham fellow and my dear aunt and the story I'd begun to tell got drowned out and we'd have to start all over again.

The mistake I'd made, I explained to Walter once we reached the safety of the screen porch, was agreeing to meet Ellie in town and not somewhere a safe distance away. I'd likewise made the mistake of allowing Rosalyn to put a phone into my hand, perhaps because the past, the play of the past, had a way of charming me out of my right mind, and I remembered Big Howie, at that same table, placing a live phone in my hand so that I could call my mother and she and he could lock horns. Ellie had been a four-year-old then, a sporting little girl wide-eyed before the spectacle of her father and her uncle-aged cousin going head to head. I hadn't seen or talked to Ellie in years. She had not been told her mother had sent for me. But somehow Rosalyn knew her daughter was home that day with time on her hands, and once I had her on the phone, I told my cousin that as chance would have it I was passing through town. Ellie wasn't out of her twenties yet, but already you could hear a trace of a liquor slur in her voice and, when she laughed, a certain hoarseness and hollowness that went deep. Jim . . . Cousin Jim . . . she repeated my name, professing delight which I chose not to doubt. Isn't this wonderful, Jim! How long's it been? No, I don't want to know. Jim, I'm so happy you're here! What do you mean you're just passing through town? Not if I have anything to say about it, you're not!

I glanced at my aunt, who could not have been privy to what her daughter had been saying, but at just that moment Rosalyn gave me an imperative little nod, and I made the mistake that would undo my efforts and dash my aunt's hopes. I said it was true, unfortunately I *was* just passing through town, but I had time for lunch so why didn't Ellie meet me somewhere and why didn't she choose the place. I glanced at Rosalyn and she nodded, so it was both of our mistakes. Oh, Jim, oh, Jim, Ellie moaned, the girls are with their father today, and they'll want to see you, too, it's so cruel you're in such demand, but if that's the way it has to be . . . and she named the place, an old columned home on the outskirts of town, there before the Whalens had arrived, antebellum I assumed, where a nice breeze always blew under some old oaks, and why didn't we meet there if my schedule was so busy and that was all I had time for. I looked at Rosalyn, mouthed the name of the restaurant—the Chambers House—and she nodded, so it was both our faults.

I don't understand, Walter said.

You will.

It was indeed an old house with many small rooms because rooms and people were smaller back then, but with a wide entrance hall running from front to back, and at the back a staircase to the second floor passing diagonally overhead. I arrived before Ellie and was lucky, or unlucky, enough to get a free table at the back of the hall with a direct view up to the front door, which had been left open. There was a screen door to keep out the flies but not the breeze, and it was through that screen door

Lamar Herrin

I got my first look at Ellie in these last six or seven years. And it was down that hall, with old family photographs hanging on the walls that I had not even glanced at, one family being enough for me then, that I watched Ellie walk, not unsteadily but somehow still feeling her way, like someone unsure of her mission, until she saw me and broke into a tremulous smile.

We kissed on the cheek, I held her, then held her back, gazed at her and, I suppose, did "dwell in her eyes," which were easily her most fascinating feature, quite large, or maybe the rest of her face just seemed more drawn than I remembered and her complexion had lost its bloom. Regardless of what stage of her life you placed her in, Ellie did not look well. Of course, her marriage had broken up and her mother was nearing the end. Soon she would be alone and easy pickings for a man like Leland Oldham. In her haste she had misapplied or overapplied her makeup, and the base was flaking, which made her look a little parched. To be sure, women in correspondingly small towns up north did not wear much makeup, certainly not as much pancake base, and I suddenly felt a deep sympathy for this young cousin of mine, one step ahead of some terrible unmasking. She wore a yellow pants suit and a florid blouse, which only made things worse. Except for a tiny locket around her neck, no jewelry, and in that she was right. I didn't see how jewelry would help.

Before I could speak, she practically shouted out her greeting, as though from one hilltop to the next, another southern characteristic. How *are* you! *Tell* me the truth!

I told her I'd settled in up north where things were not as chilly as you were led to believe, but that I was sad to see her mother declining so, and asked her, in a quieter voice, just what the doctors had said.

She lowered her head and shook it, then raised her eyes to mine. First her brother, then her father, and now her mother. Among the vanished I could also include her husband, I suppose. It's so, so sad, Jim, she said. She won't go to the hospital. There're clinics that might make her more comfortable, but she remembers all Howie went through and says she's not going to drive herself crazy like that. The doctors are the last people she wants to talk to. You've seen how she is.

I've seen how worried she is, she's worried about you, I was about to say, but I thought we should eat before I got into that, and that, I told Walter, was another mistake. Walter said he still didn't understand, and I told him to wait, Ellie and I had to order, we had to be served. She ordered a quiche of some sort, which she only picked at as every so often she half twisted around in her chair to glance up the hall to the front door, where any other restaurant not worried about being quite so old-time would have taken that screen door down, forgone the breeze, and allowed air-conditioning to do the job, but that was not the restaurant that Ellie had chosen and Rosalyn had okayed. We both had iced tea, sweetened, oversweetened, which was another way you knew you were in the South. The waitress came to clear away the plates. There were various pies, which we declined. I leaned in over the table. Ellie kept glancing back up the hall. She'd gotten jittery. She looked weaker in that moment, as if she hadn't eaten in days.

I know, Walter said.

You do? What do you know?

I know what's going to happen. I understand.

You're sure?

Do you want me to tell you?

I gave it a moment's thought, real thought, considered the consequences, which were not inconsiderable. Walter as narrator would not be one to sidestep an issue. I had heard him work in court. No, don't do that, I said. Here's what happened.

I went back to where we'd stopped the conversation when I was on the point of telling Ellie that her mother was worried about her in ways she might not want to admit, and in the presence of her daughter might not want to let show. I understood Ellie had a job now, a commendable job helping disadvantaged children, and that there was a man in her life, an older man with quite a large family, whether a widower or divorced, my aunt Rosalyn didn't know. I spoke slowly but conversationally, centering my concern on Rosalyn, not Ellie, it was Rosalyn's last days we were talking about here, it was Ellie's mother's quickly declining health that was the issue. And in that context, I risked interjecting what I presented as observations, concerns of my own. I told Ellie that any mother in the best of health might have serious reservations about what Ellie was getting into, a man that old with a family that large and a past that—well, that uncertain. But, I supposed, a mother terribly sick might find she could think of little else. At the end we all feel a need to put our affairs in order, and a mother maybe even more so, especially when she's worried that her daughter might be making a serious mistake, and at the end there'd be nothing a mother could do. I was not above reproach when I said all this, I knew I was overstating the case, but I also knew there was every chance in the world that Rosalyn had a right to be worried and that finally you had to play the odds. I put what was a blunt question as gently as I could. Did Ellie plan to marry this man?

She turned to look back down the hall to the door and narrowed her eyes as though trying to see through that screen. Then she looked back to me. She'd been such a charming child when I'd first met her, half-hidden behind her mother, looking up at this bearded cousin come down from the North. With those eyes, and all that color in her cheeks. Forget fishing, come catch *me*! she'd taunted. Let's play!

I don't know, Ellie half whispered, her voice hoarse. Maybe. We've talked about it. Then she reminded me, You know, I'm a mother, too.

I needed reminding. Members of extended families tend to get fixed in one of their roles, and for me, I had to confess, Ellie Whalen was still a child.

I know you're a mother, I told her. I'm thinking about the girls, too, I'm thinking about my aunt's granddaughters. You're not all she's worried about.

In a lowered and only halfhearted voice, Ellie said, Mother worries too much.

You're all she has left, can't you see why she'd worry, here . . . at the end?

Make her comfortable, relieve her of her worries while there's time left, don't make a mistake you'll carry with you for the rest of your life—I was on the point of saying all of that. I might have gone on, You'll pass by her grave and hate yourself for what you denied her at the end. Don't let that happen, don't do that to yourself, Ellie. Instead, another question occurred to me, the right question, and it must have brought a scowl to my face. Do you love this man, Ellie? I said. Before she could answer, I persisted: How do you love him, Ellie? How can this be?

People say that faces go blank, but I'd make the distinction. I'd say that faces go vacant, which isn't the same. Ellie had vacated her face and stationed herself somewhere else, and I found myself peering, looking for the right light and the right angle, and you'll never guess, Walter, who I thought of then. Do you remember the other Ellie, the spirit waif of Hollywood? In the midst of all that stale and single-minded ambition, the girl

I knew who flitted among it all like a hummingbird, little iridescent Ellie. Do you remember her?

I remember, Walter said, and I'm not interested. That was Holly-wood. We're done with that. What did Ellie Whalen say when she came back, when she "reoccupied" her face?

She never fully reoccupied it. She was a little dazed. I might have struck her with a precisely calculated blow. She said she thought that she did. And I said, Love him, Ellie? Really? Not the circumstances, not as a defense against all that's ganging up on you, but this man, this . . . Leland Oldham?

And hearing his name spoken amounted to another blow, coming from me, both an outsider and, generationally considered, someone pres-ent at the start of it all.

Back when the snake struck, you mean.

Walter, I should never have told you that story.

No, you probably shouldn't have, but you did. Too late now. So back to the matter at hand. When did Leland Oldham show up?

Did he?

Ellie had to twist around, you didn't. You were sitting with a direct view of that front door. You would have seen him coming first through the screen, Leland Oldham materializing from behind that black mesh.

Out of the blackness, Walter?

That's what she'd been waiting for, wasn't it? That's what had her so edgy. And your "mistake" was in letting her choose the restaurant, which she could then communicate to Mr. Oldham, who would certainly be keeping tabs. Not that our Ellie wanted him to come barging in. Just to feel secure, she had to know that he knew where she was. It had reached that point.

You're good, Walter. I never doubted it.

So when did he?

Not before I had a chance to make my case, and Rosalyn's, to not marry the man, a man old enough to be her father with a family of all but grown children no one knew anything about. I urged Ellie not to do that. She had her own family to consider, and by that I meant her girls. She was vulnerable, she was on the rebound, he was twice her age. If she didn't see how someone could be wooed and falsely won from behind a front of church-sanctioned good deeds, I did. All sorts of scoundrels had sought the sanction of the church. History was full of them. Leland Old-ham—and I paused again on the name—might not be one of them, but there was a modern-day way to be sure, we no longer had to be victims of history repeating itself, and in the most reasonable tone I could man-age I began to talk to her about prenuptial agreements, which I presented as commonplace, a modern-day given, in no way indicative of distrust, especially when there was a large and complicated sum of money involved that Ellie, as a tribute to her father and all he'd accomplished, should want to protect. We were so used to thinking of money in the abstract, as figures in a bankbook or on a computer screen, figures that go up and go down, that we forget that it was her father and then her brother who devoted their flesh and blood to that business. Whalen Apparels at one time had been the livelihood of the town, all of us in this family of ours, out to the most remote of the cousins, had thrilled to what her family had accomplished, going right back to World War Two, which we had won partly due to the uniforms and parachutes and pup tents that her father had pitched in to produce. I didn't want to exaggerate, I said, but Ellie's inheritance was that history, and her mother would rest so much easier if she knew that her country's history and her family's part in it would not be forgotten, that it would be protected, that it would be left intact. So, if she must marry, would Ellie please have a prenuptial contract drawn up, it was simple, it was routine, it was what everybody was doing nowadays, and her mother would be so relieved, it would be such a loving kindness to her there at the end . . .

Dusk was gathering. You heard not yet the loons but the remaining canoers paddling for home. Walter quietly freshened our drinks. The wicker crackled quietly, not so much in agitation or suspense as in rhythm with our breaths. The tinkling of the ice that had yet to melt struck the cleanest and clearest of notes.

You should have sold encyclopedias, Walter said.

I did.

But you didn't sell her.

I thought I had.

What made you think so?

She loved her family. But one of the liabilities of being born so late in her parents' lives was that her family was dying off all around her. She could protect her inheritance, defend it against so much death, or she could let someone else take care of it and suffer the consequences. What she didn't really understand was that her family wasn't just her immediate family, it was all of us, it kept reaching out.

So she was debating it, Walter said. She was vacillating. Draw up a prenup and please her mother. With a prenup, even though she married she remained in a Whalen. The town had a Whalen left, a real Whalen, second generation, straight from the patriarch's loins, and the family fortune remained intact. Rosalyn would no longer be around, but that wouldn't stop nephews and nieces and more and more distant cousins from making a sort of pilgrimage to an otherwise unremarkable town and holding out their arms.

Walter—

El Dorado—and those golden eyes.

You were right. Leland Oldham did indeed show up, and I saw him first through that screen—

The toad.

He was short, but not squat, pudgy but not really fat and not round. Dark-haired and balding, but through the screen I couldn't make out the features of his face. I had to take Rosalyn's word for it that he had a goatee. It must have been very sparse. He wore a sports shirt and pants that might have come from the Whalen plant. He'd arrived at a moment when Ellie was not twisted back around, but there was no doubt Leland Oldham saw me see him. He stood there until . . .

Until Ellie saw you looking and read the expression on your face.

I was probably squinting to make out what I could. And probably tightening my jaw.

And then she turned around.

And a cloud shadow passed over her face. She seemed to let out a long breath. She risked a glance at me, and I felt for her then. She was like a spoiled child who couldn't help herself, who knew she was asking for just one more little favor, after which she promised to behave. She did say, I'll be right back, please don't go anywhere, with a hoarse flutter in her voice, which she needed to clear and try again, and then she walked up the Chambers House's main hall to the front door, more steadily than I expected.

And didn't come back.

Oh, she did. Five minutes later. She wasn't out there long. Under one of the live oaks, I suppose, which a hundred miles farther south would be hung with tatters of Spanish moss, blowing in the breeze.

With her beau, the toad-man, with that little wisp of Spanish moss hanging off his chin.

She came back, she smiled, she went on, Oh, Jim, it's so good to see you, so, so good, don't be such a stranger, practically breaking into song as women down there often do when they have nothing more to say.

Or maybe the toad slipped her something from his flask out under the Spanish moss.

There was no Spanish moss.

Rolling in the kudzu?

Walter—

I'm sorry. I just hate what's going to happen. I've told you. I'm very partial to your aunt.

Ellie came back. The check came, and it came to her. They knew her there. There was no way I was going to be allowed to pay. She paid with large bills, two twenties, one might have been enough, and that did occur to me, that under the oaks Leland Oldham had slipped her the twenties, which she had at hand, that already he was that much in control. I said, Ellie, please think about what we talked about. There's no reason to marry now, you know that. And if you do marry, there's certainly no reason not to have a prenuptial agreement drawn up, it's a mere formality, your father and your brother wouldn't think twice, in fact they'd be amazed if—

And she cut me off, she interrupted me in the quietest of voices, conversational, as though out of consideration she needed to remind me of something. It may be a formality up north, Jim, she said, but we're different down here. She smiled. She wasn't taunting me. She'd been talked to. She'd gotten some coaching outside. Tell me the truth. Isn't that why you keep coming back to see us? Don't you like us the way we are?

It was only when we were outside that she named him and identified him as the shadowy man behind the screen. Leland was so sorry he couldn't come in. He had to run. He'd love to meet you, though. Can't you stay another day? Then my littlest cousin, pouting, slipped into the little girl. Oh, why can't you, Jim? I smiled and shook my head. You're just being a tease, she said. You always liked to tease, especially when you grew that beard.

So you do remember that, I said.

You looked like a man from the mountains.

My beard was trimmed, I said. Mountain men don't trim their beards.

Now everyone has one. Please come back. Promise me. Please do.

Ellie, I came to see your mother. I forced her to meet my eye. It's very possible I might not see her again.

She flinched, but recovered. She was brittle but she didn't break. In fact, I believe she was convinced I owed her something, which I didn't dispute. How could anyone in our family dispute the fact they were in debt to the Whalens? And I don't mean for just shirts and pants. She said, I want you to promise me one thing. I'm not saying there'll be a wedding, but if there is, I want you to promise me you'll come. You missed my first one, you know.

Well, judging by the outcome, Ellie . . . , I said, trailing off on a sympathizing note.

Which she picked up on, the sympathizing, that is. She tried to laugh, but the laughter caught in her throat so that, more a sigh of sadness than a laugh, she had to try again. This the daughter of a woman whose laughter rose as cool and clean as a spring from the inner earth that no one in the family thought would ever run dry.

In the end I didn't even attend my aunt's funeral, I told Walter. How in the world did Ellie think I'd come see her marry the toad?

What are you saying? Walter was genuinely nonplussed. You attended her son's funeral and her husband's, but not hers, your favorite aunt?

I failed her, I said. It was as simple as that.

How *can* it be that simple? What were you thinking, Jim?

Neither the funeral nor the wedding. Thrift, thrift in absentia, Horatio, which I wasn't sure Walter would pick up on, lawyers, unlike certain princes, not being prey to thoughts accompanied by their counter-thoughts, otherwise how could they ever argue a case to a conclusion, much less win it? But it didn't really matter, because it was in that moment that we heard a series of slashing chords coming out of the near darkness, at which point, in answer to Walter's question, I said, If it isn't Byron Wainwright trying to play "Rite of Spring" on his cello, I have no idea what it is.

But of course Walter was right. It wasn't that simple. The family gathered for the funeral, and if I wasn't the only one missing, I was the one that mattered, and it was talked about. It wasn't her daughter's marriage to a man she found loathsome that had tipped my aunt into her grave—for, as in *Hamlet*, the funeral preceded the marriage by a month—but it was my acknowledged failure to protect her daughter and her daughter's fortune that brought on her end. I was told my aunt had given up. Not that nature had taken its rapid course, but that she had paved the way for it. I don't know how that can be said. I'd reported back to her what had been determined and not determined at that lunch, and of course Rosalyn sank in her chair and whatever color was left went out of her cheek, but that's not the same as my aunt saying, I surrender, you win, Mr. Toad, take it all, the pot's yours. She thanked me for my efforts, she tried to get me to spend the night, her son's boyhood twin beds where Phil Hodge and I had slept were still there, perhaps unslept in since then, the room unchanged, a shrine within a shrine, the sheets twenty-five years clean, and I turned her down. Briefly, she tried to hold me there with family gossip, talk of Howie's children, three of whom had taken their millions, spent it, and scattered over the map. The oldest, Alan, had come and gone and had presently gone again, but she asked me to guess who had come back, in the wake of a failed marriage, and—and that was when I learned what had happened to Howie's lakefront house, how Laurie Whalen had realized that as long as it was known as her husband's death house it would never sell, so she took it off the market and in what was regarded as a pique of self-impoverishment tore it down, only to get all her money back by selling off the land as five narrow lakefront lots, cheek by jowl. My aunt told me Laurie had come by to see her, but it was hard on her, on both of them. Lacking Howie, and three of the four children seemingly gone for good, they had little to say to each other. My aunt had an address, a crosstown condo. Why didn't I spend the night in Howie's boyhood bed and then the next morning drive over there and see if I could find her? And how could I begin to explain to my aunt that crossing town now would be like Achilles trying to catch up to Zeno's tortoise, I could run and run and never get there, never catch up to that turtle, never get to Laurie's condo, halve the distance, halve that and halve it again, that my only recourse was to drive out of town along the route her husband had once traced on a map, Big Howie Whalen, who had wished me and my Yankee friend good luck and sent out a state trooper to see us on our way, and damned if we hadn't caught fish.

I kissed my aunt. She was slumped in her chair, the steel gone out of her eyes. Her maid May met me at the kitchen door, the same door Big Howie had been trying to reach when he'd collapsed partway up the walk. You come back now, you hear, Miz Ros-lyn be waitin' for you, which was half true and half false, or perhaps entirely true in that, snakes coming in all shapes and sizes, Rosalyn would be waiting for me to come back and finish what a little Boston bulldog had started. Or did I think life was one long series of handouts? Didn't I know there was a price to pay?

I stepped outside while Walter prepared a stew whose ingredients he'd brought from home. Byron Wainwright appeared to have played himself into submission and either sat spent on his dock or had gone back up to his house. But I didn't walk down toward the lake. I walked back up toward the car, passed it, and in the darkness started out along a path leading into the woods. Whether in or out of coverage I didn't know, but I took maybe twenty-five or thirty paces into the woods, where leaves rustled and the path felt mossy and damp, and stopped when I came to the first widening and I smelled before I could hear or see it a small stream. Then I heard it, on a frequency all its own, water slipping over shards of shale, and the smell was clean, rank and clean, earth and water and stone.

I had coverage and I made the call. The face of the phone cast its alien glow into the surrounding foliage until I put it to my ear. Elaine answered by asking, Where are you, Jim, and I told her, Off by myself, talking to my ex-wife who remains the only woman in my life while our mutual friend Walter Kidman makes supper, and Elaine laughed. Where exactly, she said, and I told her I'd just stepped into a dark wood. She was about to laugh again, but caught it. She had the sort of voice that came through clear on a phone, for which a phone served to filter off all impurities so that you heard the voice's music, and frequently I'd called her for no more than that, to listen to her speak. She said, How dark, Jim, and I told her my eyes were adjusting, it was all right, as always it was good hearing her voice, and it had been very good spending this time with Walter, whose cooking—and she interrupted me. Jim, why the dark wood? For a moment I didn't say anything, I let her hear the passing stream, the insects, the breeze in the trees, three orders of nature, wind, water, and a tiny, multitudinous pulsing of life, before answering, Just for some privacy, before we sit down to eat. She caught a second laugh. I could picture her face, she had dark eyes, which when her expression turned serious had a leveling effect, she settled the way a bird settles on a nest, she spread out and then there was work to be done, eggs to hatch, and no humoring her. Are you getting along, you and Walter? I answered, Yes. Fishing? Once. Cards? No. Sightseeing? A half-empty town. Drinking? Yes. Too much? Not so far. Yet you're passing the time. I'm telling Walter a story, I said. It was never actually a fishing story, even though that's how it began. Now it's something else. A story you haven't told me? No. Yes. A story I haven't told you. A guy story? Well, that's also how it began. And you're worried you can't keep it up? You don't want to disappoint our friend? You'll keep going and keep going and then it will be—what? A shaggy dog story, I said. Elaine said, You know, I've heard that expression countless times and never quite been sure what it meant. A story, I said, with no point and an anticlimactic end. A story that arouses large expectations and then abandons them. A joke on the listener, which some listeners never forgive. Actually, Walter brought the expression up. Then he gave me a second chance. Elaine and I held a silence. I held it, then passed it on to her. A dove began to coo overhead, a deep-breasted, chuckling sound. Finally, I concluded, the joke's on you. Your story goes nowhere. When you have a chance to end it, you don't. What goes around comes around, and before it's over your shaggy dog has bitten you in the butt. Walter would never do that, Elaine objected, he's not going to allow your shaggy dog to bite you in the butt, Jim. Then she didn't check her laugh, healthy and deeper in her chest than her voice would lead you to expect. What's he making for supper? Some sort of stew, I believe. Enjoy it, she said. Better go before he rings the supper bell. Before she could hang up, I said, I might call you again, Elaine. Don't be surprised if I do. There was a long pause as the forest sounds swarmed in, accompanied by the passing of that stream. Then she said, Do you want me to drive over there, Jim? Is that what you're trying to tell me? That wasn't what I was trying to tell her, not at all, I really did just want to hear the sound of her voice. But what I ended up saying was, Not yet.

IV

THE YEARS WORE ON. Your favorite team lost a game they'd waited years to play, and you, their biggest fan, didn't see how you could live through the following day, but you did, and then your team's loss became a footnote, a day in the team's history you taught your eyes to jump over, and life began again. Or you switched favorite teams, or found another sport to devote your fanship to. Sports scars were famously quick to heal. Most scars were if you gave them time. Some scars you might even forget where to look for on your body. Which leg? Which arm? Using mirrors you could inspect every inch of your flesh because you knew the scar had to be there somewhere, even though it wasn't, even though it was gone. Scars did not last lifetimes because lives did not last lifetimes. We all had more than one. A life's stories came in multiples, so unless someone is there to pull you back into an earlier lifetime, pull you back and pull you back, maybe only for the sport of it, never intending to land you for good, you could outlive your scars and emerge at last as pristine as the day you were born.

I'm assuming there was such a someone, Walter said. For the sport of it. To pull you back.

There was, but not my mother. She was too staunchly partisan and eager to pick a fight to be a source of reliable information. She fought with my Aunt Lily the day of Rosalyn's funeral, there in the Whalen house where I had last seen Rosalyn alive. They fought over a desk that my grandfather had made with his own hands and had told my mother was intended for me. Which made sense since I was the only grandchild he'd lived to see. Lily claimed her father had always intended it for her, which also made sense since the desk was as rugged and rough-hewn as Lily prided herself on being. Rosalyn, who had room in her house, had been taking care of it along with more desirable pieces of furniture, but it was the desk that my mother and Lily fought over, and it was Lily who walked away with it, leading my mother to declare that that was it with Lily and with the Whalens too. And she meant it. Big Howie had been more than she could take, no one had quite gotten over Little Howie's loss, and if Ellie was prepared to go off the deep end, my mother presumed she knew how to swim. No, it wouldn't be my mother who pulled me back. If it was information about the Whalen family I wanted, I'd have to go to my sister, and I haven't told you about her, Walter.

Only that she lived close enough to your mother to keep an eye on her.

The next town over, twenty miles away. Any closer and my mother might have swallowed her whole, but twenty miles of curving roads and a lot of farm traffic was just enough to persuade my mother to turn her attention elsewhere. My sister was married to a decent enough guy, a regional rep for a big breakfast cereal conglomerate, who was on the road a lot, and once she had her two kids in school and our mother caught up in her political causes, she took a look around to see what she could do. The important thing to understand about my sister, Walter, is that there was no end to her energy. So she had to expend it. She couldn't just let it get bottled up. And she had a hunch about things. On a small-town scale, she lived out ahead of the curve. What didn't her little town have that would cost almost nothing to bring about? It didn't have its own art gallery, it occurred to her, somewhere local artists could show their art, presenting their town and its surrounding countryside in its best light. No overhead, except literally what was up there, little spots trained onto the walls. For next to nothing she opened such a gallery. She managed to get some community funding, and when that still didn't all add up, she engaged quilters in town and turned it into a quilt gallery, too. Of course, quilts took up a lot of room, so she expanded into the empty space next door. And when that brought in viewers but still not sufficient revenue, she opened a coffee shop, which soon became a coffee shop with someone posing as a real barista, who invited you to smell the beans as he ground them, so you could sit and admire the art, smell and drink the coffee, flirt with the barista if you were so disposed, for my sister did hire a Latino-looking guy with a handsome black beard, and eat the pastry baked locally by neighbors of yours. And when that still came up short, my sister got hold of some cookbooks from a restaurant called Moosewood and introduced a vegetarian menu in her town, in effect daring her customers and townspeople not to find tasty—and healthy—something not slathered in meat gravy or fried to a sickening crisp. When the restaurant (cum art and quilt galley, cum barista-ground coffee shop) caught on, she had the inspired idea of inviting townspeople to submit vegetarian recipes of their own, one of which she would feature each week, with the winners brought in to act as honorary chefs and their photographs displayed in the window. And when that began to make her money and she had a stack of recipes and photographs to fall back on, my sister had another idea, which made her considerably more money and stayed squarely within the compass of her small town.

At first it seemed a step backward. She'd noticed that her townspeople couldn't resist yard and garage sales and spent their weekend mornings driving, in a herded sort of way, from one sale to another. My sister might have fixed on the nosiness and the small-minded acquisitiveness in this craze, but chose to view it communally instead, and asked herself what if people were being driven—as they drove around burning up gas—by the need to escape their same-old lives and get inside somebody else's for a while? What if they wanted to renew their lives by entering, piece by piece, object by object, the lives of others, who happened to be townspeople of theirs? Why wasn't this good? Why wasn't this a form of sharing? Why wasn't this what a community was all about? So my sister rented yet another space, a much larger one, and created not a bargain basement center but what she presented as a redistribution hub, where townspeople were invited not to donate but to put up for sale pieces of their furniture, clothing, kitchenware, crockery, anything really except machinery, and not records or books, there were plenty of places where those could be bought and sold, and maybe not sporting goods, either, like golf clubs, old baseball mitts, or fishing gear, but anything else, really, decorative objects, lamps, silverware, tableware, the bric-a-brac and knickknacks scattered throughout our lives, for which the owners could always be paid cash (minus the center's commission), but why not take a better deal on store credit instead, so that the person with something once dear to sell— dear but not defunct, that was the key—could replenish his or her life with something once dear to a neighbor of hers? My sister did not call her redistribution center a center of "used" anything. Nothing she took in on consignment and nothing she sold was ever referred to as "used." It had only been "previously enjoyed." Except for old tools, like shovels and pickaxes, and maybe those sporting goods, too, she pretty much put garage and yard sales out of business in her town. The downside was, as her business took on a life of its own, she needed a new outlet for that energy of hers and, with her husband traveling and her children behaving and her aging but still active mother a town away, she eventually found her way back to what was left of the Whalens, that is, to Ellie and her two girls, plus Leland Oldham and his four freeloading sons—yes, they were all boys—and began to feed information to me, pulling me back in.

Let me stop you there, Walter said. Your sister sounds like a real enthusiast, maybe for the town she lives in just a little bit larger than life. Without ever having laid eyes on the lady, are we sure she can be trusted for reliable information?

Who are you addressing here, Walter, a judge or a jury?

Neither. Just a friend who's making his case.

His case?

Telling his story.

I trust her, I said. She may have a somewhat expansive personality—

Which you believe you can gauge.

Which I believe I can gauge. And which allows her to reach out to more and more family members. When I talk about nephews and nieces and cousins galore, I'm talking almost in the abstract. I may be the oldest, but I'm also the most distant and the least in touch. My sister knows all those kinfolk. Every summer there were huge family reunions up at the Whalen house on the lake in the mountains. After Big Howie's death Rosalyn had to build a second, larger house to accommodate them all. My sister and her children attended those reunions, but as soon as I got out of school and away from all that, except for one occasion I did not. My sister—

Name, please.

Jean. Her business, her "redistribution hub," was called Jean's Junction. Children, Nicky, for Nicholas, and Mary, for the Virgin Mary, I suppose. Her husband is a very gregarious Irish American, Garrett O'Higgins. When she's needling him, or when she's really pissed, she'll accuse him of mumbling Vatican-speak or papal nonsense. Take off your beanie and sit down, we're ready to eat. That sort of thing. Actually my brother-in-law is a sweet, cheerful guy, a mass-goer only on sentimental occasions. I imagine when he's off the road on the weekends, he and my sister have a fine time.

Now, that may be more information than I need, Walter said.

The point is, during those two-week reunions on the lake my sister is an all-inclusive sort. So she's privy to what's going on.

The toad?

In that we were like-minded.

And couldn't you have told her, I don't want to know, go down there if you have to, take your kids, splash around in the lake, take out the boats, water-ski, roar in and out of coves and ride the waves, then sit out in the evening on the terrace as the lake smooths out and the light turns that dusky orange and things get so quiet that the boathouse begins to creak, and you can hear a fish striking halfway across the lake, and some kids all the way over there, yelping their last before they're sent to bed—that is, couldn't you have told her, You go down there and take it all in but leave me out of it.

My god, Walter, you've been there!

'S no different up here.

That's where you're wrong. Down south, any paradise regained is only a poor substitute for the one that was lost.

Paradise lost? Paradise lost? Are we talking the Plantation South here, the Old Order, the weary but contented slaves singing low and mellow across fields of cotton whiter than white? That the paradise you have in mind? I don't think so, Jim.

Of course not.

Then why not tell your sister—

There's nothing left to tell now. It's all over. History.

Well, I'm beginning to gather that. Yet here you are, doing the telling.

That's that little pickerel's fault. If you hadn't offered to take it off the hook, and it hadn't given me that sideways look out of its eye . . .

So let's go catch some more pickerel and you can stare them down and lay it all to rest.

Funny, I said, but it may be the best idea you've had yet.

So, shall I get out the tackle?

There's an undertow, Walter—

In this lake? Look at it, have you ever seen a more domesticated body of water?

—and my sister knew it, but she had this kind of exuberant nature that rode over everything. She could kick free from any undertow. But about the toad, you can trust me, we were like-minded. We all occupy little worlds we cast large. If you could surround yourself with enough WPA artifacts, you could probably ride out the rest of your days content and convince yourself it was all like that. I remember a child's slide in a park in Cincinnati from my days there. Cincinnati is a hilly place. This slide was carved out of stone, and it took you all the way down one of those hillsides. At the bottom there was a little plaque. A WPA product. Indestructible, Walter. You owe it to yourself to go slide down that side. It'll keep the child in you alive. I had no real choice in the matter—my sister didn't either—our little world was the Whalen world, the Whalen magic, that's the way it was, but just don't let a toad come along and take it away from you, and take away your littlest cousin, the child of your favorite aunt, whom you failed, in the bargain. A toad shouldn't be allowed to do that.

You're preaching to the choir here, Walter said. That's one toad that shouldn't have been allowed to cross the road.

I am told—and unless I say otherwise, it's my sister whose word we're going to have to take—that Leland Oldham sat in the front row beside Ellie during my aunt's funeral and let loose with audible and visibly wracking sobs. His sons sat in the second and third rows and didn't try to outsob their father but were giving it their bereft best. Ellie sat stunned, Jean said, and let the Oldham family do the grieving. At the cemetery, Leland stood beside Ellie at the graveside, and it was Leland who got his hands on the clods of dirt and, when Ellie demurred, threw them in, maybe one for each Oldham, which made a drumroll effect on the coffin lid. According to Jean. Rosalyn was buried on one side of her husband, her son on the other, each with his own marker and all within the wingspan of an enormous marble monument on which the letters WHALEN were engraved. There was, of course, a burial plot left. My sister wouldn't say, when the ceremony was over and they'd all turned and headed to the cars, that Ellie was being led as though to her own execution, only that she seemed powerless to move independent of that Oldham squad, that she was pale and shaky and seemingly sedated, not yet drunk, that would come when they were all back at the Whalen house, where various little confrontations would take place, including my mother's with my aunt Lily over that desk. Ellie's fair-headed daughters were with their father, who seemed to be keeping them at a safe distance from the Oldham clan, but that might have been a chance piece of staging. Really, all Jean could swear to was that there were the dark-suited and unhealthy-looking Old-hams, as though they were all awaiting their day in the sun, with Ellie among them, and then there was everybody else, which included the Pritchard girls, the Pritchard girls' families, and the town at large, none of whom was unaware that only one Whalen was left.

But back home at the Whalen house, my sister kept a close eye on our cousin Ellie, and Ellie sat in the parlor in Aunt Rosalyn's favorite chair, a rose mallow wing chair, and with her flanks shielded by the chair's wings allowed Leland Oldham to bring her drink after drink and did get drunk. My sister was there in case Ellie tried to get up, but she didn't, she didn't seem to have it in her or any need since Leland kept her glass full. He filled his own, too. Eventually I got more information about how he'd shown up in the Whalens' town. The charity Leland Oldham ran through the church was a church affair in name only. It had been endowed by Big Howie, and it had actually been set up before Little Howie died, so that he knew about it, too, and its purpose was to get disadvantaged boys and girls off the streets and out in nature where they could get their lives off to an undiseased and undisfigured start, and it bore Little Howie's name—well, both his and his father's name, as if one emerged indistinguishably from the other—the Howard Whalen Youth Crusade, the "crusade" part perhaps coming at the insistence of Reverend Crawly, who wanted to give it a religious cast. It wasn't just boys and girls learning the ways of white-tailed deer or largemouth bass, it was the deer and the bass and all of nature as a step toward the Christian awakening of their souls. A crusade that, with the Whalen deaths occurring in such quick succession, Reverend Crawly tried to run out of his office until he had some breathing room and could find someone to permanently direct it for the church. The endowment would support the appointment of a director, and it only seemed fitting that Ellie Whalen be asked to lead the search team in honor of her brother and her father and the name they both bore in benefit of the town so that its youth—

Wait, Walter said. You're going to tell me that Ellie led a committee to appoint a director for this charity her father had set up and which her mother professed to know so little about . . .

Because Rosalyn knew, as far as her daughter was concerned, what a shameful end it had accomplished.

And Ellie took on the job because it honored her father and brother and it got her out of the house where her marriage was falling apart . . .

And because she was her father's little girl and because her brother had set the bar so high.

So even if it was a committee of three, say, she as a Whalen was a committee of one, and she took it seriously enough to look around her part of the state, and maybe a state or two away, kudzu states all, so she looked under the kudzu and . . .

You can quit drawing it out, Walter. You know what happened.

She found the toad.

He had the experience. Scout camps, Y camps, a charitable string of successes to his credit, that sort of thing. Yes, she recruited him and he came.

Which Rosalyn did or didn't know about?

Hard to say. Probably did but didn't want to admit . . .

A man old enough to be her daughter's father . . .

If she'd been fathered at a normal age.

Which, of course, brings us to the question of why Ellie was put on this earth to start with, not that Reverend Crawly would want to speculate on that. Not if it meant accounting for the toad and his brood, as if they too were part of God's plan.

I'm not sure how much the good reverend knew of the Oldhams. At first they kept a low profile.

Meaning they didn't go roaring around town in black Cadillacs.

No, that only came later. Or something to that effect.

It did, did it? Walter expressed real surprise. I believe he'd grown accustomed to imagining Big Howie, and only Big Howie, with his girth, and his small shrewd eyes, and his plump manicured hands on the wheel.

Much later, I said. Ellie, too.

Ellie? Driving around town in one of her father's Cadillacs?

If not a Cadillac, something equally grand. It became a sort of sport, like a sighting around town. You had to be in the right place at the right time.

And we're not. Not in the right place at the right time.

We left her sitting in that wing chair, Walter. Her mother's favorite. Shielded both to the right and left, and in front of her—

Sits the toad.

Except when he's getting up to refill her glass. Hers first, although he doesn't forget his own.

And other Oldhams are spreading through the house, down to the youngest, that sullen teenage kid probably stretched out where you once were, in Little Howie's bed, when Rosalyn—

And the Pritchards. My sister and her family, the good-humored Mr. O'Higgins and their two well-behaved children. My aunt Ruth and her three, grown themselves and a daughter with children of her own. But not Ruth's sailor husband. He'd been the first to pass away, as if he'd gone off to fight yet another war and left the faithful Ruth behind. And my mother along with her sister Lily, who it turns out in her own scandalous, good-humored fashion couldn't live without a war and was stockpiling materiel in every room in her house as though to withstand a final assault, one item of which was to be that desk. And so many more, Walter, up and down the generations, the Whalen house never so full, and food, of course, you'd think you were at one of those Sunday southern buffets, an assembly-hall-sized affair, table after table—

You're sure? Remember, you weren't there.

I don't have to have been. I don't have to take my eyes off my cousin and the man there to refill her drink to know what's going on in that house. All I have to do is imagine the worse possible outcome to a life spent trying to give all the excess away to know how it was piling up—

And how quickly it would disappear?

My sister said Ellie looked both overwhelmed and, seated there as she was, as if she'd come to take control. Everybody passed by her chair before they left, and every time Ellie's spirits began to sink, Leland put a drink into her hand. He got her drunk and got her through it, my sister said. He drank himself, as if to show her the path. It was his modus operandi. Before it was over, he might have been showing her how to breathe. You had to look past his toadness, Walter. There was some deep, centered, zealous principle operating in the man that made him commanding and that, while you were sitting there observing him, made it impossible for you to sneer or laugh. He wasn't a Rasputin. This wasn't the world's high stage. This was small-town chicanery, and my sister knew

107

small towns, but on that stage Leland Oldham was formidable, a real for-midable, steady-eyed, little son of a bitch. My sister said it didn't take two minutes to see how things stood between Leland Oldham and Ellie. He got her drunk, held her up (in her mother's favorite chair), and got her through the afternoon. He got drunk, too, drunk on her drunkenness, you could say, except there was no doubt he was putting away as much scotch as she was. He'd been recruited to run a charity out of the church and, by all accounts, was making things happen. But no one there in the Whalen house that afternoon, maybe not even in the toad's own family, actually cared anything for the man or didn't see how things stood. Rosa-lyn had been right, and it needed to have been proclaimed. Engraved on her marker: I left my daughter in the arms of a scheming, unscrupulous, father-aged scoundrel. Someone should have been there to prevent it, but both my husband and my son were dead. Someone else, a survivor, say, who had a debt to pay.

A low blow, Walter said.

I know, I said.

We need to stop this for a while.

Step free of the undertow?

Jesus, Jim. A helluva way to start off the day.

I will say this, Walter. When my sister said there were two people held in ill repute by the time that funeral reception was over, I didn't doubt her. One of those two people was sitting before her, working his will on her cousin, whose mother had just died and who looked as for-saken as an orphan on the streets. The other was a thousand miles away.

All right, Jim. Enough.

That was how my sister, speaking for the family at large and for selected townspeople, had paired us off. Leland Oldham because he was there, behaving as he did, and I, my aunt's favorite nephew, because I wasn't. Because I'd chosen to stay away. Bedfellows, in Little Howie's boy-hood beds.

Jesus, Jim, enough!

I didn't disagree. I let Walter talk me into the car, and I let him drive us around. It was a perfect day. A breeze, a mild late-summer sun, late enough in the season to take the glare out of the light and lay it mildly over the land. We proceeded down valley roads with streams running alongside, and when a vista opened before us, we saw how the trees had begun to turn until you lifted your gaze to the higher reaches where the pines and spruce and hemlocks remained a yearlong stony green. There was really no reason not to continue driving like this, with the windows down and something gently bracing in the cool warmth of the breeze. I had the luxury, not Walter, of closing my eyes. With something like a blessing in the breeze. We stopped for lunch somewhere, sat out on a terrace with a valley view and, down below, a stream providing a quiet current of white noise. Up on the hillsides stood what once had been rustic summer resorts, perhaps still were, you'd have to get closer and look more closely, and we chose to stay down in the valley's fold. But gradually the hillsides sloped down to meet us, our particular valley began to level out, and we were at the mercy of a geological event and looking out on what seemed to be an inland sea that a glacier in its grinding retreat north had dug out and the streams had filled with a water so blue you wanted to breathe it down, let it ride through your body on your blood and clean out the residue. Pleasure boats crossed it, then in the clear blue light were lost to view. Lake George, named not for our first president but for his nemesis, the English king. The Sagamore was down there, too, which clearly had an Indian ring. Bygone luxury time-captured for the present day, not just a faithful replica but the thing itself, and before it rose before us I asked Walter if he'd mind very much returning to where we'd come from, along a different route if he preferred, which would end up being the same, one route as good as another, the shallow valleys steepening again, the streams freshening, the sky darkening only a bit, the winding then straightening then doubling back of the stream as it braided its way up the valley floor, and we were gradually lifted back into it, not the real Adirondacks, only the foothills, once again. We crossed a modest bridge the WPA had built, whose iron girders were a rusted red but stout enough to hold us up, the bridge bridging the stream that flowed out of the lake that Walter's vintage cabin stood on.

We took out the canoe but left the fishing rods behind. We tried paddling as a team—Walter in the back, I in front—straight up the center of the lake to see how well we would do. Lakeside neighbors might have thought we were training to compete, but against whom and for what prize? It took a while to get it right. I alternated strokes on the left with strokes on the right, but with such back-and-forth energy that invariably I pulled us in opposing directions, as though we were tacking up the lake and not striving for a straight course. Walter was the real canoer. He advised me to paddle on either the left or the right, whichever suited me and for as long as my strength held out, and let him take care of the steering. Or did I want to steer? Coming back, of course, I could. So I tested my shoulders and arms and back on the right, reversed hands on the paddle and tested them on the left. The jerks to the right and the left the canoe made as we proceeded up the lake were the equivalent of the dodging feints a boxer made as he advanced through the rounds. The farther we went, the narrower in their range those jerks became, until Walter was almost able to steer us in a perfectly straight line while I, ten years his elder, alternatingly discovered a fund of strength in my right and left shoulders that gave us sufficient forward force.

We were out perhaps an hour before the normal canoeing hour and had the lake to ourselves. There came a moment in our performance when our rhythm seemed so clean, almost so effortless, that I found myself expecting to hear applause from spectators stationed along the shore. If not applause, because there were no spectators, of course, then a click, which current cameras didn't make or made so quietly the picture takers themselves could hardly hear it, something from the old days, then, befitting a canoes-only lake, a young man and a young woman out for a chaste afternoon of picture taking, with the camera itself as a sort of party favor in exchange for the young woman's consent, if you could believe such a thing. A Kodak party. Black boxes. A preacher with eyes as dark and swift and unsparing as a shutter's lens. A Reverend Pritchard and a quartet of Pritchard girls. A succeeding generation, a firstborn and a last, roles someone had to play. Click.

I laid my paddle across the gunwales and we floated, never to a complete stop but just perceptibly toward that exit stream. I felt it in the shoulders and the back, and I felt caught in a current so modest it was unworthy of the name. There were houses on the shores, and people were quietly about, people, excepting their grandchildren, roughly our age, in keeping with a secluded lake eons old and still holding on, and I told Walter that it was a shame we hadn't brought swimming trunks, because after the pull that had gotten us this far, all I really wanted to do was slip over the side. Walter, who'd steered and not paddled, but would paddle us back, volunteered to turn us around and with his own body shield me in my nudity from the closest cluster of houses if I really wanted to get into the water, and he said it in such a way he seemed to be wondering if I could be taken at my word. So I stripped and slipped over the side, as ghostly pale, I suppose, as I had been in my life, what I could see of myself in the artic embrace of these northern waters. I swam some strokes, modestly keeping the canoe between myself and that closest cluster of houses, but as one stroke led to the next and the iciness of the water relented, I thought I could swim for it, that it was something a body like mine could still do, and I did strike out for the opposite shore with eight, nine, ten powerful strokes, timing my kicks, probably splashing more than I needed to, perhaps even getting Walter wet although he didn't protest, just began to quietly follow along behind me in the canoe. I swam until I'd gotten absolutely all I could from this water, when to ask for more would have been to beg, then I signaled for Walter to pull alongside and tried my best not to capsize us as I climbed up into the canoe. Walter asked how the water was, and when I told him he didn't know what he'd missed, he assured me he did and for that reason had remained high and dry. Accepting the pain in the upper back and right down the spine, I half lay in the bottom of the canoe, as though I'd been thrown there by a fisherman eager to add to his catch, and allowed the sinking sun to dry me while Walter, who neither insisted nor resisted, both paddled and steered us back to his end of the lake. If Bryon Wainwright had been out on his dock, I suppose I would have made the effort to dress myself, but he wasn't, so I was able to get up to the cabin carrying my clothes, dry off, dress, and be back in the chairs looking out over the lake by the time Walter had appeared. He brought the bottle and the ice and he, perhaps more than I, had Leland Oldham on his mind.

As Hamlet said, yes, "the funeral baked meats did furnish forth the marriage table," and no, they did not marry in the Whalen house, and not in the church, but in an old home squarely in the center of town where weddings and receptions of all sorts were held, and no, neither my sister nor my mother was there, in fact the only member of our side of the family present was a cousin, a daughter of Aunt Ruth and her sailor husband, after me the next oldest in the Pritchard line and a close friend of my sister's. Close? How close? Walter asked. A confidante, I said. To be trusted? I'm getting it thirdhand now, you understand. That I can't tell you, Walter. I believe so. Her name was Harriet. Her mother, Ruth, and Rosalyn always had a special bond, even though they were six, seven years apart in age. Lily came in between them, but when it pleased her, Lily was a maverick, who had her good and bad days, and my mother had been the disciplinarian when her mother failed to be and her father was away—

Except, Walter reminded me with a wink, when a thin Howard Whalen had come for a wooing walk in the woods.

I told Walter that, like anybody else, my mother could relent, but Ruth, who'd sung those love songs on the radio as a prewar girl, and must have believed every word, was constancy and sweetness itself, and Rosalyn had need of her as the Whalen fortunes waxed and waned—

But mainly waxed, Walter said, correcting our course again as if we were still back in the canoe, and I saw no reason to disagree. But I added, The thing about Ruth was that because of her husband's job with that oil company, she always lived some distance away, and Rosalyn had to either go to her or wait till the summer when Ruth brought her family for those two weeks on the lake, which could sometimes be extended to three, if it was pure abiding sweetness Rosalyn wanted, and, believe me, there were times when she did. But there's no reason to go back into that. We've reached the wedding now, which my cousin Harriet attended, and she told my sister that Ellie, who was taller than Leland Oldham and half of his girth, pronounced her vows as though from a pulpit, summoning a strength into her voice, really a note of defiance, except no one was present that day she needed to defy. Harriet was there because she was fond of Ellie, fondness and sweetness running in her blood. Reverend Crawly did not marry them. Harriet was not quite sure of the authority of who did. If the word "God" was spoken, it was by rote or mumbled or employed as a figure of speech, the way you might invoke the forces of nature to shine down on this day. It was a civil compact, with no escape clauses. Oldhams were present guarding all the doors. Ellie's daughters were not. And it was done in an old house at the center of town, with a wraparound veranda and rockers rocking a little, as though just vacated, in the ghost of a breeze.

Then what happened?

He took it all. He ruined her.

No! No! Walter protested, covering his ears. I mean what happened right then. After the wedding.

Then? The sun shone down, I suppose. Ellie had a cream-colored suit on, her light brown hair was done with a part, she had taken her time with her makeup, her lipstick was a coral red, either she'd had a good night's sleep or somebody had worked some magic, for the honey-gold in her eyes shone out of the green with a steady low luster. She was slender, svelte if you imagined her stepping out of a forties fashion magazine along with the likes of, say, Lauren Bacall. If her father had been there, he might have fallen in love with her in place of her mother, or in addition to her mother. She did not look as if she had held a shotgun or a fishing rod in her hands in her life.

All this for the toad?

Harriet told my sister and my sister told me that Ellie hadn't had a drink all day, not until the wedding supper, which Harriet also attended, so she was reluctantly forced to conclude that her younger cousin was riding a wave of happiness throughout the day, and it wasn't until after the supper that that wave came crashing down. Then a haggardness took hold of her as if she'd spent a cold night out in a storm. She couldn't keep it up. Leland Oldham seemed solicitous of her then. He kept feeding her the wrong medicine, of course, or the medicine that suited him, the best scotch Whalen money could buy, from the start no less than Lagavulin 16, Walter, but he also seemed aware of what had blossomed and then wilted before his eyes, and he had to shore up his conviction and go to work on her again. Harriet, who'd had her own rocky marriage, not hills and valleys but craggy peaks and ravines, told Jean she could see how this was going to go. Did Leland Oldham love Ellie Whalen? Enough to want to restore her before she came apart again and he picked up—and banked—the pieces? Without him, he must have reasoned, she'd have no one to put her back together, and without her he'd have no pieces to pick up and bank. So he made good on his vows and went to work.

It sounds like you're saying they made a team.

If they did, it's a goddamn shame!

He got her drunk until her only recourse was to turn to him.

She came from a drinking family, Walter. Her father had been a heavy drinker, at least during the cocktail hour when I was a boy. But when Rosalyn announced she was pregnant with Ellie, notice that Big Howie sobered up. He must have heard that as the voice of God thundering in his ear—I'm giving you one more chance! Rosalyn, of course, stopped drinking too. Ellie's father dies and Ellie turns to the drink her father gave up when she came into their lives. The only difference, scotch whiskey instead of bourbon. When Leland Oldham appears to take over as director of her father's endowment, the Howard Whalen Youth Crusade—after Ellie's appointed him, that is—and it turns out he's a bigger drinker than Big Howie ever was and can portion out to this daughter-aged benefactress/boss of his her daily allowance of liquor, which as a sort of sympathetic overseer he will join her in consuming, and they become so like-minded in their drunkenness that they actually marry and, putting their drunken heads together, dream up ways to spend Ellie's seemingly inexhaustible fortune while everyone else, I'm talking about us, the family at large, is forced to stand off on the sidelines and watch the debacle unfold because there's only one game in town and only two players left—well, yes, Walter, I guess that's what you can call teamwork.

Good God, Jim! Walter exclaimed. I thought that swim had cooled you off. Then he couldn't help himself. Here, he said, have a drink.

I did cool off, I said. I sobered right up. That poor little girl born so late into her parents' lives. Her unconscionably rich parents. And I took a long slow swallow of the bourbon.

And her little girls? Ellie's?

You shouldn't ask.

Is there a safe question left? Walter said.

Now, that's a good question. The right one, as a matter of fact. Are we into safety?

In that moment, with no warning, no plodding footsteps, no clearing of the throat, no scraping of the stool, from behind the bush and down on his dock, Byron Wainwright began the evening's recital. Down tempo, no tempo, nothing aggressive, drawing the bow in the lower registers back and forth against the strings. As though trying to catch and keep his breath.

Go inside? Walter said. Go out for supper? Separate him from his cello, bring him over here?

Remember, Walter, after he surveyed the scene he turned his back on us.

Make up? Make peace?

To your question. Her daughters remained with their father, and they kept it out of court. Jennifer, the older, had a head on her shoulders and when the time came managed to save the trust fund Rosalyn had left her.

Somehow Leland got his hands on Tracy's, she's the younger, maybe he told her he'd turn her million into twenty million, I don't know. Scott, their father, should have been more protective, but he was overmatched. Or disgusted—blinded by his disgust. He remarried and, I suppose, had his hands full. I really don't know.

And Walter reminded me, The thing about toads is that food comes to them. They blend into their surroundings. They sit there in their squat. Frogs go jumping, toads don't. They sit there and grow warts. They snatch flies out of the air and get bigger and bigger.

Here's how I'd make a case for Leland Oldham . . .

How you'd defend him?

I'd look at those four boys and I'd ask, Why hadn't they stayed with their mother? It became available knowledge in town that their mother didn't live far away, another town, maybe just over the state line. Remarried? That I don't know, but why did Leland have them all? Four boys, Walter, with whatever strains that causes in any family. The rivalries, the bullying, the sulks, the alpha of the litter and the runt. Short of having a genius for the thing, how do you keep a family like that intact? Leland Oldham took it on himself, which, from an outside perspective, seemed in line with his profession. And if you were doing justice to yours, your profession, you'd have to ask the court to give him a break.

Maybe, but I'd hold my nose while I was doing it.

Well, he wasted no time. A week, two weeks after he married, he had all four of his boys set up with trust funds of their own for considerable amounts.

This is from what's her name, Harriet, to your sister to you?

With a time lapse. By the time I learned of it, two of his sons were already out in the world. One had bought into some fast food franchise, I believe, and begun to make a fortune of his own, which he would eventually have to share.

When? When would that be?

When his father had pretty much gone through Ellie's.

Which I believe you called "inexhaustible."

By any normal standards it was. But we're in a world of sickness, here. You understand that, don't you, Walter? Disease, Walter, for which there was no known cure. You could go over the world, as Little Howie had, looking for some way to clean that tumor out of his brain, and it wasn't going to happen. The drinking allowed you to forget it a while, and the drinking made sure it was going to get worse. What's left? There's a boys' and girls' camp up in the mountains, within hailing distance of the first house that Big Howie and Rosalyn built up there, where we had our earliest summer reunions, and as you pull into that camp there's a life-sized bronze statue of a large man holding a fishing rod in one hand and his other arm around the shoulder of a little girl. Leland Oldham had a convenient commemorative streak in him, and he was always appealing to the little girl in his wife that he kept feeding booze. Whoever sculpted the statue caught the chubby-cheeked boy in Big Howie, and the proud father, and the lord of all he surveyed, and the little girl was squarely planted under her father's arm. Leland commissioned the work. The camp has long since passed into other hands, for as Leland exhausted Ellie's fortune he exhausted the foundation's as well, but as far as I know the statue is still there. The day it was unveiled happened to have been the day we buried my mother in the town in which she and her three sisters had been born and brought up, from that camp in the mountains a good two hours away. It was also the first time I saw Ellie after her marriage, and the first time I saw Leland Oldham when he wasn't a shadowy, toad-shaped figure standing behind a screen door.

I paused in my narration, left it for Walter and, I suppose, for Byron Wainwright, who had found a rhythm and was sawing lugubriously away, and went down to the bottom in my Adirondack chair. My back and shoulders were sore, and the pain branched up into the back of my head, which had nothing to do with the afternoon's exertions. Or with the bourbon, which could never finally get the best of me.

Walter said, Let's go up to the cabin. I'll make a fire. We'll pretend it's that cold outside. The temperature is due to drop anyway. We'll steal a march, Jim, that's all.

There's a phrase, I said, you don't hear every day. Steal a march, get around in your enemy's rear. I'll drink to that, and I held my glass out for Walter to clink his against, which he did. I don't think Byron Wainwright heard that clinking of glasses. If he did, he played right through it as we left the field to him.

A cold fireplace and the first fire of the season, for which some birch wood had been stacked off in one corner of the screen porch. I expected smoke to back up into the small living room, which would have driven us back out onto the porch or onto the terrace and within range of Wainwright's cello, but we were lucky that over the summer no birds or raccoons had nested in the chimney and it still drew. Once Walter had gotten it started, the crackling of the fire overrode Bryon Wainwright but overheated the room, causing Walter to size down the fire until we could comfortably sit before it and what we could hear of Byron Wainwright was no more distracting than the creaking of the wind in the limbs of trees would have been, had the wind been blowing with any kind of force. We shared the bourbon, and when Walter produced, as though from his sleeve, a deck of cards, we played a little two-handed poker. A wheel of chips had been left on a shelf by the fireplace, and the chips had a weighted, worn vintage, perhaps dating from the time this cabin had been built. We played five-card stud and five-card draw, games quick to conclude, each chip from a stack of ten worth a dollar. After I won Walter's first stack, I won his second on unremarkable, adequately drawn cards, and I suspected Walter had his mind elsewhere or was suckering me along. At one point I said, We were pretty good paddling up that lake together, but you're not holding your own now. And Walter asked to be cut some slack, claiming that we all had our lapses, but finally admitting he'd been left on the brink of my first firsthand account of Ellie and the toad as man and wife and supposed that was where he still was. We were sitting in twin easy chairs, too small and too close-fitting to lounge in, and playing cards on a collapsible cane table not much bigger than a dinner tray. When I put my cards down, I must have put them down more emphatically than I'd meant to—I hadn't meant to put them down emphatically at all—and Walter's eyes flared. There was an instant's consternation there, as if he were about to be betrayed or abandoned, and in just that instant I wondered what I had done. It must have seemed that I was laying down my cards in truth, quitting the game.

And I said, but not as though reminiscing to Walter, rather into the fire, which was settling in to a clean, steady burn, My friend Phil Hodge, who almost jumped into Cuba and World War Three, took a look at the Howies, at all four Whalens, and ended up shaking his head. He couldn't believe it even though he'd seen it, or he couldn't see how it was worth working up into anything resembling belief. Of course, we caught all those fish coming north, maybe that was all it took, a real live weight at the other end of your line, a good smallmouth, say, no mistake about it, and all the swagger and hero worship and bluster and the sticky maneuvering around a family web went out of your mind.

Then I turned from the fire to Walter, and Walter said, Phil Hodge is no longer your friend, Jim. You've been out of contact with Phil Hodge for forty years. He may be dead. He may have moved south to retire. He may be fishing those very same lakes. Fishing the jumps. Or, via Canada, he may have traveled down to Cuba and been seduced by the place.

All of which I admitted was true, my only point being that Phil Hodge had had a good closeup look at the Whalens, found them preposterous or, perhaps, just touchingly out of date, shaken his head, and as soon as that cop who stopped us had waved us through, had gotten on with his life Whereas you, Walter . . .

Yes, Jim?

You seem to be taking it all to heart.

Do I?

And if truth be told, it's a bit—surprising.

If truth be told.

Well, I'm trying, I said. After so many years, it's not that you pick and choose so much as your memory picks and chooses, and what court would hold a man my age accountable for each of his memories? Some things stand out, others fade back, any of which might be true. The things that stand out might make a better story, that's all—

And Walter interrupted me. What makes you think that that isn't what a court of law is all about, who, which side, can tell the more convincing story? Juries get tired and distracted. Just like judges. They all want to hear a good story. Of course, they'd all like to hear it firsthand, not what a cousin of the sister of the accused happened to observe.

The accused?

To draw the parallel, Jim.

Phil Hodge got it firsthand, shook his head, pulled in the fish, and walked away.

That's because it wasn't his story. His story was almost—three times on and three times off the plane, wasn't that was what you said?—jumping into Cuba, and almost, almost helping to start World War Three.

That would have been some story, I said, if anybody had been left alive to hear it—or tell it.

Whereas your story, Walter said, is you. Oh, you have a cast of characters, some more familiar than others and some out in left field, but you *are* my friend, I'd go so far as to call us teammates—

Teammates?

Canoeing teammates, card-playing teammates, guys getting away for a weekend in the woods teammates, bourbon-drinking teammates, we could be right there on the label with the Beam brothers—

Those are fathers and sons, Walter, I said. And one nephew.

But we're brothers, and to emphasize the point Walter freshened my glass and took a long drink from his own. I began to suspect the bourbon had loosened his tongue, Walter not having been born to it. And we have a sister, a sister-in-law, he went on, but we could keep the law out of it. We have Elaine. And we could bring Molly back in by the back door. You should have seen your friend Molly—

Also known as your wife, I said.

And your friend, you should have seen her when we left you and Elaine out on our patio that evening so the chemistry could begin. Being more discreet, I wanted to go sit in the living room and let nature take its course, but your friend Molly—

And your wife, I remind you again.

—wanted to peek out from behind the patio curtains the whole time at what became, I guess, your courtship. And Molly won. I kept her from cheering, but it *was* sweet to see, Jim, we couldn't hear a lot, nothing, actually, you were keeping your voices low, but we could see, and when you touched Elaine's hand that first time, or she touched yours, that was a moment to remember.

I challenged him. What do you remember? Tell me about it.

We'd taken away the plates when we went inside, but drink glasses were still there. And a couple of hors d'oeuvre dishes we'd missed. The citronella candle was producing a flickering effect. Your hands, your right hands, were on the table. You were talking—but relax, I told you we couldn't hear what you said, I wouldn't have let Molly get away with that—and smiling and looking in each other's faces, then one of you—and Molly and I differ on this, too—reached out, and when I say "reach" I mean twelve, fifteen inches, and covered the other's hand. You never took your eyes off each other's faces, and you clearly continued talking, but your hands had a life of their own, and before long—if you ask how long, I'd guess a minute, but time has a way of going slowly in moments like that, both for the principals and the observers, maybe for the observers most of all—your hands turned over onto their sides so that one wasn't covering the other, and there was no gripping and no strain, and what I really remember was that you never took your eyes off each other, off each other's eyes, but your hands from that moment on were—I guess the right word is "bound." Molly wanted to cheer, because, well, you can imagine, Molly was the one who had it all worked out, but I put my hand over her mouth and pulled her back into the house and from that moment you and Elaine were alone.

My memory was that Elaine and I had found our hands like that as we'd gone on talking about the key points in our lives that had brought us to that table, and neither of us registered surprise, which did come as a surprise, although the evening had begun to cool and a little act of intimacy of that sort felt more instinctive than anything else, the giving and taking of a little animal warmth.

In that moment I confessed to Walter, You know I talked to Elaine last night briefly . . .

And Walter smiled.

You were making supper, I said.

Jim, Jim, Walter half sighed, half sang, the bourbon now clearly having its way with him, I don't care what you and Elaine have done in the eyes of the law. Believe it or not, there are times when I don't care about the eyes of the law.

We're fine, Walter. Better than ever. I know it seems strange.

Strange? He pulled up in his chair, then settled back down. Strange? he repeated. He began to laugh, but the laugh caught in his throat, and I thought about taking possession of the bottle, preemptive possession. A brief abrasive passage from Wainwright's cello got through then, and as if in protest, the fire popped, which seemed to put Walter on alert.

Strange, he said, is whatever's going on between Ellie and the toad, that's strange, that's downright incomprehensible, not you and Elaine. He looked at me sharply then, angry if what I had put him into was a position to beg. He said, I want it firsthand now. Not your sister and not her cousin. No branch on the Pritchard family tree. No little dead-end twig. You were there. Firsthand. He paused, grimaced, then gained traction again. Your mother's funeral, is that what you said? Damn, Jim, I'm sorry. What did that goddamned toad do?

Once again I felt like laying my cards on the table, and once again wondered what I was doing, what I had done. Walter, I said, it's not worth your attention, it's not worth going on. It's a sordid, sad affair, that's all. Forget it. Textile empires rise and fall every day. New England first, then down south, and now in every offshore haven where the workers barely earn enough to stay alive. One day it may come back, I suppose, the way those pendulums swing, but forget it for now. The story's here, it remains right here, FDR, the New Deal, and the ever-enduring WPA. A slide, Walter, that will be there till Judgment Day! Go to Cincinnati! You owe it to the boy in you to go sliding down that slide!

Merely invoking the WPA was apparently enough to sober my friend up, to deliver him back to familiar ground. But remember, he said, you didn't have FDR and the New Deal and the WPA down south. Not so they counted. You had right-to-work laws, the old plantation plutocracy turned to textile mills and apparel plants, and the Big Howies. And maybe you had favorite aunts uncomfortable with all that excess, who wanted to give it away, but what you really had were toads. I'm sorry it's over your mother's grave, Jesus, I am, but that's what I'm waiting to hear. Tell me about the toad.

But it wasn't over my mother's grave. Leland Oldham never got closer than a hundred feet of my mother's grave. And my mother had been within days of reaching her ninety-second birthday when she died. Lily had preceded her and, of course, Rosalyn years before that. Of the Pritchard girls, only Ruth was left, and the last few months before my mother died, she had almost become a match for Ruth in her tolerance and equanimity and her songbird's sunny disposition. During those last months, when you walked into her room, my mother greeted you with a kind of floating sparkle in her eyes, as if she were stargazing. My sister and I looked at each other and wondered why she couldn't have been like that always, that sergeant-at-arms of a preacher's daughter. No one seemed more at ease with her impending end, which would overtake her in her sleep and leave a smile on her lips. What in the world—or well beyond it—was going on? My mother's death was almost a cause for celebration, and it was in that spirit that we made the trip down to her native town and were standing around the gravesite when Ellie Whalen now Oldham came hurrying up, accompanied by her two daughters, hurrying in such a way that my sister and I both looked back to where she'd started

121

from, and there beside his car, not a black Cadillac is all I can tell you, Walter, stood Leland Oldham, I had to believe. A short, narrow-shouldered man, with a paunch and a loose-fitting sport coat, dark glasses—no goatee that I could make out—and an unsteady stance in the sun beating down, tracking his wife as she approached the gravesite shaded by the awning we'd all gathered under, as if, although I doubt he'd ever fished a day in his life, Leland Oldham had given the fish he'd hooked too much line to play with and now feared she was about to get away. He was a trifling figure, hard to take seriously. Nonetheless, he came close to ruining my mother's funeral. If he'd accompanied his wife to the gravesite and sat with us under the awning while the current minister from the town's First Christian Church made a few farewell remarks, he wouldn't have. It was the way he remained back there beside the car as though he had a stopwatch running that threatened to erase from my mind that aura of sweetness and sublimity my mother had achieved at the end. My sister was not so affected. And my cousin Harriet, who was also there, had seen Leland Oldham in action too many times to be taken by surprise now. As far as Harriet was concerned, he had our cousin Ellie not on a fishing line but on a good reliable leash, and what else was new?

It all slowed down, we bowed our heads for a final prayer, then when we raised them Ellie came rushing up to me. I'd barely had a chance to greet her two daughters, whom, it was true, I really didn't know, when Ellie grasped me in a hug as though she had something vital she wanted to whisper in my ear. She gave off not the smell of liquor but an anxious sort of heat, a sort of caustic sweetness as her perfume broke down, and I sensed she was holding on to gather strength before she attempted another run back to their car and the husband who had his stopwatch on her.

She said, You didn't come to *my* mother's funeral, and you didn't come to my wedding, either, Jim, but here I am! And as she concluded her little canned remark, which she half sang, she seemed to gather the strength that would allow her to pull back and look me in the eye. And allow me to look at her. Her green and gold eyes were larger than I remembered, which is to say, more stark in their hollows. She'd added a sparkling bronze burnish to the lids. She now had the pronounced cheekbones and chin you might associate with some predator, or with someone preyed upon. She couldn't hold her smile. It was as if some seismic wrenching had taken the face of the little girl I'd first seen half hidden behind her mother and left her with this outcropping of bone and this alien mineral luster around her eyes. Surely I was overreacting. But I remembered the last time I'd seen Little Howie as he suffered the deformities of his disease, I remembered his protuberant brows and lopsided head, and I thought, What is it about this family, what have we all bought into?

I said, Mother died very peacefully, Ellie. I'm glad you could come, if only here at the end. And, after glancing once more back to their car and that seemingly inconsequential figure standing there, I added, It would be nice to get away for a few minutes and talk. We have things to catch up on, don't we?

Oh, Jim, she said with a staged sigh, you don't know what day it is . . .

I was about to restate the obvious, as though my little cousin were more oblivious than I could have believed, it was the day we laid to rest the firstborn of the Pritchard girls, when my sister came up to Ellie, followed by Harriet, and children of theirs, all pleased their cousin had made it just under the wire, and I turned my attention back to Leland Oldham, who in the glaring sunlight had begun to pace back and forth the length of his car, no longer looking our way but at his feet, as though he was counting each step and would hold the tally against his wife. I took it as long as I could and was about to walk over there and engage my cousin's husband in conversation when Ellie slipped away from various kinfolk just long enough to say, Wait, don't do that, Jim. Wait on me.

And Walter, sitting half slumped before the fire, a full slump being hard to manage in these small chairs, said, "Wait on me"—those were her exact words?

That's what I remember, I said.

Don't do *what*, Jim? I wonder what she thought you had in mind.

Ellie spent a few more moments with my sister and her family, but it was as if she had a hand on my arm the whole time. In fact, she might have. And when she actually started walking back to Leland and their car, I know she had her hand there, up on my left biceps, and its purpose was to slow me down. She wanted to tell me why she and her girls had had to come running in and why they now had to go running off. Besides being the day of my mother's—and her dear aunt's—funeral, she wanted to tell me what day it really was. Which would also explain why she was so late in arriving and perhaps a hundred other things. It was, she declared, dedication day for that statue at the entrance to their summer camp for needy boys and girls, the statue of the man with a fishing rod in one hand and his other on the shoulder of a little girl. And what a coincidence that that dedication would fall on the same day as Aunt Esther's funeral. That was why Ellie had to be in two places at once. It's was Leland's baby, that statue—she didn't say that, but that explained why he was pacing off the minutes until he could get up there for the unveiling, when he intended to present the statue as a big fat sop to his wife.

Your word, Jim.

My word, Walter. But all the rest was what she said. It did not correspond to her grip on my arm. That was an anxious, urgent grip, and it did not let up. We weren't fifty feet from their car when I slowed our pace and when Leland Oldham—

The toad, Walter said.

All right, the toad, my cousin's husband, stopped pacing up and down and, motioning his stepdaughters on, managed to get them into the backseat of their car. I said, Ellie, what is it? And under a fluttering pant in her breath, she said, I may need you, Jim. Not today, but sometime.

What do you think she meant? Walter said.

I don't know. She sounded a little scared, but she also had an adventuresome tone to her voice, as if she contemplated some big step, as if she might need to consult me for one more foolish investment of theirs.

He wasn't beating her, was he? That wasn't what she meant?

No sign of it, Walter. Rather, beating her with the booze. That was leaving its marks.

So what did you tell her?

I stopped and looked down at her. She was taller than her husband but not as tall as me. She'd put her sunglasses on, and it took me a moment to find her eyes. Leland was maybe twenty feet away from us now. He was impatient, angry. That statue was his pet project. Anything I said to his wife I would have to say in a whisper, a stage whisper, which I was going to take a certain pleasure in doing. When the time is right, I finally responded, you let me know.

You'll remember I was the oldest in that generation of the family, Walter. It was a bit of a drama, something of a *Godfather* moment, with the toad standing there, ready to roar off and leave my mother's funeral under a cloud of his exhaust. Of course, he was worried he wouldn't arrive back in the mountains on time. Of course, people would be waiting. Out of deference to his wife, he'd created this gap in his schedule. And, of course, there was the remote possibility that I'd been wrong about him all along, that he was in reality a bashful man, felt out of place, and was reluctant to intrude. That that was why he hadn't accompanied his wife up to view her aunt's casket and to offer condolences where they were due. That as an outsider he knew he belonged back with the car, like a chauffeur, or, for that matter, somewhere outside the big house, behind a screen door. But I'd be damned! I spoke slowly, and loud enough for Leland to hear too. I said, Then we'll see.

Then we'll see?

Then we'd see what measures I would take. I don't mind telling you, Walter, I felt like a bit of a fool. But it was *my* mother's funeral, Leland's big day was up in the mountains, a good two hours away.

Then we'll see, Walter repeated, each word loaded and deliberately delivered, right between the eyes. I almost like it. Noncommittal, but keep your head down. How did Ellie take it? How did the toad?

She didn't release her grip on my arm, not at once. But it quit digging in. For a quick moment her mind seemed to go elsewhere. Maybe she felt embarrassed, as if she regretted having to beg. I felt something of that in her hand as she loosened her grip. I leaned in and kissed her on the cheek, but I was upset, too. She owed my mother more than she'd given, showing up the way she had at the very end of things, running her little girls up there like interference—

Of course, she could say you'd owed her mother, too.

She could.

Isn't that what you told me, Jim? You were the only notable absence at Rosalyn's funeral, after all she'd piled into your arms.

I took a deep breath, not suddenly but finally very tired. Walter, please understand. I hadn't seen Ellie since I'd met her for lunch and urged her, as Rosalyn had asked me to, not to do what she then did. I'd done my aunt's bidding. Now if her daughter found herself in a fix, it was of her own making. If I felt foolish, it was because of the tone of what I'd said—and the staging. But she'd brought the staging down on herself, hadn't she? Leland hanging back there like that, Ellie rushing up like some movie star with a fifteen-minute opening in her schedule before she went rushing off to her next photo shoot up in the mountains. Running her two little girls out there like movie extras being paid by the hour. I really don't want to think about it anymore. I don't know why I brought it up. We were playing cards and I was skunking you—

Unfazed, as if he hadn't heard a word I'd said, Walter quoted me, "When the time is right, you let me know. Then we'll see." I like it, Jim. Cards close to your vest, but they're the right cards. I like it. I'll drink to it. Walter held up his glass, but it was empty, and I did have possession of the bottle now.

I think we'd better eat, I said.

We will, we will.

We were going to steal a march, get in the enemy's rear. Is that where we are?

Tell me where the toad is and I'll tell you.

You know where he is.

Did he shake your hand? Did you shake his?

I didn't have the chance. He opened the passenger door and got his wife inside, and then before I could even approach him, he got around to the driver's side of the car, and that's where he was when he mostly mumbled, I'm sorry for your loss.

He did? He said that? And then you were going to shake his hand?

I don't know. For Ellie's sake, I might have.

Even though you told her she was being played for a fool.

I don't think I ever used that word. I'd said that she was making a big mistake, that she owed it to the memory of her father whose fortune, if she didn't get a prenup, she was going to waste—

But who would be immortalized in a statue soon to be unveiled, and she would be immortalized at his side as his pre-alcoholic little girl—

OK, Walter. It's all true. Let's give it a break, find something to eat. It's been a long day.

I'm glad you didn't shake his hand. There was absolutely no call for that.

Not even to get in the enemy's rear?

The goddamn toad got away, to live and fight another day. Walter chuckled at his own remark, but also at the prospect of having the toad around to play with another day himself. Except that the following day we were due to return home. I didn't remind Walter of that. The fire popped three or four times in quick succession, and that roused him, brought a relishing look into his eye. How'd he drive off, Jim?

You mean did he gun out of that cemetery, leaving a streak of rubber behind?

No, toads don't do that. But our toad might have. What was his parting shot?

No parting shot.

No? No parting shot? He let you have the last word?

I didn't say that. It was a small-town cemetery, up on a little knoll. It was full and pretty much forgotten. People were no longer buried there. Unless you'd been thinking well ahead, or your father or your grandfather had, and had bought an ample family plot years before. My grandfather, James Pritchard, the celebrity preacher with the gleaming black eyes, had thought far enough ahead to buy up four burial sites, in addition to those where he and his wife were going to lie, two on each side of theirs. Four for the four Pritchard girls, I suppose. But my mother as her father's enforcer had somehow gotten them all. I don't know how. Probably none of her sisters cared. But my mother and father were buried on one side of my grandparents, and on the other side were the sites reserved for my sister and me. Jean, who didn't spend a lot of time dwelling on death, just laughed it off and said something like, Fat chance! But we played along with my mother, who in her last days kept musing very uncharacteristically about the blissful eternity we had coming when we'd all lie side by side again. She claimed to remember times when my sister and I as children had gotten in bed with both of them and the four of us had floated away in some earthly rehearsal for the eternal rest we had coming, which, given my sister's and my age difference and my mother's and father's clashing characters, and for a dozen other reasons, could never have happened. But we let her believe it, and she probably floated away that night she died dreaming she had her family at her side. And you want to know, Walter, what this has to do with the toad and his parting shot? Nothing. There was no parting shot. In that long-past-its-prime cemetery the narrow roads among the family plots weren't asphalted, they were all overgrown gravel, and Leland Oldham and his Ellie drove away so slowly and so quietly I could hear every pebble crunching under his wheels. I didn't miss a one, Walter. Which began to seem like a little eternity of its own.

V

What is 'ums? And "is 'ums" became "isums," which was the word Mama Grace used—because I did, she insisted—to refer to pancakes when I stood beside her at the stove and waited to be served the first stack. I do remember using that word. But even as baby talk, its derivation seems hard to believe to me, and maybe the word had something to do with that racist cast of characters associated with pancakes in the South, with Aunt Jemima and Little Black Sambo, to name two, and maybe I inherited it from them. What is 'ums? We're having isums today, Jimmy, and you get the first ones. How many can you eat?

My grandmother stood at the stove. A cast iron stove with a built-in griddle on top. A wood- or coal-burning stove—I'm not sure. At times I think it's my first memory, and other contenders—one of me playing somewhere up north in the snow, another where I'm mounted on a pony dressed like Cowboy Joe, but not one that has me trailing along behind a little bug-eyed dog named Bing—come from family snapshots, where I'm cherubically round in the face and cheeks, still looking fresh-born. I see my grandmother, it must be summer because she has the flimsiest of slips on as she stands before the stove, the flesh in her upper arms is bare, she's a tall woman and her hair is piled up, making her taller still, and the perspiration is fresh on the nape of her neck, fresh and clear beneath the caught-up hairs, and I am waiting like a dog down below for her to tell me what isums are and to be served the first stack. Since my grandfather died when I was one, she could have been into the second or third year of her widowhood by that time, which means that my cousin Harriet would have been born, and probably Little Howie, too, but surely neither of them had stood behind her at the stove—behind her and way down there—as she flipped isums and built a stack worthy of her first grandchild.

The isums carried over and became a sort of code word between my grandmother and me, and by the time the war had ended and the soldiers and sailors and Lily, my WAC aunt, had come home, and the Whalens, their business booming, had built their cabin up in the mountains on the lake and we'd had our first family reunion there, Mama Grace was still standing at the stove making pancakes, only on an electric stove now, and I was still entitled to the first stack. It wouldn't be long before Little Howie would demand that honor for himself, but as the firstborn, first memories belong to me. My grandmother towered above me at the stove, rosy-fleshed in those beginning years of her bereavement, some all but transparent fabric falling over her shoulders and her ample hips, the batter-scent and the flesh-scent getting mixed up into the same stack. As a young woman she'd made an effort to attract attention; now it took no effort at all. Click.

But it quickly became Little Howie's world up there in the mountains, and he learned quickly, to swim, to fish, to boat, to pop birds out of the trees with his BB guns, to seine for minnows, to catch crawdads, to distinguish between poisonous and nonpoisonous snakes and to scare everybody with the nonpoisonous ones, to back boats out of the boathouse and to nudge them in, to gig for frogs, and with that same frog gig to spear a good-sized boathouse bass three feet under the water, as I once saw him do. Every year he seemed to be more adept at more things—he couldn't have been over twelve when I sat and watched him repair a balky motor that had stalled on us out in the lake—and then more willing to teach others without making a boastful display of himself while doing it.

I was always surprised, not to say amazed, at what his parents consented to. It was Little Howie who was allowed to take out the speedboat and show not just me, his elder by two years, but much younger children in that ever-enlarging family, how to water-ski. Howie himself, who all but lived on the lake during the summer, while the rest of us spent on average two weeks there, had had enough water-skiing thrills, but we his cousins needed to learn, and one by one as we got up and got our legs under us and began to speed along the surface of the water, almost, it seemed, to fly, we looked up ahead and there sat Little Howie at the wheel of the speedboat looking back over his shoulder at us, with never a broad smile but a proud and almost private one as if we now belonged to his club.

Or he'd load us all onto the houseboat, and some of the adults too, and take us for a tour of the lake, passing various boat docks, some of which were like little town centers where you could pull in to get gassed up, stretch your legs, go shopping and have a bite to eat, pointing out certain sites, big houses built up on bluffs, railroad trestles, parks with boat ramps, unremarkable streams entering inconspicuous coves but yielding good fish, picnicking areas where we could stop and sometimes did to eat our lunch, fingers of the lake leading off to various towns with attractions of their own in case we were interested, really back-of-his-hand stuff for Little Howie, who was a child prodigy when you added it all up. And, before we'd head back, he'd pull us up below the dam, which rose in a towering concrete crescent above us and where we could feel the current quicken as Howie pitted himself against that massive structure and those built-up depths and gave us all a little thrill before opening the throttle and pulling us back out. He didn't talk a lot, not even there at the end when we'd reached the climax of the afternoon, for the lake spoke for itself and all we really needed was just something to joggle our memories here and there for the next time we ventured out. The dam explained the how and why of the lake but not the what, not what the lake meant, not for the family that gathered there each summer for two weeks. I was the first of the generation that my namesake James Pritchard had grandfathered when he'd picked his wife out of that mostly pleasure-seeking Saturday evening congregation, but when we convened each summer, that generation had added to itself, so that every family reunion became a celebration of a past, a present, and an ongoing future, and the lake, which Little Howie Whalen had taken the measure of, was like our grand baptismal font.

There was a long dock leading out to the boathouse, long because there were periods when the water was low, and in a boathouse built too close to shore, the boats, unless they were raised on hoists, could become beached. The long dock allowed you to get a good running start, not to the boathouse itself but to the float fastened alongside, off which you could dive into water that was chilly only on first contact, but after which was as suited to you as the water out of which you'd been born. Some of the grown-ups complained that it smelled faintly of gas—and boats did

131

run up and down our finger of the lake to a ramp at the end—or that it left an algae-like film on the skin, but this was the excuse aunts and uncles used when all they wanted to do was sit on their chaise lounges in the shade of a catalpa tree, on a strip of lawn between the house and the retaining wall, and sip their iced tea, or in the evenings their cocktails, and be entertained by their children as we jumped on and off that float or water-skied by.

Occasionally one of them would venture out to the float to swim. Uncle George, Ruth's sailor husband, was a big man, six feet five inches tall, it was said, and he was the one we welcomed with cheers, because he always shouted, Man overboard! before cannonballing into the water, which created a huge cratering splash. Afterwards, if you were lucky, he'd tell the story of when the Japs torpedoed his ship and he really had to jump overboard, which made him lucky to be alive. But here he was, and he'd be damned if it wasn't a beautiful day! Ruth didn't like for him to use that sort of language, especially around us, and she wished he wouldn't keep telling those war stories to impressionable young ears, but one morning, when they'd left their bedroom door open so the air could pass through, I happened to glance inside and saw them in bed, Uncle George sleeping on his side and my aunt Ruth clinging to his back as if she were the one who'd fallen overboard and was holding on for dear life. Uncle George could seem massive and Aunt Ruth had never been petite. But, together, they buoyed themselves up.

We all knew about her youthful career as a songbird, but I never heard her sing to him. My mother played the piano, and when she struck a chord and her sisters were present, they knew to gather around. But there was no piano up at the lake. Up there the grown-ups spent their time talking, they reclined on their chaise lounges deep into the evening, and, depending on the day I'd had and the mood I was in, as the oldest of the youngest generation I'd sometimes hang around. They told stories, the same stories, year after year, unless one of the four sisters happened to be absent, which was frequently the case, and then they told stories featuring that missing sister. I wouldn't hear those they told about my mother, since when I was there she was too, but her bossiness was so notorious there wasn't much left to tell. And, generally speaking, her three younger sisters didn't begrudge her her bossiness since Mama Grace had been an equally notorious soft touch.

Rosalyn, being our hostess and benefactress, rarely got stories told about herself. When Big Howie was there, for the sport of it my mother would tie into him, but that frequently had something to do with politics, which on a summer evening with the swallows swooping over the lake at sunset, dipping their wings into its lustrous orange glow, could have a jarring effect, as playful as my mother and Big Howie might try to keep their little confrontations. My father didn't always go to the lake with us. Before going into business he traveled for a living, was, it seemed, his own boss, and rarely gave himself a vacation. He sold granite to monument companies. He was not a high-powered salesman type, not at all a quick talker, and he let the granite sell itself. Granite from Vermont, granite from Georgia, gray granite with swimming black specks and red granite straight from the iron-enriched earth. When he was there in that line of chaise lounges drawn up before the lake, he usually found himself seated beside Aunt Lily, who, with her provocative swagger, amused him no end. She was the mystery sister, and how a woman so up-front and open to attack could be mysterious was a mystery in itself.

She had married late, a man twenty years her senior—a marriage of convenience, it was whispered, whatever that meant—who, not being an outdoorsman, more of a banker type, someone who would have a vault nearby he could step into when life got too raucous outside, rarely came to the mountains. Why in the world he had married Lily, and vice versa, her sisters soon tired of talking about. Since as a subject of conversation Lily was waywardness personified, her sisters saw the folly of trying to account for her and talked about something else. She still intrigued her mother, as though Mama Grace before she died was determined to figure Lily out, but Mama Grace also knew when she was beat, and I decided, as far as Lily was concerned, the missing figure was her father. Mama Grace would shake her head and mutter some baffled endearment under her breath, but my grandfather, James Pritchard, would have picked Lily out of the congregation with his pinioning black eyes and sat her up straight.

She'd been in Australia at the war's end and had brought me a boomerang. When I had the arm for it, I launched the boomerang, expecting it to fly around me in a huge circle before falling, like an exhausted bird, at my feet. Instead it just kept flying away. What kind of hoax was this? I wondered. Something that could trace a great, world-encircling arc before returning home I'd bought into, and the failure of the boomerang to perform as advertised might have been my very first loss-of-inno-cence moment. But then I remembered that Aunt Lily herself had sailed off and basically gone around the world and come home, so I'd been able to shore up my innocence with a bit of symbolic reasoning. The boomer-ang was her totem, her charm, you didn't throw the boomerang so much as you threw yourself, and when you circled back if you were lucky you landed here, up at the lake, with your family spread out in one long front row as the sun set over the water. I told Aunt Lily she was the boomer-ang lady, which caused her to smile her big opened-mouth smile and to say, Bud (her name for me from the start), I'm going to change that to the Boomerang Babe, if you don't mind. It suits me, don't you think? And then she gave me her hoarse, hooting laugh.

It was a laugh that could scare the fish, and she was the other adult who would make appearances out on the swimming float attached to the boathouse. She wouldn't run out the long dock to get a head start, but when she appeared out there, she seemed to be riding the winds of some sort of release, so you never knew what to expect. She wouldn't always jump in. Unlike her sisters, she never wore a bathing cap. She had crin-kled ginger-colored hair, which she kept short, also unlike her sisters, whose hair was a wavy shoulder-length black. Some days she'd stand there on the float and make critical comments about our swimming styles and attire, and other times she might dive in over us and with a powerful kick swim straight out into the lake, in which case the message she was send-ing us, her nieces and nephews, was clear. Get your money down, because the odds were good that this time she wasn't coming back! When she finally stopped, she'd be out in the middle, swimming-wise in a world of her own. There were houses and boathouses across the lake, housing other families, in case she wanted to make a run for it, but she always came back to us, and cautioned us as she pulled up onto the float. Don't you dare swim out there where I did! I saw a fish out there as big as Uncle George with a hungry look in his eye! Then she went back and took her seat in line, frequently beside my father, whom she never failed to amuse. From his time on the road he must have seen a number of women who reminded him of Lily, just as those women out there, thanks to Lily, would remind him of home. My father had a long face, he was lanky and long and could always use a smile. Lily obliged. She was the swing char-acter in the family. The boomerang babe.

When I wanted a break from the lake and the family, it was simply a matter of choosing any of the streambeds flowing down off the hills and following it back up. There were hiking paths up there where I almost never saw anyone hiking, and sooner or later I'd branch off onto one of those, but the streambeds were full of stones, so that even if it had rained recently and water was running down, you could make your way up, and these streambeds always gave off a deep breath of earthy coolness even in the middle of the day. If you got hot from your effort, all you had to do was find one of those especially cool spots and stand there without moving, without making a sound, and a breeze in the pines and the scent of pines would come down to find you. Birds took their turns calling, a whistling sort of screech, probably warning each other there was an intruder in their midst, but if you stood still long enough, they quieted down. You weren't really an intruder, but they didn't know that yet. Eventually you began to hear whippoorwills and jays and the low chuckling coo of doves. There was a constant shrilling of cicadas, but that was a curtain of noise you could slip behind and into the presence of quieter, more intimate sounds. Something was always scampering away, there was always a woody ticking of some sort or maybe a stray gust of breeze in the pinecones, some insect would buzz by your ear, and there was a quiet settling sound, as though the earth itself were settling, but which was probably just the settling of your own breath. And, of course, there were snakes, there was an ever-nearness of snakes, but if you stuck to the streambeds and the paths, the snakes, with a thin rustling slither, as though keeping their half of the bargain, would move back into the brambly underbrush. The smell of that underbrush was so fresh it was rank, it was manless and rank, as if in a thousand years a family reunion had never been held anywhere near there, as if you could travel a thousand miles and get no farther away than you were at that moment from that large family gathered on the shores of that lake, probably no more than a hundred yards down that streambed. But I was young, and a little wilderness went a long way.

And I loved returning from my excursions. As a boy I was a loner until I'd gotten my fill, then I wanted to belong. The family kept getting larger and larger, and for the longest time no one died. Even as a young girl my cousin Harriet had a detached, unflappable way about her, which made her a reliable playmate, if not a very active one. She picked things out about the adults, though, which made her seem wiser than her years.

135

She was the next oldest of the children, and would be the cousin in whom I confided. She had gotten her father's height, a girl's share of it, and something of his long ruminative face. She had sleepy brown eyes, which served as a decoy because she was keeping an active eye on everything.

As a girl, more than a talker Harriet was a gossiper of a few well-chosen words, which you had to coax out of her, but which she took pleasure in, in the effort you made. Lily, of course, was easy pickings, so easy she made a mockery of gossip, but the way Big Howie had Rosalyn under his control and the way Rosalyn escaped it once her husband's back was turned allowed Harriet to take potshots at her uncle from behind the shield of his wife, so Big Howie's gaucheries could be made to seem like a little boy's. Using any of the Pritchard girls as shields behind which their husbands could be ridiculed was something Harriet was very adept at. Lily's banker husband (although that was not what he did, just how he behaved; he made his modest living as an accountant) was like a dog Lily let out to do its business and let back in when he learned to scratch at the door. Lily's husband had a son from a previous marriage, and the one time Lily brought the two of them to the lake, they seemed like a species from another planet. They struck a stance and stayed put until Lily took them home. Her own father, Harriet claimed, could be whistled down if her mother suddenly became untracked, which could happen. It was as if Ruth had woken up one morning and said, Where am I now? and when Uncle George spoke the name of a place his wife couldn't even pronounce, she told him they'd strayed too far over the map. They needed to go back to the lake to touch base, and here they were.

It would be years before Mama Grace sat me down and told me the story of how her husband had picked her out of the congregation and held her there with his eyes until he could propose at the church door, but her daughters must have known that story and taken its cautionary lessons to heart. Matinee idols posing as itinerant preachers preying on innocent young girls with picture taking on their minds—what all that meant was that the Pritchard girls needed to be on high alert and, in the public eye at least, to keep up the farce of keeping their husbands cowed.

More children came. Harriet had a brother, little Bobbie, three years younger, who was a pistol, a firecracker, and all of that. Then a sister, Beatrice, little Bea, so pretty and happily behaved that you questioned your memory once she'd become a normal, active, stubborn, spoiled and noise-making girl. And my sister, of course, was included in there, five years younger than I, but I never forgot that I was the oldest, the first-born, with certain obligations I imagined I had to fulfill, a position that not even Little Howie with all of his gifts could claim. I drifted off and I drifted back. I counted heads to see if more children had appeared, reassured when none had, but I knew the day would come.

For a while the question became Lily, and Lily was the sort of woman you could put the question to directly. All right! Let's see! Cards on the table! Are you going to reproduce or not? But no one bothered to ask the question or even hint at it in a joking sort of way, because Lily in the guise of a pregnant woman, with a pregnant flush to her skin and a pregnant rounding out of her bones, no one could imagine, much less imagine her husband performing the role of procreator. So then the real question became the one that everybody had been asking themselves since the Whalens had built the cabin and invited family up here: When would Little Howie have a brother or sister? The Whalens rebuilt the cabin, modernizing and extending it so that the original cabin became a sort of off-at-the-end nucleus of what was now one long train car of a house, painted a cedar red, with new bedrooms and baths off to each side, room to sleep up to twenty, and the question of how to fill those rooms was never far from anybody's mind. We still sat in front of the fireplace in the original cabin, the trout and bass mounted on the walls stayed there, a bearskin rug remained before the hearth with the bear's head attached and the teeth still bare but completely domesticated now, and on the rainy afternoons—part of the risk you ran, rain in the mountains on summer afternoons being close to the norm—we assembled jigsaw puzzles or played cards on the screen porch, canasta and hearts and old maid, until the rain ended and we were let loose back into the lake.

It was mostly the women playing cards, and it was mostly then, with the competitive juices flowing, rather than when they were all sitting out before the lake and the setting sun could soothe their spirits, that the most telling stories got told. It was on a rainy afternoon on that porch that word escaped my mother's lips that Lily was not exactly childless, not technically at least, and that a gasp escaped Ruth's lips, not at the news, which she seemed to have known, but directed at my mother for revealing it before one of the children, for there I sat on a nearby daybed, as my generation's spokesman, with now, perhaps, another cousin to add

137

to the count. But mum was the word, and it wasn't until much later, in fact after Lily died, that my sister in going through some of her things found a photograph of our aunt in her WAC uniform holding a baby in her arms, actually holding it up as though proudly presenting it to the world, and the look on Lily's face was radiant, even though the quality of the photograph was poor and the intervening years had dulled whatever luster it had once had. But I asked myself: how was anyone to know if this was Lily's baby or not? There was the better part of a year it took for Lily to travel back cross-country from San Diego to her hometown, time enough for her to get pregnant, if that hadn't happened overseas, and to give birth, but that delay was chalked up to Lily feeling her oats, with her father dead for four years and her mother too loving and obliging to take offense. Lily, it was believed, was out seeing something of the country she'd just helped to save. When she finally appeared before us, she came bearing gifts, a boomerang for me and down under mementos for other family members, and with a big grin on her face that meant, in case we'd forgotten, We won! We won!

If, I put it to myself, after all that death she'd seen in the Philippines, she'd gotten off the boat and held a baby in her arms, that didn't have to mean she'd given birth to it, did it? Even though she might have spent the better part of a year out West soaking up the sun, it could have meant, We won, we won, and here's fresh life to prove it. Somebody's fresh life. A twig on somebody's tree. Jean secretly hoped it had been Lily's baby, even if she'd had to give it up for adoption or something like that. But only after, as Jean imagined it, a long, jubilant one-night stand! Yet that look on our aunt's face in the photograph could also have been the look of a victor, celebrating with the nearest fresh life at hand. Knowing how impulsive my aunt could be, and how winning, too, I could imagine Lily stepping down from that troopship in San Diego, with crowds there waiting to welcome their loved ones home, and persuading a young mother to relinquish her baby for just one moment, for just one snapshot from the thousands of cameras that must have been on hand out there. Or, since there were no Polaroids back then but an abundance of Brownie cameras, and Lily was still, after all, her mother's daughter, it could have been a snapshot taken with Lily's own camera, perhaps a hand-me-down from her mother, which Lily had carried through the whole horrid course of that war in anticipation of this one moment, when she could step off the ship onto free American soil and hold up a newborn baby to represent them all. Why wouldn't Mama Grace have loved that? Why wouldn't we all? I could have made the case to all my cousins if I'd thought of it, or if I had dared.

Click.

But I'd shown myself to be discreet, and for all those years mum continued to be the word until Jean, who'd make a nice living sorting through and selling once prized possessions, came across that photograph and showed it to me. It was only then that I told her what as a boy I had overheard our mother remark to our aunts. But by the time Jean had found that photograph, more babies were probably being born out of wedlock than within it—in fact, by then "wedlock" had become pretty much an archaic word—so to get the full dramatic impact of the situation, you'd have to be willing to put yourself back in those times, and who, Jean wondered, would want to do that? What times! Yes, the family lined up in front of the lake at sunset telling their tales, it sorted itself out until only the good stuff was left, and it cast a nice glow, but—wedlock? Young lady, I'm going to wed you and lock you up for the rest of your life? And for a couple of generations at least you could count on that lock holding? Is that what we'd all bought into whether we knew it or not? Well, unlock the locks and bring me your heirlooms and let's start spreading all this good stuff around. What a family, and none of us ever met the preacher man who'd turned the key.

I did, I reminded my sister. I was one year old. He'd been famously handsome once and wanted to spare me the sight of what he'd become.

Jean laughed. Then, with a certain cemetery plot in mind, she said, Just don't expect me to be lying for all eternity at his side.

And with another cemetery plot and another monument with an even broader wingspan in my mind, I responded, You know what would have made a difference? If our grandfather had lived a few years longer and gotten to know Little Howie. Who better to introduce him to the great out of doors?

Jean laughed.

I am referring to the great, wedlock-free out of doors.

Little Howie?

Seriously, I said.

Seriously?

When you come down to it, I said with a straight face, Little Howie may be the only remarkable one of the bunch.

Little Howie?

Little Howie, I repeated.

Matching my straight face, my sister replied, Now, there's a novel idea!

But there was really nothing up there on the lake Little Howie couldn't do, and do as though born to it, which made him as a teenager a natural, perhaps the only natural I'd known in my life, and how was he not going to make a lasting impression on me? But I did not go on in this vein to my sister. I really don't think she would have understood. If the world for those summer weeks was that lake and the pleasures you took on it and the tasks you first had to perform to make those pleasures real, then there was only one man equal to it all and that man was a boy—and I certainly didn't reveal any of this to my sister, who, like our aunt Lily, had a good hooting laugh of her own.

Fishing was at the heart of it, of course, but I also had memories of going out with Big Howie to fish, just the two of us, Big Howie in his swivel seat back in the stern of the boat, like his son making selective casts up among the stickups by the shore, Big Howie with all his girth letting his flicking wrists do the work, a cast here, a cast there, it was his world, he'd gotten here first, and to use an analogy my sister might have hooted at again, but this time with pleasure, marking his spots with each cast as a dog marks his, warning other dogs to go find their own place to pee. But he didn't catch fish. He'd talk to me during his time. Unlike his son, Big Howie was a big talker, and as I got older his talk would become more boastful, about the good things he'd done for his town, and for the colored folks, especially the colored folks, the firewall, in effect, he'd built around his town as the country'd begun to heat up, and every so often with a delicate flick of the wrist he'd shoot a little double-jointed Bassmaster spinning plug up into the brush, twitch it, make it dart this way and that, a big man with chubby, short-fingered hands and a pencil-thin rod held at ten o'clock, masterfully retrieving a lure as he recited his life's accomplishments, but he didn't catch fish, because the fish, I came to realize, were indifferent to his boasts. In a way, he could make a case for all this being his, all this shoreline, every cove we cruised into with the electric motor barely making a purr, but the fish preferred someone who could get down among them, take on their ways, feed as they fed, work the shoreline as they did, and dart to the kill while continuing to cruise, and that was Little Howie, who rarely said a word. Naturals don't talk, they become one with their prey, take on their prey's ways, deer, bear, long-horned sheep, it didn't matter, it was pretty clear there was a bond of sympathy there, a willingness to step out of your skin and into another's, just as Little Howie could be said to have stepped out of his skin when he measured me for a suit that fit as naturally as a second skin of mine. When you fished the jumps, you got wild; when you fished the stickups along the shoreline in these secluded coves, you got as quiet as if you were out for an evening stroll. Big Howie recited his life's accomplishments in case, as the oldest of my generation, I'd want to make a record for future generations to consult. Only occasionally opening his mouth, his son caught fish. He taught by example, but there was just so much he could teach. Make yourself one with the fish, one with the deer. I remembered him following those narrow deer paths in the woods below his house. Even as a boy he was not trying to get anywhere. I followed along behind him and came away with my arms scratched and my shirt torn by the briars. Little Howie, with a deerlike fluidity, slipped through.

With those clear blue eyes of his, you saw right through Howie. It was unnerving only until you realized he was offering you, if your nerve held steady, the whole natural world. Did Howie know this about himself? That for all those years up on the lake as the family grew and cousins brought friends who became boyfriends and girlfriends once puberty had been breached and a whole new class of activities had taken hold, did Howie know that he was providing an avenue into the only world that would at last matter? Probably not. Almost certainly he didn't. He'd become a shirt and pants man like his father, he'd marry the prettiest girl in town, have himself some kids, and buddy up to his high school friends out on the town square. While still a boy up on the lake, he'd put on a target practice show with his pistol and his bow and arrows if he felt his little cousins weren't giving him the admiring attention he deserved. He always had a supply of cherry bombs around if things were too quiet for his taste. Even before he had his driver's license, he'd grab the keys to the family car and run it up and down the road. He'd run his father's Cadillac, too, when Big Howie was there. If he went into a sulk, he did his best to impersonate a black hole and take everybody with him. If little cous-

Lamar Herrin

ins—and some big ones—began to stray into the boathouse with all its enticing boating and fishing equipment, its rods and reels and various landing and seining nets, its minnow buckets, its gigs and its spear-length boating poles, its life preservers and cushions, its water skis and tow ropes and all that shiny speedboat paraphernalia, a magical world in there for a kid who was only used to exploring his own garage, Little Howie might run them out. He was, for those who chose to see him in that way, insufferably spoiled. None of that had anything to do with my lasting impressions of him and the part that he played in my life. I would have gladly relinquished to him my honorary first stack of isums if Mama Grace had still been on the job. But she was too old to stand in front of a stove for any length of time and occupied her position out in that line of chaise lounges, except she had to sit in a cushioned straight-back armchair and safely in the shade of that catalpa tree with those long, cigar-like pods hanging straight down as though in the pull of a gravity-enriched earth.

The last year I went with my parents and sister to the lake I was on the point of turning eighteen. No one in the family had died, and still others had been born, but the sense was that by the summer of my eighteenth birthday that generation of the family was complete. A late-comer like Ellie wasn't given a chance. I was set to go to college and leave all this child's play behind me. I took a few long walks up into the hills, which were not so steep as I recalled them being, the streambeds not so wide and the stones situated not so far apart. There was a current but nothing like a rushing one, and I quickly got a sense of how things had been scaled up and then scaled down as I passed through my childhood to arrive at where I now stood. In a commemorative state of mind, I breathed it all down, the pine trees and musky, mossy odor of the dampened and dried, re-dampened and re-dried earth. When I struck a path, I stayed on it for a while, working my way around the brambly underbrush the snakes made home. I didn't see a one, but all I had to do was stand motionless long enough for the treetop-to-treetop screech of the birds to go still and I'd begin to hear that quiet thin rustle the snakes made, unlike the quiet scampering rustle their small prey made, or other small animals seeking the safety of their holes.

Before I made my way back down to the road, I came upon a cabin built back in the woods, which years later I would recognize as Little Howie and Laurie's first lakeside residence although the lake was down a

142

rutted drive and visible only at a distance through the trees. It was something like their honeymoon bungalow until they built higher and grander on land more sweepingly located, with a panoramic view of the lake. None of that, of course, I knew at the time. I'd heard family talk about Laurie Kingston, for she and Howie had been sweethearts from junior high on, but not from Howie, and not even from the family as they occupied their chaise lounges in the evening and in a family forum told their stories. I'd heard it privately, perhaps from my mother or sister, perhaps even from Mama Grace, for whom sweethearts had a special appeal.

When I reached the road, I turned away from the Whalen house and walked on a ways more to Coggins's bait shop and lunch counter and boat dock, where we often pulled in to get gas for a boat or to have sandwiches and Cokes or, when Little Howie wasn't on the scene and we didn't want to dig for worms or seine for minnows, to buy bait. A father and son ran it. Their faces were swollen and baked, their eyes sun-narrowed into slits, they were heavyset and smelled like boats and gas and fish and bait, and at a quick glance the only way you could tell them apart was by the burnt baldness of the father's head and the bristly crew cut of the son's. Big Howie paid them something every year to keep an off-season eye on the house and the boats. In turn they were more than obliging to every Whalen family member who showed up, to the point at times of seeming servile, and I'd become curious about them, these not quite official employees of Big Howie's, and mildly fond of their folksy ways and all their fishing lore. I stopped in to say goodbye and sit at their counter and have a last Coke. How're they biting, what are they hitting, how deep down, what time of the day, and the crappies, and the bluegills, and the walleyes, what about them, and how about the jumps, middle of the day, middle of the lake, anybody doing any good there? I told the father, whose name was Buck, I was about to go off to school and probably wouldn't be coming back, which caused him to nod skeptically with his lips pressed tight as if he were holding back a howling laugh. He had the key, he reminded me, and anytime a Whalen had a hankering to spend a few nights up here, all he had to do was stop by. If Coggins Senior wasn't there, Coggins Junior would be. I didn't remind him I wasn't a Whalen, because he would have shaken his head and in his own set-in-stone way would have said, Oh, you're a Whalen, all right.

I wasn't even a Pritchard. I was a McManus, but on that side of my family nothing even faintly resembled what I had on this side. I had an uncle on the West Coast that I had seen three times in my life, and he had a daughter from a busted marriage he saw infrequently and I had only seen once. Grandparents equally indistinct. Since there were no family reunions, there were no family stories, and if my father knew one, he wasn't telling. The continent, once you crossed it, became a great tabula rasa, if you wanted to think of it that way. California could have rewritten its state motto to read: "We do do-overs like nobody in the world!"

It really wasn't until that summer I turned eighteen, when I doubted if I'd ever come back and when it was too late to do anything about it, that I realized just how beautiful the Pritchard girls were. I suppose I had to be eighteen to pay the right kind of attention, and they, my mother and my aunts, had to be on the full-blown point of losing it all. They had gotten my grandfather's black hair, all except Lily, they had gotten his high cheeks and versions of his straight prominent nose and his strongly modeled chin, and Rosalyn had gotten his dimple there. They had all gotten the best bone structure available, on which they had gotten Mama Grace's faintly rose-flushed skin. All except Lily. Or, Lily had gotten it all raw and she made sure she kept it that way, so to see the four of them side by side, you saw Pritchard beauty both sheltered and unsheltered, cared-for and weather-worn, as though in peace and in war. They got their mother's blue-to-gray eyes, all except Ruth, whose eyes were as dark as her father's to go with the darkest brows and the very darkest hair, which made you wonder if there wasn't a Latin strain to the family. None of the sisters had gotten cheated feature-wise, stature-wise, stamina-wise. They had soothing voices and full, even joyous, but unabrasive laughs, all except Lily, whose joy *was* abrasive and whose pleasure it was to rough things up. None of them stood in a slouch. And not one of them looked as if she was about to go tiptoeing off. They belonged where they stood, and when you saw the four of them side by side, the Pritchard girls, as commanding a get as a roving preacher ever got out of a Kodak-crazed girl, the earth they stood on belonged to them. The great sadness was that their father never got to see them as I did that summer I turned eighteen, when beauty began to mean something to the boy I'd been, at which point I realized that the moment it reached its peak, beauty began to steal away, that there wouldn't be another eighteenth year for me and another reunion on the lake, that this was it, and in my eagerness to be gone I should be willing to take the loss like a man. That was how I saw my aunts and mother that last summer I was there—as a preview of that loss. Beautiful women, daughters of their pretty, flirtatious mother and striking, flirtatious father, who in summers hence would lose it all. I would see them together again, at weddings especially, most memorably Little Howie's, but never as I was seeing them there that summer I turned eighteen. My mother had those widely spaced eyes, really the only feature distinctively hers, which I fantasized her father had left her so that she could keep his entire family in view when he was off preaching to other congregations eager to hear what he had to say—"For the unbelieving husband is sanctified by the wife, the unbelieving wife is sanctified by the husband: else were your children unclean; but now they are holy"— and which, lacking such eyes myself, I had expropriated to view the four of them there. The Pritchard girls on the way to losing it all in the year that I, one child out of many, but the firstborn, in a family whose children were deemed by scripture to be holy, turned eighteen. Beautiful women. Damn, I'd tell myself in the voice of a young man who would one day lay claim to having seen it all. Look at them there! Damn it all to hell!

Click.

But I did come back. I came back after both Little Howie and Big Howie had died and Rosalyn in the last years of her life built a house that was like an ocean liner cruising into port and from whose prow you looked out over the lake. Its only purpose was to gather everybody together there in protest, and in celebration—the two would never again be separated in Rosalyn's mind. All my cousins had married and had children—many children, it seemed. I too had married, but so briefly that children hadn't made a peep. Even though my cousins' children did their best to fill the house, space was left and Rosalyn was counting heads. Children's heads— new life. My sister was there with hers. But not my mother that I recall. Aunt Ruth was, first widowed in the family and so a source of consolation for her younger sister. Mama Grace had died. Lily, who'd never really been married as the Pritchard sisters knew and lived the word, was also widowed and her stepson long disappeared, but none of that mattered. It was for the children Rosalyn had built such an enormous house. Ellie's daughters were not there. That might have been the summer that Ellie was getting her divorce. Little Howie's children, grown except for one, had scattered, but there were children left, surely there were enough children left out there to fill this new house, which featured a loft on top of a loft, and semicircular tiers of rooms.

I stood it for two days. I think my sister had tipped me off, in a worried tone, as if Rosalyn was going to need support. I never heard her laugh, not as I knew Rosalyn to laugh; I heard her greet newcomers with a sort of welcoming urgency and, impressively, I heard her name names. Many names. These were numbers she was calling to her defense as if she knew someone soon was going to try to take it all away. With my sister acting as a sort of knowledgeable secretary, I made an effort to meet all these new young cousins of mine, but they were as strange to me as I was to them. They wanted to get into the lake, they wanted to run wild, and there were moments when the house and its portion of the lakefront seemed rife with enough energy to give birth to more of its kind. Moments when Rosalyn might have looked down from that prow-like deck cantilevered out over the road and said, Keep it up, keep it up, forget anything you've heard! This is your captain speaking. Play, dammit!

I got the key and went down to the original boathouse, at the end of that long dock, took the fishing boat out and just sat there in the middle of the lake without, as they say, wetting a line. I sat there until all that combustion of childhood on shore had died down. I sat through an afternoon rain, then more sun, and the rocking wakes of larger boats returning home. For a while I gazed at the new house crowding up through its avenue of trees. It was far too large, it seemed stranded there, stopped short in its quest to reach the open seas. The old house was closed down, the row of chaise lounges lined up in front removed. None of this should have been allowed to happen, I told myself. As firstborn I should have been consulted. Someone should take it away from her, someone should snap poor Rosalyn awake. Say it was her father's fault, with all that talk of children made holy. Or the little dog Bing's fault, intercepting the snake in midair, saving the child. I remembered Little Howie, one with the fish, one with the animals and birds, slumped on his sofa, a pablum smear left unwiped beside his mouth, looking more beastlike than human in that moment but pleading a case for God. But who wasn't pleading a case? I suppose seen from the prow of that new house my aunt had had built I made a spectacle of myself out there in the middle of the lake, pleading for a return to the way things had been, or just being standoffish and better left alone. Two days later, with no notice being taken, not really, I was gone.

Now I sat looking down on a lake that was a puddle in comparison, a little blue glacial afterthought, around which weekenders and retirees had pitched their camps many years ago and never bothered to renovate or enlarge, when Walter Kidman appeared on the terrace with a breakfast tray, which he set on the glass-topped table between us, sheepishly, it seemed.

He said, I'm afraid I had too much of the Beam brothers last night. Sorry if I got out of hand.

And I said, I'm assuming we remember they're not Beam brothers. They span two hundred years.

Indeed, in direct descent—except for one nephew, Walter recalled, cheering himself. There you go!

We ate breakfast silently, in the multi-throated warbling of the birds. It was an overcast day, but humid, warm, windless, as if a southern weather front had moved in. Meteorologically, very hard to account for, considering the crisp, cool evening we'd had after I'd taken that swim and we'd gone in to sit before the fire. It was a Monday, the day we were to leave, but Walter had not said a word. I was retired, he wasn't. I had no idea what awaited him at home, what was on his docket, if that was the term he still used.

He poured us coffee. Strange to be toasting with cups of coffee, but we held ours up between us as if we'd come to our last hour here and a toast was on our minds.

Walter said, with a mix of vehemence and forbearance, and a touch of fondness, too. That goddamned toad!

A toast to the toad? And I replied, What you have to understand is, it really was a paradise up there as long as I was a boy.

Walter made a sighing, sympathizing, growling-with-anger sound.

And I told him about it. About my aunts and their families, and about their husbands as they came off the road. About my cousins, all my junior and all but one willing to assign to me the supremacy I deserved. I tried again to acquaint Walter with Little Howie, but this time up in his element, where the boy became a man, and where even as a boy, once we got past the cabin and the jigsaw puzzles and the card games in the rainy afternoons, and that row of chaise lounges in the glowing evenings, he was our entrée into that world. And I tried to make Walter understand how a world like that one up in the mountains only became truly and

Lamar Herrin

fully available in the wake of a war, it took a war to get back what before a war might have meant little more than a pleasant two weeks out of a year. And it took getting down close to the fish, eye to eye with the fish, whose world the lake was and which you fished for in an effort to join them. A crusty father-and-son team, by the name of Coggins, who performed the role of gatekeepers. A woman standing by a cast iron stove with you down below her, waiting to be fed. Isums. What is 'ums, she said I'd said.

Isums? Walter repeated. And what are isums?

The first food I remember putting into my mouth.

So what is thems? What are we talking about?

Pancakes, I said.

Ah! Walter said. Then shook his head. You and Little Black Sambo. Jesus, what a world down there!

Don't worry, Walter. It's gone now.

That goddamn toad!

Don't worry about the toad either.

Once he took it all, he took off?

Something like that.

For a moment we sat before the water, down at the end of this little lake. It felt and sounded like Monday down there, we'd gotten up late and people who'd come for the weekend had gone back to wherever they'd escaped from. I assumed that didn't include Byron Wainwright, but until five in the afternoon we were free of him. It was so quiet there at our end of the lake, in that humid, windless morning, I felt I could get up and walk out upon the water, that the lake would permit that liberty since we were the only ones around and could be counted on not to say a word. It was that kind of morning.

I could tell you about it, Walter, I said. It won't be firsthand.

Not even a glimpse or two? Not like at your mother's funeral?

It will be secondhand but mostly third. Through cousin Harriet, through my sister, and on to me. If you're willing to settle for that.

You saw him standing back from your mother's funeral, keeping a stopwatch on his wife. And you heard him driving off, pebble by pebble. And that was it?

Yes, I said without hesitation, that's the deal.

Ah, and behind that screen door.

I'm not even counting that, Walter.

148

Because that could have been any toad-shaped man not quite ready to step into the big house.

True, I said. It could.

Hmmm, Walter said, as if weighing the pros and cons, considering the entertainment value on this Monday we were due to go home.

And before he could decide, I said, You could probably tell it yourself. Think of the various ways a man with a chip on his shoulder and a whole lot of weaknesses to feed could waste a fortune, and don't leave out a single one. Maybe there were a few original touches in there, but they don't amount to much. Here's an image. The passengers disembarking from a ship and the rats clambering on board. You want to take it from there?

I'll pass, Walter said. Then reconsidered: Better said, I'll take a pass I can use later on.

A big house, I went on, like an ocean liner my aunt had built after her son and husband died. She was determined to keep it all going. Every summer she sailed into port, docked, and invited anyone remotely connected to the family to come spend two weeks with her. It was an extravagant house. She got, I believe, two summers' worth out of it, maybe a third, I'm not sure and it really doesn't matter. The summer after she died, Ellie took over. In the name of her mother she summoned the family back to the big house, but she also gave in to her newly wed husband and allowed Leland to invite what he could cram of his family into the original house, that cedar-red one with a line of chaise lounges facing the lake. The same two weeks, Walter, and it's not hard to see why. My sister and her kids were there, Aunt Ruth came with her two daughters, Harriet, our pipeline, and her sister Beatrice, and their kids. And there were others. My mother, smelling a rat, and Aunt Lily, who always smelled one, stayed away. Leland's kin filled that lakeside house up with aunts and uncles and cousins all from the same town in the next state over, and his kids too, a couple who had kids of their own, even that sulky son of Leland's, the one who might have stretched out in Howie's, Little Howie's bed after Rosalyn's funeral—

Where you slept too, Walter reminded me, perhaps just to show me he was staying in touch.

That's right. Richie, "Little Richie" they called him, so somewhere there must have been a big one.

Jesus! Walter said. It never fails, does it?

You don't want to take it from here, Walter?

Let me make one guess. The toad had one of those boisterous southern mothers, who could go toe to toe with any man—

Amazing! You've got it, Walter! I'm impressed. Married to who?

Some stock car racer gone to seed? I don't know. Or some no-neck football player, a lineman, a tackle, never took his helmet off, Bronco somebody.

Close, I said. Leland's mother's name was Sammie, or that's what they called her, and her husband was known as Sarge because he'd spent twenty-some-odd years in the army, where he'd been the company cook. He was not Leland's father. Leland's father had been run off or run over or run through and good riddance. Every day Sarge would cook up a pot of something, chili or stew or pork and beans, something like that, and from the deck of the new house you could smell it cooking and you could smell it coming, for he always sent a pot up—

A Trojan horse sort of offering?

Walter!

Don't flatter me, Jim. It's pretty obvious how you're setting this up.

You can see it, my sister could, too. And Harriet. Ellie, it's hard to say about her. She was straddling the distance between those two houses. In one summer Leland's kin overran the red one. Cars everywhere. Motorcycles gunning up and down the road. Children who never stopped screaming, so their mothers and fathers screamed, too. Music blasting. Terrified fish. For a year, I think just one year, maybe two, Ellie straddled those two worlds, but nature abhors a vacuum, and as soon as our family stopped going to the lake, Leland's family, multiplying by the day, moved into the big house Rosalyn had built to keep it all going, and from this point on we're pretty much in the world of hearsay. Except for Harriet. Harriet, out of loyalty to Ellie, tried to keep going, even though she might leave her children behind. Remember, she was the only member of the family who'd gone to their wedding. She was a quiet sort, not really mysterious, but she kept her own counsel and you knew she knew things. But she'd always been like that. When we were kids, I'd go to her to catch up on what I had missed. She'd tell you, but maybe only the part she wanted you to know, I could never be sure.

Our pipeline, Jim?

She liked a good story, Walter, but if my sister didn't want to take on the role, we probably couldn't have a better eye on the Ellie and Leland show than Harriet. And somehow she insinuated herself into Leland's good graces. It even got to the point where Leland employed her.

So we have *our* Trojan horse, too.

You wouldn't want to say that about a lady.

Sorry. I keep forgetting we're no longer up north. Employed her how?

We're getting ahead of ourselves, Walter. First there's the toad on the lake.

It was horrible, inexcusable, what Leland Oldham did in the name of the Whalen family, how somehow he tapped into the goodwill the Whalens had built up over the decades up there until he'd run it dry or until he'd poisoned the well so irremediably that no one who valued his life would drink from it again. He played the fool but played it so aggressively the last laugh caught in your throat. He played the fool with such utter irreverence that the fool became the fiend.

So I told Walter about Leland on the lake where my cousin had taught us about boating and water-skiing and fishing, of course, but fishing as it were from the fish's-eye view. But Leland Oldham never touched the fishing boat, he went straight to the speedboat, and instead of teaching his nephews or nieces or any stray kids of his how to get up and stay up on water skis, to earn their pleasure in the streaming open air, he found some kind of sub-sized surfboard—a boogie board, he called it—and pulled them up on that. And swung them off. He was drunk. He veered back and forth in the open lake and whipped his family members off that board. Then he swung back by them with that board flying at the level of their heads, and the miracle was that no one was ever hit by it and no one was ever reported drowned. He drank constantly and took his delight in sending nephews and nieces and probably his own surly son through the air. He had another board, which he called his banana board, that he could crowd four Oldhams onto and quadruple his pleasure by whipping all four off. According to Jean, the kids loved it for a while and then began to get scared, and Leland had to browbeat them into coming out onto the lake with him.

In that year of the overlap Jean went out with him once. But this was on the houseboat, along with Harriet and a couple of her kids, and also Sammie and Sarge, who brought a pot of his cooking along, and Jean said that something as pokey as a houseboat Leland ran at open throttle, if nothing else so that he could swing right and left and ride his own waves. He drank like a drunk out to keep a mean streak going, like someone who'd gotten his hands on something and he'd be damned if he'd give an inch or ounce of it up. He didn't drink straight from the bottle—after all, he was the captain and had his own mug—but he threw his empties overboard and fouled the water. Sammie and her Sarge were one step behind him. Except they were bursting with their own brand of delight. Imagine, Jean said, someone who'd lived her whole life hearing stories of the leisured life of the very wealthy and suddenly found herself living it. And, according to her son, with no end in sight. Why wouldn't she be giving vent to some kind of howling pleasure? Jean could make a case for the rowdy good-natured mother and her man. Leland, she said, was a more devious sort and had grievances that ran deep.

Everybody's got grievances, Walter reminded me. Grievances are the cheapest thing going. You'll never win a case pleading your client is in the grip of his grievances, whatever they are.

Ellie, in one of her sober moments, told Jean that Leland had suffered horribly from his father's neglect, more than anyone knew, and that he loved Ellie because her father had loved her so much. He loved father love and what it could do.

Which was probably why, Walter surmised, he became a scoutmaster or campground leader or whatever he called himself. He wanted to give other little underloved boys and girls what he hadn't had himself. Put up that statue of the big man and the little girl and case closed.

They ran that camp for a few years. There actually was a camp back there, Walter. Little Howie's first cabin became a kind of headquarters, I suppose, there were streams, beautiful trees, I spent time back there before Ellie was even born, it was its own world . . .

Until?

Until they had to sell it like everything else.

What else did they have to sell, Jim?

Cars.

So Leland, the toad, was a used car salesman on top of everything else.

He liked old cars. Vintage, mint-condition cars from the Roaring Twenties and the thirties. No Rolls or Mercedes or Jaguars, nothing like that. Al Capone cars with running boards and those bulbous headlights and rumble seats. He built an enormous garage for them down beside the red house, ground we'd played on as kids. Six cars in all before he had to sell them off. And he ran them around that lake on roads so narrow you'd have to pull off if you saw him coming. Drunk as a lord, of course, but for a while being married to a Whalen got him a pass. Waving at everybody, my sister said, and for a while people waved back. It *was* a show. One of the cars was bright yellow, a color no gangster ever painted his. Whether he thought of himself as a gangster or not I don't know, but he probably did think he was one of the untouchables. There was a tackle and bait shop down the road, a dock a father and son ran, and Leland used to spin in there, scattering gravel and roaring out, just to let them know the lengths to which someone with a lock on the Whalen fortune could go. He spent a nice chunk of that fortune on those cars, Walter, you have no idea what one of them could cost, and then one by one he had to sell them off. His empties he threw out beside the road.

Fantasy land, Walter said. But then it had been a sort of fantasy land for you, too, up there, Jim.

It's not the same. But you know that already.

I do, indeed.

Leland, your toad, was not uneducated. He'd been schooled. He could do numbers. He looked at that Whalen fortune and really believed he could see no end. He was drunk on it. I'm not sure he even needed the booze. Or you could think of the booze as something like the fortune's lifeblood, for figure out what a fifth of Lagavulin 16 costs compared to a paltry pint of blood and right away you saw the difference. Of course, he'd have to pay to keep Ellie drunk, too, but that was an operational expense to keep it all in his hands, an expense he could probably write off as a tax deduction, and to keep her defenseless and drunk he'd do her the courtesy of staying drunk himself, too, just a bit more functional and a step ahead to keep the whole enterprise going. But it was self-indulgence of the most reckless sort. They took a trip west, went skiing in the Rockies, down, I suppose, the slope reserved for drunkards, became so charmed with the place that they bought a bed-and-breakfast out there and tried to persuade Harriet to run it, which she did for a while, before they had to sell it off. They took the house that Big Howie and Rosalyn had on the coast, an enormous house that Ellie had some childhood memories of, although nothing like those up on the lake, and upgraded it, sparing no expense.

Lamar Herrin

This included building stables for horses it's hard to imagine them riding. Everything pristine. Ellie was so grateful that she bought up surrounding tracts of land that came up for sale and put them straight into Leland's name, she was so, so much in love with her man, as Jean reported Ellie had said to her, making a cooing, booze-slurring sound when she said it to me. Soooo, soooo much in luuuvvv.

I get the idea, Jim.

The idea, Walter, was nothing compared to the lavish fact of the matter. You'll have to take my word for it.

Which I have up to now.

Well, I drew breath and said, this sort of thing went on, and Leland kept setting his family up, too. Not just his sons. Some cousins he picked out from the goodness of his heart, a favorite aunt. He had a heart, but think about it in military terms and Leland, the toad, was building perimeters of defense, he was surrounding himself with recipients of his largesse who would defend him to the death.

Something like what Big Howie and Rosalyn surrounded themselves with. Don't take offense. Something *like*, I say, not the same.

I'm not taking offense, Walter.

Good, because I truly dislike the toad, I detest the toad, and Ellie, if we could ever trace her back to little Ellie . . .

Walter trailed off, expecting me to pick it up. For a moment I held off. Little Ellie before the toad and her fate had found her. Ellie when anybody other than the toad had wandered down her life's path. Relieve her of the toad. Give her a fresh start. Perhaps that was the tack we could take as we drove back home, which would have been the sensible thing to do. There wasn't much more we could get out of this lake. Nothing moved on it now. The air remained settled, heavy, thickening in its warmth, air right out of a humid summer's day of my boyhood, which I had left behind the day Phil Hodge and I, as a couple of sixties casualties in our mid-twenties, had turned the car back around, bid the kudzu and a state patrolman out to do the big man's bidding goodbye, and headed north. Walter and I should get into his car, turn the air-conditioning on, and go back home. Later I'd retell it all to Elaine, reach this point, and with a touch of gallantry that she was used to and might still credit, admit I hadn't been able to wait any longer to get back to her, and here I was.

But it wasn't going to be that way, and it wasn't because I was being

154

pulled along in the toad's wake. The day came, Walter, when the tide turned, the waters receded, however you want to think about it, and they were confronted with bare sand, strewn with the flotsam and jetsam of all the passing boats. They weren't broke, but they were close to being grounded. The land they bought down there on the coast they had to sell back, at a loss. They sold the horses, held on to the house, and closed it up. If you remember how Howie, how little Howie expanded the business, going offshore, going international, winning converts every step of the way, well, now the film was running in reverse. They came back to the Whalens' hometown, sold the property on that nearby lake with the twelve-hundred-mile shoreline, and retreated to the original Whalen house. Ellie's daughters, Jennifer and Tracy, stayed mostly with their father, who had remarried and moved to a town just far enough away that rumors of the excesses and outrages their mother and stepfather were committing didn't reach them on a daily basis. Jennifer had her money, the inheritance Rosalyn had left her, safely socked away, but little Tracy—

I can imagine, Walter said.

Probably not. Or at least not how Ellie consented to it, urged her younger daughter to place her trust and money in Leland's hands, he was such a good, wise man. For proof Tracy had only to look at the camp for deprived children Leland still ran. The camp's mission was to rescue deprived children, not to exploit yet-to-be-deprived ones.

A convenient front they set up for themselves, Walter muttered scornfully.

I'm not sure it was entirely a front.

And they kept that camp going?

Through the Howard Whalen Youth Crusade foundation and on the strength of that statue out front, they did. The camp was one of the last things to go under. Eventually Leland raided his own foundation and ruined it too, but the statue . . .

Overgrown, hung with vines, kudzu . . . Walter allowed it to materialize before his eyes.

No kudzu up in the mountains, Walter.

Shame. I had an image of the toad being strangled by the stuff.

I took a long settling breath while Walter entertained his image. Then I took another. It was northern air I was hoping to breathe down, not this utterly improbable, sultry southern stuff. It did occur to me that

155

that might be air that only I was breathing, that like so much else, air was in the nose and lungs of the beholder. My friend Walter would be happy to tell me, No, Jim, this is Adirondack air up here, pure, utterly unladen air, take a deep breath and come up clean.

Instead I said, The image of the toad you want to summon up, Walter, is of a man riding around the town where his wife's father made his fortune not in one of his Al Capone cars, and not even a Cadillac, but in a Humvee.

You mean a Hummer, Jim?

No, I mean a real military Humvee, built low and wide and jacked up on those oversize wheels, the thing itself, minus the machine gun mounts. Color of the Arabian sands.

Spanish moss blowing in a Humvee's exhaust?

Spanish moss farther south. I thought we settled that.

Don't be touchy. I need to visualize the thing.

Big Howie drove down the street in his black Cadillacs and they tipped their hats. Leland Oldham drove down the street and they ran off and hid.

Drunk?

To one degree or another, always, Walter.

Am I supposed to imagine him driving that thing through the black neighborhood too?

I think you can imagine him driving it everywhere.

Dressed in fatigues?

'S up to you. Everybody'll have his own image of the toad in mind. Click on the one you want to keep.

Now that he's gone.

Now that he's gone.

Even though he may come back.

Unlikely.

Now that nothing's left.

There was always something left, and something left to defend. However late, there were duties left to perform. No statute of limitations expired on them, I was about to add when I heard, as though on the mind's ear, a long dirgelike chord, struck perhaps from Byron Wainwright's cello, which took a moment to fade, the air being so heavy and so still.

Good, Walter, I said. Keep going.

Less than nothing? All the Whalen money gone. His wife a piggy bank he shook every coin out of and then cracked open for good measure. His kids got theirs and took off. His family did. The cash cow ran dry. His mother and her Sarge were left in a sort of game-show daze. Why hadn't they taken the sure money and stopped there? Everything her son and his rich girl bought they had to sell at a loss—a film running in reverse. But the theater was empty by now, the empty bottles rolling down the aisle . . .

Have your fun. I asked for it.

You did give me that pass, Jim.

And I'll give you another one. But just let me know when you want me to tell you what happened.

I'm ready, he said. But hang on, and he suddenly pulled himself up. Be right back.

It occurred to me that, early in the day as it was, he might be going inside to bring out the bottle and the Beam boys. Instead Walter returned with a pitcher of ice water and two glasses. He said, This heat! Where in hell did this heat come from?

So you feel it too?

He shot me an incredulous glance. If we couldn't agree on the air we sat in, how were we supposed to agree on anything else?

He poured us two glasses of ice water and we each drank a half. For an instant the ice water—not unlike the Jim Beam—went to my head. I waited for it to clear, aware that until it did I couldn't be held entirely accountable for what I said. My friend was an attorney, an attorney for the defense, in matters of confidentiality, yes, as sworn to secrecy as a priest. But an officer of the court, nonetheless.

I waited until I was clearheaded and then put it on the record. They moved back into the Whalen house, I said. For maybe two months they did nothing. Perhaps longer. Except drink their increasingly modest fortune down. Leland rode through town in his Humvee, it seemed with one idea in mind: to make himself as unbeloved as he could. A string of investments he'd made—and no one was clear on this, not even Harriet—went belly up. The investment that counted, though, never failed him. He invested in his wife. In her drunkenness. He invested in the booze that kept her that way, and he kept control of her life, her fortune, the foundation that had brought him into her life. Summer by summer they kept the camp for disadvantaged kids going, and they kept their version of the family reunions going up at the lake. Occasionally Leland went over and acted like a camp master. It was something he could still do. He knew nothing about nature, plants, animals, birds, and butterflies, the great out-of-doors, only that it was out there and somehow beat a disadvantaged life on the streets, and if he could put a group of kids who'd been shortchanged in contact with it long enough, something good might come of it. Some alternative to the way they'd been might begin to take root. At a certain stage of his drunkenness he felt such a stirring himself. Unless he was imagining it. He'd look at that statue of the founder and his little girl he'd had erected at the entrance to his camp, a man in fishing garb with a fishing rod in his hand, and a little girl who bore a resemblance to his wife, and make the argument to himself that children should take the example of that hugely successful outdoorsman to heart. Grow up to be like him, and never forget to keep a sheltering arm around a little boy, or in his case a little girl. He'd smile and tell himself that that statue represented the best investment of his wife's money he'd ever made.

But he was living on islands, and since he never got in the water, no one was sure he could even swim. One island was up in the mountains, another was down on the coast where they'd restored the Whalen home there, the third was the Whalen home back in the pines and dogwood trees in the town the Whalens had put on the map, and there may have been a few islets scattered here and there, Harriet wasn't sure about that, there had been such lavish spending back at the start. But the tide of their debts was rising fast, and those were the only land masses Leland and his wife had left. They managed to sell the house on the coast, at a significant loss. They retreated to the lake to lick their wounds. Another reunion took place, and the fruitfully multiplying Oldhams showed up and ran amok. Harriet was there to keep an eye on Ellie, and during that time our Oldham, the toad, sought Harriet out. He had a plan. He wanted to pay another tribute to his wife. The toad, when he had to, could muster a humble sort of gallantry that might fool most people, if not Harriet. He wanted to open a business back in the Whalen hometown, not manufacturing and selling head-to-toe apparel wholesale, those days were past, those days belonged to Big Howie and his apparently born-to-it son, but an apparel business nonetheless, and since what most people looked at first to tell one article of clothing from another was the label, Leland's company would dedicate itself to designing and then stitching in the most appealing labels money could buy. In the higher-priced range they could do a sort of embroidering. They could make labels and monograms that would outclass the clothing itself. There'd be an art in this, and there'd be a moment when Ellie would come to see it as the crowning touch to the empire her father had built. What did Harriet think? Did she think enough of the idea to come work for them to see it get off the ground?

Walter stopped me. He raised his hand and took a breath deep enough for both of us. The air, if anything, had become more oppressively heavy and hot. Why, he said, wouldn't the Chinese or the Bangladeshis or the Sri Lankans or wherever the clothing was then being made have thought of the same thing? The label a work of art, the clothing itself a piece of shit. Did the toad research this?

How do you research a brainstorm, a bolt from the blue, Walter? Exercise outfits, all that high-end sportswear. You could even stitch "Made in the USA" on it and it wouldn't be an outright lie since the label itself would be homegrown. This was something Ellie's father—

—your uncle—

—by marriage, never paid much attention to. Who bothered to design a high-end label back then? That I know of, Little Howie didn't do it. I've still got that suit he made for me, and I can't remember what the label looked like. It's an old idea, Walter, but embroider it, in stylish gold thread, in some Old World font you could get off the Internet—

Not too stylish, not too Old World. Not if we're talking about a sweatshirt.

The point is, he was going to do it, the toad was. Harriet never believed in it for a minute, but in the beginning she allowed herself to be roped in. To get it going, though, Leland made a colossal nuisance of himself with the Town Board and the Planning Committee to get them to give in—I'm not sure why. Probably because he wanted to locate it on land too close in, not zoned for business, or because he wanted it done yesterday and would run over them in his Humvee unless they hopped to it. What I do know is that he sank every cent of little Tracy's money into it, and it wasn't until Tracy came of age and asked for her inheritance that Ellie found out what her husband had done with it. Leland blamed a couple of thieving salesmen for embezzling them and their labeling business into ruin. Harriet said there might have been something to that, one man's thievery inspiring more of the same, but the story she told was of Ellie sending out word to cousins, no matter how remote, to come by the showroom so that she could pile the most artfully labeled sweatshirts into their arms. These were all factory rejects—I'm not sure why. I wasn't there. Badly labeled, mislabeled, labels whose thread was unraveling by the time they reached the showroom floor. When Rosalyn piled shirts and pants into our arms, if we'd told her the labels were coming apart, they weren't worth the thread they were stitched with, she would have kept laughing and piling it on. Ellie took it hard. Perhaps she'd wanted to be her mother then. Perhaps she'd wanted it so that, regardless of what her husband said, she could give it all away. She drank herself into a stupor every night. Leland, angry with the world and with all the ungrateful dollars that had eluded his grasp, did put his wife to bed before he passed out himself. That was the one investment he'd managed to protect, all that scotch paid off and his wife's day came drunkenly to an end.

My sister, Jean, saw her once during this time and said the cheerful front Ellie tried to keep up seemed ghoulish, she was like a member of the walking dead gossiping on about the most embarrassing trivia. How could she talk about her daughters, about Leland and his children and grandchildren, as if they were a normal family with all their endearing little ups and downs? The instant she stopped talking, she'd have to look around and admit she was absolutely alone. So Jean and Harriet and Beatrice had to let her talk, and they'd get phone calls at almost any hour of the day or night. While the *Titanic* was sinking, Ellie chattered on. Or she'd call one of them while driving through town and neighboring towns with her speaker phone on, and tell you everything she saw beside the road, and everything that everything she saw reminded her of, until, inevitably, something would remind her of something close, something dear, she'd go into a nosedive and begin to cry. It seemed as though the road gave her the illusion she could drive out from under herself, she could give it an extra burst of speed and roar through whatever hick town and leave her sadness behind her, until she couldn't anymore. She got pulled over in a neighboring town. Not for the first time, but this time she happened to have Harriet on the speaker phone and Harriet heard it all. The cops knew Ellie in that town. They might not have recognized her in the flesh, what little flesh she had left on her bones, but they knew of her, probably knew who she had the deep misfortune to be married to, and the cop who stopped her had his partner drive her the ten or twelve miles back home while he followed in their patrol car. They gave her a serious but still subservient talking-to, and Harriet, who might have intervened and pleaded for her cousin, heard it all and didn't have to say a word. Ellie got let off. Later Harriet tried to talk some sense into her, but by then the evening's scotch had had its way with her and her speech was so slurred she might have been speaking under water. It didn't make any difference. It was a tale of woe Ellie told, a monologue interrupted by a few self-applauding and sentimental observations. Harriet didn't believe Ellie realized how fast the money was running out. Leland might disgrace himself, but the following day his reputation for being an inspired investor was restored. That didn't keep the investments from failing, or businesses from going under, or creditors from hammering at their door. Ellie was not at home.

As I said, they sold the house they'd remodeled on the coast plus a few other properties they owned. They were down to the Whalen home and the houses on the lake. And the camp, which Jean insisted, getting it through Harriet, continued to thrive, not so much as a moneymaking concern as a bulwark of respectability. But even as Harriet was making that claim, Leland had begun to raid the foundation's coffers, which was the same as stealing money directly out of Big Howie's pocket, just as Leland in assuming Big Howie's place had stolen his daughter. And Jean, for one, put the pieces together that Harriet had left jumbled, that we as children might have left jumbled on the puzzle table up there in the mountains, when an afternoon rain ended and the sun came back out and all of us, all the cousins, in impressive numbers long before Ellie was born, were allowed to go running back into the water.

Walter held up his hand, not as though he had a question to ask but a contribution to make. You're back where you began as children, he said, and somehow that camp for orphaned children, for disadvantaged children, is like a stockade you can all retreat behind when things in the outside world get too tough.

Really? I said.

What's it doing up there anyway? As coincidences go—

I've never seen it. I've never set foot inside it. As far as I'm concerned, it's all hearsay. I've been told that Little Howie's original cabin up there

161

is now the camp headquarters, but I've never even been in it. The closest
I got—

I know the closest you got. Your cousin's wife lifted her head off the
pillow and with her hair falling across her cheek wished you good luck
fishing and you went out and caught a lunker in her honor, the last time
you had Howie around to show you how it was done.

Walter!

I've been listening, Jim. It hasn't just been the Beam brothers. It's
been the Pritchard girls feeding into the Whalen saga and leading you by
the hand. It's been paradise, as you said yourself, and paradise lost. And
here we are with the toad squatting where a Whalen once stood and the
last child of the last of the Pritchard girls wasting away on the bone. And
a camp for deprived—or was it disillusioned?—children standing close
by. Just how much disbelief am I supposed to suspend?

I had no answer for him, but the heat was suddenly all over us. All
over me but all over Walter, too, for we both reached for the pitcher of ice
water at the same time. I poured, Walter's glass first, and a little slopped
over the rim. But it was my throat that was parched. I was about to propose to Walter we suspend this story while I regrouped when he asked the
single question I couldn't answer, not yet, and couldn't avoid.

When did she call you, Jim?

Me?

She's called all the cousins and rambled on, pleading with somebody
to tell her it wasn't true. So when did Ellie call you?

I lived up north, I answered evasively. I was out of her range.

I haven't forgotten what she said. "I may need you, Jim. Not today,
but sometime." And there at your mother's funeral—you called it your
godfatherish moment—you told her, "When the time is right, you let me
know."

I looked out over this small lake, from the end at which we sat down
to the other. Nothing was out there and nothing broke the surface. Pickerel swam below, I knew, as sharp-toothed as tiny crocodiles, but this
strange heavy heat lay over the lake like a closed door.

Walter concluded, Then you'd see, you said.

And I faced him. His small, eager eyes held steady. He was a friend,
at this stage of my life my best friend, and I must have believed my best
audience. And he was an interrogator. I suddenly felt the need to consult

my ex-wife Elaine, whom Walter and his wife had placed in my path. I could leave Molly out of it, but the truth was I loved them all. They were family, and it was not as if I were trying to build a bridge between them and what I had forfeited down south. That wasn't it at all.

I breathed deeply. Walter, I said, we aren't there yet.

First came the interventions. There came a time, I told him, when Harriet and her sister Beatrice and my sister Jean accepted an invitation to a summer reunion on the lake, only instead of two weeks they made it one and they didn't bring the children, who were grown anyway and no longer interested in childish outings. But the three cousins went with a plan, and after the first night of listening to Ellie ramble on, the next day they took her into a bedroom and locked the door. Locked Leland outside. Jean told me the house, the big house, the one Rosalyn had had built in the wake of her son's and husband's deaths as sort of a citadel and an ark, was now swarming with Oldhams and hangers-on, and that the only descendants of that celebrity preacher James Pritchard with the commanding black eyes were locked in that room. Jean said that Ellie began to panic when she realized there was no bottle in there with her and no way outside where shouting children were running back and forth to the lake, as she had once been a shouting, carefree, and much heralded child. Her three cousins were the picture of sobriety, and sparing no words they informed her what she had done to herself and what her only recourse now was. They were three elder cousins of a like mind, whose smiles were no longer fond and forgiving and who didn't cave in. It was a sort of mutiny, if Ellie wanted to think of it that way, and in these closed captain's quarters they were taking control of the ship. Jean said that Ellie started to cry, but once she saw that none of her cousins was crying with her, she stopped. They hugged her and told her they loved her, but they didn't sugarcoat it for her. They loved her and, confronted with her addiction, intended to save her life. If she had anything to say for the life they were intending to save her from, now was the time. And Jean said that Ellie didn't fight it. Why should she, if she expected Leland to bust through the door and save her? Jean said she might have been wrong, but there came a time during that session when, instead of looking at the door or out the window for relief, Ellie looked at her three cousins in the most humbled way and appeared to give thanks. It was an instant's recognition, and Ellie seemed to be saying in that instant that her life was in their hands.

Her older daughter Jennifer, Ellie was informed, was on board too. But this intervention they were subjecting her to was a product of the second generation of the Pritchard girls. Before it was over, they'd shown her the brochures of a rehab center up north where they had already booked her in. It was the best that Whalen money could buy, and it would be hard on her. For four weeks she'd be lumped in with other abusers of other families' love and trust, spendthrifts of other people's fortunes. She'd open her eyes and see versions of herself everywhere she looked. Doctors, the best doctors, would be on hand, but the medicine that worked would be what she saw of herself in those other miserable souls around her. That's what was being asked of her. And after what seemed hours and hours of this, a very chastened Ellie agreed. Jean repeated she could have been wrong, of course. Ellie might not have been all that chastened. Then when Ellie became as hard on herself as any of her cousins had been and agreed to go that very day, if someone would drive her to the airport and put her on the plane, Jean might have been wrong again. Four weeks alone, with more of her desperate and deeply humbled kind, and when Jean said she would drive her, Ellie went to pack, with Jean folding and then handing on her clothes. And when Jean decided at the last minute to fly with her to a northern state without not a breath of southern comfort in the air, perhaps wrong yet again. She turned her younger cousin over to the nurses and doctors paid to save her and flew back. She represented the last contact Ellie would have with anybody from her past life for four weeks, and Jean was utterly wrong about that. During her return trip their planes might have crossed in the sky. Leland took a hotel room in the town in which his wife's rehab center was located, and day after day until the four weeks were up he managed to sneak Ellie's allotment of scotch into the center or to sneak his wife out. By the time she got back to her town, he'd gotten her drunk again, and somehow en route from the airport to her house she got lost. Why had Leland let her drive? But why not, he'd saved her from those meddlesome cousins of hers and those officious know-it-alls up north. She was back on familiar ground. Her daughters drove over to look for her and, after searching the town, found her just inside the gate to the Whalen estate, not crashed into a tree but brought to a halt there nonetheless. Sleeping, so glad, so happy to be home.

Okay, Jim, Walter said, pleading it seemed for a pause in this heat we had somehow called down on ourselves. I get the idea. He'll hound her to the ends of the earth, and she'll wake up hung over back where she started.

Only the next time she didn't make it home. She drove out early in the morning, stark naked, not driving erratically, the opposite, in fact, the windows down and the wind in her hair, stopping for all the lights, signaling for her turns, around and around the town square. Naked as the day she was born, her bare left arm hung out the window as though to sample the air. I guess it was the bare arm that seemed to be beckoning other drivers to follow, for when the police stopped her she had gathered her own little motorcade. The police threw a blanket they had in their trunk over her. They admitted she was coherent but insisted she belonged in another world. I don't think they ever tested her blood alcohol level. They probably assumed she was on some mind-bending drug. It's always possible, I don't know if she had slipped onto drugs or not, but it's just as possible she'd woken out of a blessedly happy dream, a dream she refused to part with and committed herself to taking with her out into the world. A dream from her pre–Leland Oldham childhood given an early morning tour around town. This time, though, they did take away her license for public misconduct, dreaming naked, I suppose, in the early morning air. Although I'm not sure she was ever charged. She'd never driven more responsibly. They probably just turned their heads and said, Put your license in my hand and please keep yourself covered while we take you home.

All right, Walter said. Ellie was Lady Godiva, but who was Peeping Tom? You know the story?

I know the story. The Peeping Tom would be us, I said, wouldn't he, Walter? He would be everyone drawn to the spectacle, cheering her on. But not her daughters, they tried another intervention with her, and this time Tracy, the younger, the one that Leland had robbed of her inheritance, was squarely on board. She wanted to be a doctor, do premed, go to med school and do doctoring, save somebody in a family where the doctors had not fared well—and she and her sister got together and sent their mother to dry out, but this time in a rehab center down south. Same result, Leland got wind of it and busted it up, and in retaliation Tracy might have killed a patient before she saved one. She hated Leland with a passion, and she hated the part of her mother that clung to that hateful man. Leland's children—and remember, he'd set them up—then forced him into a detox unit, and for a while that seemed to have stuck. He discovered he could keep his wife's addiction more efficiently in order when he was sober, but it put him at a distance from her and it probably made him realize he preferred, rather than not, to have her to cling to as they both went down. That children's camp didn't close, but it passed out of his control. Another church took it over and didn't want a drunkard wandering proprietorially over its grounds. The statue stood, but Leland himself became persona non grata. He and Ellie hunkered down in the Whalen house and put Rosalyn's huge house on the lake up for sale, thereby not ending the summer reunions but ending them on such a massive scale. They still had the original lake house with the long dock and boathouse, the only one I cared anything about. As their debts piled up and second and third mortgages they'd taken out came due, the moment arrived when the bank threatened to foreclose on the original Whalen house, the one I'd driven down to with Phil Hodge hoping to show him a good time, and the one Ellie had gone to sleep before after her harrowing experience up north. Which, I suppose, was the other house I cared about. So in fact there were two.

I stopped there, but it was Walter who drew a long pensive breath. The heat had continued to gather. It occurred to me, such were the preemptive powers of storytelling, that I could take the Whalen house away from Leland and Ellie, too, before the bank did. At the last minute the bank might have relented—deferring to the Whalen name and all the benefits the Whalens had brought to the town—but I didn't have to. I could make it one away from a clean sweep, and the house I would allow to stand would be up on the lake, originally a small cabin and then extended, stained a cedar-red, with a boathouse at the end of a long dock containing not just boats but all the tools and playthings needed to thrive out on the water. Walter, I could hear myself saying, when it got down to that house with the chaise lounges lined up facing the lake, sunset, the swallows swooping, the fish splashing, the doves settling, neighbors across the way pulling into their docks, that long, long pause with the water stained darker and darker shades of orange and pink and red as the sun set and the stars began to blink on, when that moment came that a whole family occupied those chaise lounges and seemed to breathe as one until you heard your aunt laugh and the stories began to be told, it was precisely at that moment, which could last a long time, Walter, an entire childhood, the evenings being so mild and slow to fade, that toads were declared off limits, that toads with their bloated bellies and horny warts were deemed unimaginable in the presence of the Pritchard girls, where everything was beautiful and bountiful and aboveboard, and so given to extending itself through all the years.

But then Walter expelled the breath he'd drawn, drew another, and I turned my attention to him. It was then that Ellie finally called you, he said. It wasn't even half a question.

Yes, I said.

What did she want?

She wanted to talk, just to go on, her monologue as the other cousins knew it.

How did she sound?

She was trying to keep her voice light, nothing more than a late evening chat, but she was dragging it along.

And then it stopped.

You're right, Walter, it did. And then I asked her if she was still there.

And?

She began to cry, hiccup, whimper, stammer, blow her nose.

And drink.

I heard every swallow and I heard every tinkling note the ice made— before it melted. I'd been warned by my sister that once she'd made contact these monologues could go on.

And now, finally, it was your turn. What did she want? Money?

No, she was like Leland. She never thought the money would run out. Even when it did, she refused to believe it. There was always money.

Poor rich kid. So she just wanted to cry on your shoulder.

That and to reminisce, to let one thing take her to another, tying one thing to another as if in that way she could make a safety net that would catch her when she began another free fall. She even mentioned that lunch we'd had when I tried to convince her to sign a prenup.

She did? Just another reminiscence?

I thought so, but as she kept talking I realized that the real reason she didn't sign a prenup was that she was too proud. She could take care of her money, she could hold her liquor, she could educate her daughters. She could get square with her mother. But the truth was, she couldn't do any of those things. She was weak and she was lonely. Very lonely. Of all the reasons people drink, finding a way to live with your loneliness may be the one that counts. Drunk, you have company. Drunk, you can get along with yourself.

Really?

There's more than one of you then, Walter.

I see.

Drunk you feel more in a family mood, as if you were conducting your own little family reunion.

You're not referring to the Oldhams, are you?

No.

Maybe not even the Whalens.

Maybe not.

You really mean the Pritchards, and since you were the firstborn of your generation, Ellie had worked her way up the Pritchard family tree to you. That's why it took her so long to call you.

You're very astute, Walter. Very good.

And it wasn't just a shoulder to cry on or an authority on reminiscences to consult. She had a favor to ask. The last born to the firstborn, to make the circle complete.

It wasn't as impersonal as that.

Of course not. She remembered as a little girl reaching up and touching your beard.

Ahhh. I let out a breath I'd been holding, a light laughing pant. But it brought the little golden-eyed girl back again, as she darted in and out from behind her mother, my favorite aunt. It was devastating the way memory worked, but only because life was, every step of the way. From there to here, devastation.

And, Walter continued, she remembered you standing up to her father. As a four- or five-year-old she wouldn't have been left with much more than that. The touch of your beard, the giggles it gave her, and you and her father confronting each other as equals, with neither side giving in. Her father is dead, and so is her brother, but in her world of drunken lights and shadows, it's as if her father is alive again through you, you're the back side of his front side, or vice versa, but drink enough and sink down far enough and you might as well be the same man. What did she want you to do?

Walter, I cautioned him, this heat is getting to you.

You're right, Jim, it's bad.

We could jump in the lake, cool off, then turn the air-conditioner on and drive home.

We could.

We could get Molly and Elaine and go out for supper, then sit out on your patio and . . .

Count our blessings? Walter said.

Something like that. They are numerous, our blessings.

You stood up to the Big Man, Jim.

And as a reward we went back North and got to catch all those fish. End of story.

You, the oldest of the cousins, stood up to the Big Man, and the youngest of the cousins took note. That young, you don't calculate the chances or break down the percentages, you remember the outcome.

The outcome was we got run out of there.

With your honor intact.

What would a four- or five-year-old know about honor?

Everything! You became a hero facing another of her heroes, and it turned out both of you could win. You'd traveled down south with Phil Hodge to show her that, how to keep two heroes in your head at the same time.

Like, how many heroes can you balance on the head of a pin?

Big Howie on the head of a pin? I'll need to consult the Beam brothers on that one.

Walter, it *is* time to go back, you know. We're the only ones left out here.

There's Byron Wainwright.

Before he cranks it up again, for God's sake!

Jim, your story has come full circle, but it's not the end. Remember her grip on your arm? In the cemetery, at your mother's funeral? If you're anything like me, you can still feel it. And then when she loosened it but didn't let go all the way. What did she want you to do?

She babbled on, Walter. And then she babbled herself to sleep.

Really?

Half the time I wasn't listening.

It took her all this time to call you, and then it was all gibberish?

Some old grievances, sentimental grievances, the way Leland's family had taken over summers on the lake and, she claimed, squeezed our family out. Certain other cousins who'd given her the cold shoulder. Topics too painful to mention, so she didn't, she talked around them, such as her children. She didn't talk about all the money they'd lost, either, or what the banks threatened to do. Childish stuff.

As if, Walter said with perfect timing—I could never forget he was a pro—when you got down to it, only the child was worth saving.

It may be that's still how she thought of herself. As if she were stranded back there somewhere.

Waiting for her hero to show up.

I smiled.

So, she wanted you to come save her. That was what she wanted.

Of course she did. That goes without saying. It's what she wanted from everybody she called.

And she'd gotten round to you.

No one makes calls that late at night, that lost in themselves, laying it all out there, meaning anything else. Come save me. Come save the child. Remember that slogan the phone companies used to have? Reach out and touch someone? All that means is come save me. It's as simple and sad as that.

I heaved up out of the chair. An oppressive Monday was upon us. A year's worth of Mondays in one. And that, Walter, I said, is the end of the story. It ended where it began. There was no talking to Ellie at the start and there was no talking to her at the end. As a family's firstborn, you think you're somebody, and you're not. The Pritchard girls are dead. The Pritchard girls' girls and boys are blurring out. The world has reached a kind of stalemate where history is no longer made. Everything is local legend now, the Howies are, and soon the copyright will expire on them and you can make of them what you will.

And the toad?

The toad is a barely distinct figure behind a screen door. That is where he'll remain.

Even though he ran off. Our toad did.

Yes, our toad ran off, he lit out for the territory, his pockets stuffed with the little that was left, but that doesn't mean he's not still squatting there behind a screen door, waiting for his princess to appear. Before too long somebody will step on him on the way out.

But not you, Jim? You didn't step on him? You let him off the hook and he's gone?

Not off the hook. You don't hook toads. You gig them. You spear them with a barbed prong. A frog gig. A toad gig. My cousin would have known.

We're not talking about your cousin now. He's long been laid to rest. Your cousin might have gigged a frog or a toad at a hundred yards. A local legend, you just said so yourself. We're talking about you, Jim. Why didn't you step on that toad?

I had no answer for my friend.

You fought it, Walter went on, and you really didn't believe it yourself, but that family meant everything to you. They were your blind spot and they were your shining light. You were a fool but finally you couldn't fool yourself. You haven't been telling me this story for the last three days just to while away the time. That was your family. And your aunt, your favorite aunt, the one who kept loading you down with clothes and laughing away all your qualms, knew it. Don't let my daughter, don't let your littlest cousin, marry that man! Unfair? Of course it was unfair, she should never have asked it of you, but you were first in line and the first with his arms held out, and it was you, you little blue-eyed cupid, that the snake had spared, and it was you who gave birth to your aunt's laugh. There were endless riches in that laugh, you were dazzled, you were hooked every time you heard it, so why didn't you step on that toad, Jim?

Walter . . .

What, Jim?

The short-haired dog got shaggy, I was about to say, I wanted to say, but didn't because it had not been a shaggy dog story I'd told him, we both knew that. Shaggy dog stories came to nothing and ended out of inertia, not where they'd begun. I shook my head instead, turned and walked down the slope of the terrace, and stepped out onto his dock. The water lay motionless, the blue showing uncharacteristic traces of a mossy green. There wasn't a breath of a breeze. The sky was overcast, and the trees overhanging the shoreline across the way deepened the shadows to the point that, if there had been bass in this lake, they would almost certainly have been feeding there, in the stickups along that shore, cruising that shore in small schools of three or four. A surface lure there, twitching in a crippled way, would have netted fish. Lacking such a lure, lacking even

Lamar Herrin

a rod and reel, at a lake supposedly lacking bass in any numbers worth
fishing for, I was still on the point of stepping into the canoe and fishing
that shore as if fishing, right now, in this northern but southern-behaving
lake would restore a balance I had lost no telling when and, given my age,
might never regain. I had to do something. If Walter hadn't been sitting
right up the terrace from me, I might have called Elaine. I had alerted
her to the possibility, and Walter, if I were to tell him, would have said,
By all means, do. Talk to Elaine. Take her hand. Molly and I might sneak
a peek but, believe me, Jim, we won't be able to hear a word. Call her.
Reach out and touch someone. Phone calls, needy phone calls, seem to
run in your family. I wouldn't deny it. I could call my sister, Jean. I could
get that protean energy, that doubt-free current she ran on, flowing down
the line. As she recycled lives in her redistribution center, as she shuffled
and reshuffled a town, she could pause long enough to bring her attention
to bear on the Whalen family once more, what can be done with what's
left, what can be done with what's been done, Jean, let's get our bearings
again, and she'd laugh, not with the windfall gaiety of my aunt's laugh,
but a shrewder, more targeted laugh, a laugh you might convince yourself
could overcome any obstacle, negotiate any impasse, make a small miracle
come true—oh, how southern women loved to laugh.

 And what could I tell her that she couldn't imagine for herself? As
families lived and breathed, they shared their stories. What could I tell my
sister that she couldn't turn around and tell back to me? Up close Leland
Oldham looked like a man who'd wasted a fortune and who'd drunk himself to a standstill and who was calculating an advantage that no longer
existed. He had a small head, like a knob. Very small eyes and folds in the
lids that threatened to overgrow his eyes entirely. Hair that had thinned
and re-thinned until what was left lay flat and discolored and looked forgotten, like a toupee from years past. He spoke with an instant's delay—
first the mouth worked, then the words came out. A whiskey-parched
voice. Shoulders that slumped. His chest had partially collapsed. He had
a tidy potbelly, the best feature about him. Short legs, a little bowed. On
an irregular rhythm he roused himself, he shored himself up, then a sad
and no longer dismissible reality took hold and he allowed himself to sink.
Toads did that, they puffed up, then they drew in. He wore khakis with
an overlarge belt buckle and a checked short-sleeve shirt, clothes that
I had worn when I was a boy. I recognized the pants and I recognized

172

the shirt. There was, there had been, a goatee, a few scraggly hairs. At his back stood a cedar-red house, once a cabin, looking out onto a lake. There was no one else, no children, no kinsmen, no wife, and on the lake at large nothing that moved, no minnows fleeing and no largemouth bass in ravenous pursuit. He was utterly alone. There was a boathouse, inside of which, it had to be taken on faith, there would still be boats. And the accessories that went with them, paddles and ropes and life preservers and down-dragging, depth-sounding anchors. Taken on more faith, there would still be towns, schools and stores and churches with their steeples and cemeteries, at the bottom of that lake. And empty streets. He might find a home there. Come evening when the swallows swooped and the doves nested and the fish rose and down the line stories began to be told, and the moon waited until the last hour before it appeared over the hill, it might be possible to go boating as though in one's own private universe, as though one owned it all, had never lost a stick of it, had only watched it grow. It might be worth waiting for. A boat ride in the quietness of that hour. Until then we took our seats in adjoining chaise lounges and, as the oldest of my generation, really the last authority left, I explained to him how this world had once been in the triumphant aftermath of a war, and how it had been overrun, trampled, befouled, made mockery of in the war that followed. I told him that story. It took the better part of the afternoon and evening. We might have looked for food, but didn't. Strangely, he did not bring out a bottle. When I finished we had a window of time, a very dark window, before the moon rose, and really the only light came from the flash of foam the fish left as they struck the surface. We walked out that long dock to the boathouse where we still had a choice of boats, and I chose the fishing boat, the Bassmaster, the one with the electric motor that made such a quiet purring sound not even the fish could hear it, and out we went, to enjoy the lake and the midnight hour when you might never know what abominations had been committed back on land. Leland Oldham professed from what he called the depth of his being that he wished it had always been like this, when everything was given and nothing left to be desired. Then, with a certain trepidation, but with the frustration and the fondness, too, with which a parent talks about a misbehaving child, he named his wife, Ellie, and still with his back to me told me of a time when they'd been out on the houseboat and Ellie, who, as everyone knew, couldn't hold her liquor, had fallen overboard, and he, Leland Oldham, had jumped in and saved her life. It seemed he was always jumping in and saving her life, the youngest of the youngest of the Pritchard girls, although that was not what he called her, but for me that was all that it took. A paddle to the back of the head, the anchor tied around an ankle, man overboard with no one to jump in and save him, and it was done. When the moon rose I was back where I belonged, and that night I slept where I'd slept as a boy, and slept well, and was still sleeping as Walter moved up behind me where I stood on his dock extending out into his small lake. It was as if he were whispering in my ear, but that was the effect of this hot heavy day when all sounds were quiet and close, as if meant for individual ears alone. Jim, Walter said, here's what I want to do. I want to go fish the jumps. I want you to take me out on that lake and show me what Howie Whalen, *Little* Howie Whalen, showed you. I want to get in the car and drive down there with you the way you drove down with Phil Hodge after he didn't jump into Cuba and unbeard the Castros. We're clean-shaven, Jim, but I don't want to go meet your family. I want to go fishing, down south in that lake. I want to fish the jumps. Can we do that, Jim? Is that asking too much? Your story's not done yet. It didn't begin with Ellie. It began with you and your cousin out in that boat and the water boiling with bass. Let's end it there. Let's go south.

I did him the courtesy of not turning around. I didn't have to turn around to see the look in his eyes, the shining expectation, no different from when at the poker table he believed he held the winning hand. Followed by that little leap of pleasure when he turned over the winning cards. You didn't mind losing a hand every so often to Walter Kidman, because with your chips in his stack Walter was happy to share his pleasure with you. We were playing poker, no more than that, and, fine fellows all, our chips were making the rounds.

I made a deliberating sound. And don't even ask, Walter said, my docket is clear.

I made another such sound, and he continued, We will need to tell the women something, you're right about that. Unless we invite them to come with us. Or we could meet them down there, for a big fish fry. Why don't we all go, Jim? Why don't we end your story for you the way it should be, with your most fervent admirers onstage?

And I made a last sound. Deeper, farther down in my chest, in a more private cavity there, a sound Walter would have heard before as clients of his placed their fates in his hands, just never from me. And this time his reply had something of Byron Wainwright's cello in it, the way Wainwright, a rank amateur but an old and lonely man, could draw out one long and passionately bowed chord. There will always be toads, Jim. Toads are something like the missing link, except they're never missing. They tell us how far back we go. There's not a garden in the world without its toad. Not a flower that's bloomed without a toad squatting beneath it. Our only choice is to forget them. Or catch them and use them for bait. Let's go fishing!

VI

WALTER DROVE. He took control—it was his pleasure and his particular pursuit—and he called his wife to explain our change of plans, plans that would include her and their good friend Elaine Sinclair were they so inclined. Then he drove. Soon thereafter we were stopped before a broad-winged stone building topped by a glassed-in cupola in the town of Poughkeepsie, a post office, one of many and one of the best that the WPA workers had either built or restored, but in this case FDR himself, concerned with the state of these old stone buildings along the Hudson, had been there to re-lay the cornerstone. Then we were back on the road, presently entering the forested hills of Pennsylvania and rising into an area that had been stripped of its first growth of hemlock, then of its second growth, which had been burned in the iron foundries there. Trough Creek, the creek that ran through those hills was called, and along its bluff ravens nested. Long before the WPA arrived to reclaim it all, and lay roads and bridge the creek and build a park lodge, Edgar Allan Poe had come to hear the ravens and be inspired, Walter thought I'd be interested to know.

We skirted Poe's death state and entered the state of his upbringing, except that this part of Virginia was West Virginia now, and we stopped before another WPA production, a pinkish limestone building with a bastion-like façade, a county courthouse in the town of Beckley, before swinging down into what remained Virginia and entering a tunnel on its Blue Ridge Parkway with its arch-stones wedged in so tightly the Romans might have built it. But the WPA had, and all the other tunnels on that

Lamar Herrin

parkway, men with pickaxes and very few power-driven machines, so that more and more men might be employed. This could go on, and it spoke for itself. We emerged into North Carolina and came at last to a stop before a structure that back in the New Deal day had been a field of play for some of the very best in the game. It wasn't all courthouses and post offices and tunnels hammered out of rock. There were beautiful national parks, and there were parks in which to play the national game, in this case a baseball diamond with a wooden grandstand roof called Hick's Field. Of course, FDR had been a fan. Had he given this ballpark to the WPA to build, to then give to Eleanor to name and pass on to her lover? FDR, Walter didn't deny it, had been a devious man.

And Walter had his own agenda in making this trip. But he turned his cards up on the table. Show him some kudzu. Show him some lakes brimming with bass. Sit him down to the table and it wouldn't all be black-eyed peas and cornbread, greens and grits with red-eye gravy. He'd eat his stack of isums, too. I could either share his boyish enthusiasm or call him on it.

He drove. The kudzu appeared, but not those fresh burgeoning swells of spring green that Phil Hodge had seen and fallen for, as if nothing within reach of his imagination could so beautifully cover such a multitude of sins. The kudzu was beginning to brown out. It lay there no less thickly but with none of its rampant aggression, as if confessing that its day was past. We were on and off interstates, and once off them it wasn't hard to find local color and local incongruities—a dog-trot house that hadn't seen a speck of paint in years, a deeply shaded yard without a blade of grass strewn with rusted tools and parts of disassembled cars, dogs plopped there, an overgrown ditch, a mailbox badly off plumb, ramshackle outbuildings of no apparent purpose built at odd angles to each other, the house itself built close to the road as if to say, stop in, neighbor, and take a load off, or slow down, neighbor, just a little more and I'll blow you away, a weather-grayed, swaybacked house raised over a black crawl space on slabs of rock and concrete, the staircase leading up to the front porch knocked askew, partially detached, some rotten risers, the porch itself without a swing, a glider, a rocking chair, or a plant, a stage onto which no one had stepped for years. But sitting up there, on the porch's edge, bent over his long legs with his feet at rest on a slanted step, was an old man in faded overalls and a meal-colored shirt, an old man with nothing less than a cell phone held to his ear, who seemed to stop speaking just as we passed and shot us an angry look. As if we'd interrupted his business. As if he'd seen one curiosity-seeker too many. As if, with our northern car and northern ways, we didn't have a clue. Walter said, Look at that, would you! Who hasn't got coverage these days! That alone is worth the trip! And I said, Walter, We don't need this, you know, we could go back. We've got Byron Wainwright. Think of it that way. And Walter replied, But you've got the fish. This is a fishing trip, Jim. A fishing story and a fishing trip, and damn it, this time we're gonna catch our share!

He had a GPS trip mapper. Once he'd passed his WPA sites, Walter had a device that would tell him where to turn and turn again, the practiced voice of a woman so flat and incontrovertible it didn't occur to you to disobey. You switched her off, and she was the same woman, the same authority without appeal, when you switched her back on. I gave Walter the number of the road up into the mountains, the name of the town closest by, and then, in a petty act of defiance, I gave him the boat dock and bait shop and lunch counter and the name of the owners back when I was a boy. It was only when our trip mapper intoned the name of Coggins's dock and tackle shop with exact directions of how to get there that I gave in. When Walter, pushing other buttons, activated his speakerphone and passed on the Coggins coordinates to his wife, who was already on the road, I knew for a certainty that we were going to be four. At that point I acknowledged the authority of the trip mapper and attended to her words as I might those of an oracle who had our best interests at heart.

Turn right, turn left, right and left, proceed up into those hills. Be patient, you'll wind and wind. Your memory will betray you. Old landmarks will have disappeared. The road will narrow, threaten to become a path. A raggedness will have set in. Have faith, the faith of a fool, of a pilgrim whose day has passed. Yesterday's holy site is today's hole in a wall. Choke down your sadness, beat back despair. Be alert for the first flash of water beyond the trees. There! Have faith, it will come again. Continue to wind, a hairpin curve, then another. Screw up your faith. A second flash, shimmering, radiant, quickly and cruelly gone! Pioneers want a vista, a prospect, a broad green world. You are not a pioneer. Piece these glimpses together. Soon you can roll down your window and smell gas on the water and the water-soaked pilings and the bilge and the boating trash and the staleness of old dock mats. And the stench of boatyard fish. A last turn and you will see boats in their slips, rocking with a tremens all their own. Moored, at the mercy of the little waves. A ticking and a slopping sound you almost never hear unless you've been away for years and just come home. Pull in. Coggins' Boatyard, Tackle and Bait Shop, Lunchroom and Pickup Grocery Store. Journey's end. Turn off your motor, sit and wait for the rest of your party to arrive.

Walter said, I'm assuming we can rent a boat here. Tackle and lures. What was it you said Little Howie caught those fish in the jumps on, a silver spoon?

A daredevil spoon, which I doubted were made anymore. Wait, I told Walter, and got out of the car.

I went looking for a Coggins and found one, seated at a table at the back of the lunchroom. There were novelties, distractions. There was a large and shiny new aluminum freezer. There were plastic accessories and plasticized menus spotted down the length of the counter. There were signs, ice-cream-on-a-stick signs, cola signs, photographs of meals that looked air-brushed. The Coggins I came to seated at the back of the lunchroom did not smell of fish and bait and boat motors as in years past. He smelled of yesterday's pizza, as the whole lunchroom did. But with those deep creases across his forehead and the tight fissure of his mouth, he was a Coggins. That was a Coggins's burnt bald head. And he sat the way Cogginses had always sat, round as a boulder, as if an erratic had come to rest there, as if glaciers had ever reached this far south. He didn't doubt himself for a minute, he'd known me at once. I was Jimmy. I was Little Jimmy Whalen, come back to these mountains. He didn't ask how long it had been, because it had been yesterday. I asked him how they were biting, and he replied they were still out there, waiting for a Whalen to come catch them. Still fishing 'em in the jumps? A Whalen might, he said. On those daredevil spoons? If you could find them anymore. He wouldn't happen to have a couple of those still around, would he?

He rolled out of his chair and hobbled into the bait shop like a man who, a lifetime later, was still searching for his land legs. The bait shop was shadowy, and I understood that this was a transaction best undertaken in the near dark. Coggins reached into a drawer and placed two silver spoons with treble hooks on the wooden countertop, whose scored and unvarnished surface you could read like Braille. I closed my eyes and ran my fingertips over it, the stories it told. When I opened my eyes, Coggins had placed two more spoons beside the first ones. That's your classic daredevil, right there, he said, with the red stripe, but Howie Whalen was partial to the silver ones. I closed my eyes again, and this time, when I opened them, two keys had appeared. That one's to the gate and that one to the house, but you ain't forgot none of that, have you, Jimmy? And the boathouse. You know where that key is. Right where Big Howie Whalen always kept it. I nodded and reached into my pocket to pay the man, and Coggins waved me off. You bring them lures and keys back and next time they'll be waitin' for you. I'll be waitin' too. You'll owe me a fish story.

We laughed. It was not easy to walk out on this man. He had stories to tell, too. I began to explain the circumstances, the friend I had waiting outside, when it occurred to me I had an additional favor to ask. Two ladies, I said, might very well be stopping by looking for directions to the Whalen house. One of these ladies had large dark and level eyes she rarely blinked. She had beautiful bones that time had sculpted in a beautiful way. Water, turbulent water, would flow around her as around the prow of a boat. The other woman would be the opposite, shorter, bouncier, curlier, a consumer of her energy and yours. These would be Yankee women, and they'd be looking for us. And, if he would be so kind as to give them directions, they too would be the Whalens' guests.

Then I turned, with my lures and my keys, even though I knew before I reached the light at the doorway I would have to turn back. I couldn't leave it like that after all these years. I owed this man. I imagined myself loading Buck Coggins down with shirts and pants, piling into his outstretched arms the postwar shirts and pants that our victorious soldiers had needed to reoutfit themselves as civilians, and I heard, more clearly than I had for decades now, the cascading wealth in my dear aunt's laugh.

But it was condolences that were in order, and as I turned and began to offer them to this particular Buck Coggins on his father's passing, and perhaps his grandfather's as well, he met me with a look of such wise comprehension and incomprehension that I swallowed everything I had left to say. What passing? What death? Maybe in that world down there where push always came to shove, but not up in these mountains. I was looking at the father and I was looking at the son and at anyone else down that Coggins line of descent. Except there was no descent. Maybe down there.

Back in the car I displayed the lures to Walter as a jeweler might.

His eyes lit up as if he saw the water frothing with bass. And the boat? The tackle? Everything else? His GPS trip-mapping woman had fallen silent. From this point on Walter looked for his answers to me. I held up the keys. And the toad was really out of it? Not as a toad, not as a figure of fable, even of fun, a figure to while away a long weekend with, but as a man named Leland Oldham who reputedly had little left except this house on a lake, where he might very well decide to throw up a last line of defense and make a stand, that man was out of it, that man who'd pissed it all away and might bring down as many as he could before he'd allow anyone to take back the little that was left, that man was really gone? Not "lit out for the territory, his pockets stuffed with what was left," but really gone, gone so that we should experience no unease sleeping in his beds, so that we could count on a good night's sleep, take it to the bank, as they say, where Leland Oldham would be persona non grata, before we woke refreshed and went out to have a fabulous day on the lake, and to silence Walter I held up the keys, swinging them before his eyes as a hypnotist might. Gone gone, I said.

Walter was a friend. And Walter had been an eager, appreciative, occasionally insubordinate listener. He stood now with his back to a cedar-red train car of a house that had once been a cabin, looked out a long dock to a boathouse with a swimming float attached, and across a lake of less settled, more turbulent water than he was used to, and said he recognized the place at once. I brought the chaise lounges out of storage, four of them, and told him he could no doubt imagine the rest that would in their heyday have extended the length of the house, and he said, Yes, it was getting clearer by the minute. There was the original cabin with its screen porch, just beyond it the catalpa tree with its cigar-green pods hanging down. Beyond it was a wall of something sweet, an entanglement of honeysuckle or blackberry brambles or wisteria vines. Yes, yes. We sat down, we reclined. The mountains across the way, the mountains at our back, the humid haze in the sky, boats on the water, returning to or setting out from the launch ramp at our end of the lake, our finger of the lake, the chugging and choking down of their motors, their exhaust mixing with the smell of fish, thickening it, creating the illusion of a lake thronged with fish, which was not an illusion, you only had to know the when and the where and the how.

Walter couldn't quite bring himself to believe it. I told him to close his eyes and breathe down that fish-heavy air. He'd done the driving for much of two days. He could afford to go off guard and leave it to me. He smiled, he settled, he didn't disagree that we'd need to conserve our strength for the fishing that lay ahead, and the last thing he said as he began to drift off was, So here's where they brought you when you were a boy. Paradise . . . he mumbled with both a dubious and an envious little laugh that never quite got out of his mouth.

For a moment—impossible to say how long—I was alone. Then Molly and Elaine drove up to the gate, which they waited for me to open. I made a tamping-down motion with my hand, for I could sense that Molly was about to lay on the horn. It was Molly's nature to rouse everybody out of odd-hour sleep. She was an empty-nester who'd never stopped waking her children up. There'd been three, and at last a grandchild, and if anybody could pick up on the spur of the moment and drive seven hundred miles south and arrive at a gate bursting to get in it would be Molly Kidman. I liked her. All of us fed off her energy, different from my sister's because Molly's obeyed no design, and all of us knew when to run off and hide. I began to open the gate slowly, my left palm flat against the side of my face, my head inclined, miming sleep. In the passenger seat, Elaine, of the unblinking gaze and a measuredness so natural to her that you could feed off her too, smiled. Molly, round blue eyes and graying red hair cut short as a helmet, made one more horn-threatening gesture with her right hand, and I allowed my left cheek to fall into my left palm as I closed my eyes, and we held our pose. Then I let these Yankee women inside and walked them around the house to where they could see for themselves that Walter Kidman had indeed fallen asleep in his chaise lounge. There was a lake out there, and, although late in the season, the afternoon had yet to cool. I left Molly with her decision to make and went back to the car, a van, to bring in the sacks of groceries I had noticed in the cargo area. I heard Elaine following me—I knew her step. But no one had spoken, not really, until we were at the car and then, at my back, at my ear, Elaine said, You wanted me to come, didn't you? I felt that you did. I turned and kissed her, and her eyes, in a pleased, unstartled way, flared. We're back at the start, I said. It's the Molly and Walter show. And Elaine replied, But this time we'll know what to expect. We'll be on guard. We laughed very quietly, and I kissed her again. Then Elaine helped me take the groceries through the cabin's front door and into the small original kitchen, where my first memory would always be of my grandmother standing tall before a cast iron skillet turning isums, building a stack, while I waited down below, never more like a dog, to be the first served. Back before Little Howie Whalen had yet to demonstrate prowess at anything other than pouting when he didn't get his way. Here. On this spot.

Elaine read my thoughts. Or she saw something in my eye, or the shine on my lips. She said, Walter told Molly to be sure to bring pancake mix. She'd forgotten, when he'd warned her not to, so we had to stop a second time on the way.

The Walter and Molly show, I repeated.

Elaine smiled. I think it's your show, too, Jim.

We plugged in the refrigerator and put away the supplies. I left the pancake mix—and it was not Aunt Jemima I saw pictured on the box, only in my mind's eye—out on the counter. There was no meat of any sort, but other than that we had enough to last us for days. In addition, there were three bottles of New York State wine. Two six-packs of beer in case the weather got too hot.

So we really are supposed to eat fish, I said.

I don't know, Jim. Have you caught any yet?

I shook my head. We took our time getting here. Walter had a number of WPA sites he wanted to take me by. It was as if he was trying to convert me, or fortify us both against a prolonged stay down here. Or maybe he was propitiating the gods, who would then look favorably on our fishing endeavors.

Roosevelt died down here somewhere, didn't he? In the arms of his mistress? Or was it in the train coming back?

Somewhere, I said. With the whole world at war, it was somewhere down here. The South is snaky, I reminded her.

Jim . . .

One more kiss, Elaine.

She kissed me with her wonted poise, laying her lips on mine.

Now, I said, let's go out and see our friends.

They were reclined side by side in the chaise lounges and Walter was in the act of telling his wife the Pritchard story as it flowed into and mixed currents with the Whalen story and brought us to where we now sat. For Elaine's benefit, although she didn't request it, he started over. The War, which was where Elaine and I had left off, with FDR's death, although she didn't mention that. The story was long, even when abbreviated, and at some point Walter suspended his narration so that Molly could bring out cold beer. He narrated with a deliberate and selectively detailed authority that any judge and jury would credit. He was bringing the ladies he'd brought south up to date and to this spot on the map. He was not pleading a case, at least not overtly, although of course he had his favorites, my aunt Rosalyn as she stood at the foot of her son's boyhood bed holding a tray of shaving utensils, for once not laughing, not piling our arms full of clothes, and my raucous aunt Lily, back from the war, the self-proclaimed boomerang babe. And Little Howie watching wheels turn within wheels in that small Dominican town of his, Bella something, and with his trusted tape measure measuring me for a suit, soon to be cut by that oldest employee with the hanging hazel pools for eyes, and Ellie—Ellie the little girl whose eyes were golden and attracted the attention of one warty, wheezing toad, at which point the sun sank below the ridgeline before us, the day's heat stole away and left us in a wind-stilled, ember-cool warmth.

It was time to eat. We sat on the small screen porch and ate an enormous salad, first course to a second course that would have to wait until the fish rose out of the lake to join us. We sat at a card table—old maid, hearts, gin rummy, canasta, but never poker that I remembered. Poker was a man's game, a war game, as was the clinking of chips, the rattle of dice, as was the panicky skitter of a little ball around a roulette wheel before it came to rest. Soldiers coming home. Troopships. Demobilized, decommissioned, newly outfitted. Shirts and pants.

Sedate, civilian life.

Old maid, hearts, gin rummy, canasta.

I cast direct glances at my three friends, one of whom had been my wife. Sitting where Pritchards and Whalens had once sat back in the pre-toad days, which could never be measured in years. It had lasted forever, and then it was as if it had never been. I closed my eyes and managed to get my hands in all of theirs, as though we were joined in a séance. I gave thanks. As little Howie Whalen himself might have, I promised fish for the following day. I squeezed, and the first to break free was Molly, who had been left hanging on what she assumed was the precipice of my life story. Then Walter, who had no choice but to gratify his wife, who had made a long trip on short notice with no WPA landmarks to set her course. I opened my hands on Elaine's and allowed Elaine to slip free too, but she stayed near.

Thank you, I said. A sentimental moment. I am a lucky man.

No, no, Walter protested, it's a great occasion, it's a trip we've had coming for years.

I could show you things, I said.

Not necessary, Walter said. You'll need to rest for tomorrow.

A boy's things. I mean I could show you where they'd been.

Peace, Jim, Walter said. He raised his hand as though to hold me off, or to offer a benediction.

Peace, I repeated.

The peace that passeth understanding, Walter said. The only kind worth settling for.

Fellows! Molly broke in, feigning a limit she had reached. Why so solemn! Let's go back out and sit in front of the lake. What's the matter with you? Do you want to waste an evening like this?

Behind the screen's mesh, it was true, the water was turning a duskier and duskier shade of orange. These were minutes that wouldn't come again, that, maybe, were worth driving eight hundred miles for. Insects struck the screen, insects wanting in, a disorientation typical of a southern summer's evening, except we were late into the season. A last boat passed, an overlarge fishing boat, rumbling as it choked down. A sheet of sound then struck up, crickets and katydids and cicadas in full chorus, which you learned to talk under and for periods of time never heard. A fish striking you would hear, and if the strike was loud enough, everything stopped. That was a voice from the world under water, and for the initiated it spoke in code. There were hungry splashes, defiant splashes, playful splashes, then attention-getting but noncommittal splashes intended to put you on alert.

At times voices reached you from across the water, a child's high-pitched plea, a man's curse or booming laugh, a woman patiently, a woman doggedly, calling her family in.

And dogs, family pets, barking back and forth as the night drew on.

Silence. The small waves stirring on the shore, the very quiet slosh of waves trapped inside a boathouse.

Elaine said, We should. We shouldn't let this evening pass.

Walter said, Let's do it. I'm bringing out the Beam brothers in case anyone's interested.

Molly said, Who are they?

A big southern family, Walter said.

Borderline, I said.

One by one, filing out, we took our seats before the water. We reclined. The stars had yet to appear. The sky was a mix of colors, deepening as we sat there, the blue thickened to the aurora borealis of a bruise. The yellows, the oranges, the reds, the mauves, before a backdrop of blackness with an endless depth of field that might never appear as long as stories continued to be told on the ground, from chaise lounge to chaise lounge. Walter, the interloping Yankee, took it all on himself. Jim, our Jim, the family's firstborn—with, you'll remember, his preacher-man grandfather and his Gibson girl grandmother—was one year old when the dying grandfather says, No, no, take the little angel away, don't let him see what it all comes to. Little Jim is taken away. Fast forward, Little Jim, our Jim, the first of his generation, is called down to the deathbed of the youngest of his mother's generation, his favorite aunt, to be set the task of rescuing the last of his own generation, a cousin young enough to be his daughter, whose eyes in the right light could be golden, eyes that cast a golden glitter and attracted a toad. If it sounds like a knot, it was, a knot of kinship that Jim neither cut through nor untied, although he tried. The toad—as Jim's aunt Rosalyn described the man, a toad with a scraggly goatee—came from a family of toads, while Jim, our Jim, came from a clan of church-founding and church-attending folk but with an eye out for beauty, nonetheless. And, such is the way of the world, the toads won. The toads squatted there and flicked flies out of the air. They ate to the point of satiation. They were of one mind. Beauty was all in the flies. Where we now sit became toad-land. Until the toads overbred, ate all the flies, squeezed out of the little girl with the golden eyes every last cent she possessed, and then the toads lost. At which point it became a matter of who had the best memories to preserve, the toad who had ruined it all or the first of that generation whose grandfather had spared him the sight—and remember, the grandfather for whom our Jim was named had been a very handsome man, and his wife had been a very beautiful woman, and someone had to keep that memory bright. And that was when Jim, here with us now, along with our good friends the Beam brothers, told me the story, which in effect brightened the memory and won it all back from the toads. You'll see. Tomorrow the fish will be lining up to bite on his hook.

Walter, with eight hundred miles behind him and his case rousingly argued, proposed a toast. To our liberator! To James, our hero!

To please him and to applaud his performance, we all clicked glasses up and down the line.

But Elaine remarked, Isn't it some kind of frog with a very long tongue that flicks flies out of the air?

Flies and filth! Walter responded. I know at least one toad who does.

And, Molly took it up, just how did James, our Jim here, liberate the place? He won it all back because he told the story and kept the memory bright? Does that make a storyteller a liberator?

Technically, I don't know whether it does or not, Walter allowed, but the field is ours! The place is ours! Look at it! Look out there! Paradise for a boy, our Jim called it. Paradise minus its toad . . .

You mean its snake, Molly said.

That's another story, Walter said.

Is there no end to them then? Molly asked.

Storytelling in the South, Elaine mused.

Correct! Walter exclaimed like a game show host awarding a prize, professing to be pleased. What you drove seven hundred miles for!

Walter stood and poured out the Beam brothers in sacramental measures right down the line. He returned to his seat. By then the stars had begun to swing up. And a waxing moon which cast its first rays over a table of water so still, so unmarred by boaters' waves or windbursts or untoward behavior of any sort, that it was possible to believe in a sort of universal suspension, in a quiet and collectively held breath. It was then in the hills behind us that the whippoorwills began to sing to each other, clear, glassy notes, three of them, the third assertive, triumphant, which you could time your breath to again. Breathe in on "will."

Those birds had been common when I was a boy, but I had not heard them much since then. I reached over and held Elaine's hand.

It's lovely, Elaine said.

When you come down to it, it's really nothing special, I confessed. There're houses up and down the shores. People roar in for a long weekend and roar out. Most of them leave a mess behind. They muddy the waters and give a good goddamn. And yet . . .

I knew there had to have been a place.

How? How did you know?

By the way everything, really everything, came up just a little bit short.

You didn't, Elaine.

That's nice of you to say, Jim.

This really is child's stuff. You know that, don't you?

Of course.

Actually, there was this child—

The one with the golden eyes.

Which obviously weren't golden, they just glittered that way. She's a sad, middle-aged alcoholic now. Penniless. Living on the sufferance of her daughters, who've done all that they could.

With a husband who abused her . . .

There was such a man.

You mean "the toad." What was his real name?

I don't even want to say it. Not here, not now.

Then don't. But get him out of your mind, too. You're here, he's gone. We're here, he's gone. Our friends Molly and Walter are here, and he's gone. How old were you?

When?

When the war ended and the victors gathered and families began to form. How old were you then?

Fresh born, I said.

Elaine laughed, warmly. She squeezed my hand. The whippoorwills sang and I breathed in.

From down the line, her patience exhausted, on an evening out of a picture book or a movie show when no desire should go unfulfilled, Molly demanded, All right! Who's going to tell me this snake story?

I took refuge in the night, on the far side of Elaine, behind a curtain of crickets and katydids and cicadas and all the insects of a southern summer night, and once again it was Walter who took on the role. For fear of underrepresenting it, he, of course, over-staged the scene. At every turn a southern pine forest, choked with brambly growth, became a bower of bliss, and huge swells of kudzu grew up to the path's edge so that a single deviation had you sinking into a feather mattress of tendrils so tender and eager and quick to include you that to fight against it would be to declare war against nature itself, as those granite-faced Puritans up north had done. And the little boy, tender and eager and tendril-quick himself, and a little dog, plug-ugly but quicker yet. And then there were two pairs of lovers, one licensed and bringing up the rear, and another taking the day's license unto themselves and speeding out ahead. Space them out, place the dog and the little boy in the center. A family portrait in the South.

Walter . . . Molly drew it out, as though taking aim, to let her husband know the risk he was running.

Virginal moans out ahead, veteran moans bringing up the rear, Walter went heedlessly on, honeysuckle or something equally sweet on the air, the cooing of turtledoves overhead, and there at the path's midpoint, with a marimba rattle and a venomous hiss and a muscular uncoiling that would sound to the little boy like a Lash Larue whipcrack on the air—

Lash Larue? Molly objected with a threatening frown.

It's Jim's generation we're talking about here. Jim?

Lash Larue, I quietly gave my okay.

—a Lash Larue whipcrack on the air, Walter resumed, and the snake struck. And the little bug-eyed dog leaped. And close enough so that Little Jimmy saw snake eyes staring right back at him—and who's to say that a drop of venom didn't fly through the air and land on his cherub's cheek—the dog and the snake met in midair. The battle was fierce, it waxed and it waned, there were timeouts and time-back-in's, and when it was over the snake lay stretched out at its entire phallic length over the ground and the dog was doing the panting for both of them.

Molly stopped it there. She turned to look down the row of chaise lounges to me.

She said, Does this bear any resemblance to the truth, or is one of the Beam brothers doing the talking?

They weren't brothers, Molly, I explained. They were fathers and sons.

Not brothers?

Fathers and sons and a nephew. Two hundred years of them. It doesn't make sense any other way.

A chain of Beams?

A chain.

And how do you break a chain?

I suppose that's what the snake was trying to do.

And would have, Walter interjected, if a heroic little dog hadn't sprung to Jimmy's defense. Of course, the mother and father come rushing up and the mother's kid sister and her swain—

Her swain?

We're out in the country, Molly. Her swain. Her beau. The man who went on to found the plant that gave us all of this—and Walter swept it up in one hemispheric gesture, the lake, the hills, the sky—that man, a swain's swain, and Jim's favorite aunt, a handful herself with a laugh that wouldn't quit, came rushing back, and that was what they found. A dead snake, a dying dog, and a little boy who had been spared, leaving one enormous question on everybody's lips. Spared for what? Spared for what? Anybody care to venture a guess?

Molly grabbed the bottle out of her husband's hand, and Walter, submitting, enjoying himself enormously, laughed. That still doesn't answer the question, he said.

Spared so that you could come all the way down here and make a boisterous fool of yourself? Molly said.

That may be true, too, Walter allowed, but that's not the correct answer. Try again.

So that you could make me regret getting within five hundred miles of you?

That would put you somewhere back north of Mason-Dixon.

So that you could traumatize—*re*-traumatize—our friend Jim.

It's an old, old story, Molly, I said. All the damage has been done by now.

Elaine, Walter said, you're a wise head. You can take the long view. Why was our friend and your soul mate spared? Think of the lifetime that lay before him. If that little Boston bulldog whose name was—Bean?

Bing, I corrected him.

Of course, Bing, Bing, named for the crooner, who sang love songs like nobody before or since. Come to me my melancholy baby . . .

Don't you dare, Molly threatened. Why did we ever wake him up?

. . . cuddle up and don't be blue. All your fears are foolish fancies, baby . . .

All right! Molly gave in. Enough of the crooning! Tell us straight out. Why was Jim spared?

Why, to take me fishing, Walter declared, overcome by disbelief. What other reason could there possibly be?

To take you fishing? Molly repeated. Eight hundred miles just to take you fishing?

The jumps, Walter said, practicing patience with his wife. To fish the jumps. High noon. You can stand on the shore and applaud.

Molly held the Beam bottle out of her husband's reach and passed it on to me. I said, Take your choice of a room. Or two rooms, if that's your preference.

The jumps? she said.

I said, Get Walter to explain it to you. Even with the state he's in, it'd be hard to exaggerate.

Molly pulled her husband up and, of course, he was nowhere near as drunk as he pretended to be. He was nimbly on his feet. He stopped, took a deep breath, and let the insect-shrilling silence rule. Sleep in and go fishing at noon! he practically cheered. Never in my wildest dreams—

You'll miss the pancakes if you don't get up before then, his wife reminded him.

Miss the isums? Are you out of your mind? I'll be battling Jim for the first stack.

The isums? Molly said.

And yet another story, I said.

There really is no end to them, is there? Molly said.

To the isums? An endless stack of isums? Isums reaching to the sky?

She smiled. No end to the stories.

No, I said. Not lined up here, facing the lake, the air like a bath you can breathe. No end.

Molly took Walter off to bed. Elaine and I remained in adjoining chaise lounges. The whippoorwills appeared to have gone to sleep. Voices had ceased from across the water, not even a dog. A fish splashed, small, incidental, gratifying only in the sense that you could go to bed assured the fish were still out there, waiting for the hour when the minnows would rise and the bass would rise after them and a fisherman might stand in their midst.

So, Jim, Elaine said. Why *were* you spared?

I reached for her hand. Walter had it right, I said. So that after all these years I could take him fishing.

And you're sure to catch fish?

No, Elaine. I have a memory, a couple actually, out fishing with my cousin when we caught them in a furious burst. The times we didn't I've forgotten. Basically, I have a memory of marveling at him.

And now it's Walter's turn to be marveling at you.

I laughed.

This cousin . . . Elaine ventured.

It's far too late to be talking about him. I paused. Elaine sensed I had more to say. What was it not too late to be talking about? It was not too late to be talking about things that spoke for themselves, the two of us sitting there, reclining, half horizontal, in the absence of earlier generations, the Pritchards, the Whalens, here as opposed to anywhere else on the face of the earth, an interlude that wouldn't last long, made possible because there were interstates and trip-plotting GPS women and aging, mostly retired men and women with time on their hands, in possession of comfortable, air-conditioned cars, and because there were faithful retainers from years past, someone like the Coggins family, who came by and in honor of Big and Little Howie Whalen kept the grass cut and the walls of wild growth cut back and the squirrels and raccoons out of the chimney and the boats in the boathouse suspended above all that would rot them, who let fresh air in and old depleted air out, and kept on hand, in case someone rose from the dead and asked for them, silver spoons and red-striped spoons that dared the devil to keep fish off the hook. But all that paled.

What couldn't be permitted, I found myself saying, was that someone would come along and let it all go to hell. That someone would speed it on its way. That's no different than going to the cemetery and before they rot digging up the bones to see how many nickels and dimes you can get for them. We've all known people like that.

Have we?

People without an ounce of reverence in their souls. Sure, we have.

I don't know about reverence, Jim, Elaine replied. There may be too much of it out there. It may run too shallow or too deep. As if in the name of reverence . . .

Elaine trailed off. We had become accustomed to completing each other's thoughts. Which could lead to testy moments or to moments of real intimacy, moments which needed little else to complete them, perhaps nothing else.

. . . people can commit barbarous acts? I said.

Or silly ones.

But irreverence isn't the answer either, is it? There's a fine line you have to draw . . .

. . . which very few people can.

Keep your reverence private?

Or know your public well if you can't, Elaine allowed.

We're private here, I said. Semiprivate if you include Molly and Walter.

But you've said it yourself, Jim. We're in a world full of ghosts. The last thing you want to do is disturb those bones. What if you left the fishing for another day? Another life? Am I carrying this too far?

It's hard to get a fish to bite, Elaine. If you'd ever tried, you'd know that.

But if they bite and won't stop? If there is something that happens, some line you don't want to cross?

I laughed at her, out loud, a little too loud. The fish stopped striking, the crickets chirping. I'd brought on a hush. I put the back of her hand to my lips. A slender hand, an elegant hand, whose darkening veins and age spots wouldn't show in this light. I told her that she would never know how much it meant to me that she would travel this far, in the company of our voluble friend, to sit at my side—recline, recline—to listen to me and help try to make it all make sense for me while she took nothing away for herself.

And she interrupted me with a quietly incredulous laugh. It had a little purr to it. It was a bit of a moan. Oh, Jim, Jim, she said, I'm taking away all I want.

And she continued to laugh.

Many years ago, I said, I sat right here with my mother and my aunts. They were all beautiful, and if you put them together, the quiet faithful one, the spunky provocative one, the open-handed laughing one, and the mostly tongue-in-cheek sergeant-at-arms one, they added up to one extraordinary woman. But not as extraordinary as you.

And I kissed her before she could laugh again or grumble that she'd had enough flattery for one day. I asked her if I might have the pleasure of her company for the rest of the night. There was an abundance of bedrooms, where either one of us might escape, but what if for old times' sake we lasted out the night, side by side, in one lakeside bed. Whose sheets would be musty, I warned her in advance, but surely we could sweeten them in our way and wake up to the morning light—and a melodious racket of birdsong—together.

I woke up long before that and carried Elaine out with me into the night. Her arms around my neck, the deep luster in her eyes. Until the last moment, when it all rose over the top and a lifetime of unseized chances and uncertain calculations went flooding away, she wouldn't take her eyes off mine. Then, as it all came to bear, more than a groan she released what sounded like a deep vacating sigh as her eyes closed and she was gone. In the immediate aftermath she always spoke my name. Not in gratitude, certainly not in reverence, but as a simple act of recognition. Yes, I had been there, I had been there with her right up to the instant she'd gone off, but in the middle of the night I did get out of bed and in bare feet walked out the long dock to the boathouse—and I had always known where Big Howie Whalen kept the key, as the oldest and the first of my generation, that was a secret entrusted to me that would take more than one lifetime to forget. But rather than enter the boathouse, I stepped down onto the swimming float. A swath of moonlight lay down the center of the lake, then scattered out on the margins to a mosaic of silvered scales. There was no wind, just little vagrant breaths of breeze looking for a gust to join. They came to nothing. All that assortment of electric night sounds was confined to the shore. I stood there waiting and listening, scanning the water and moving as the float moved on the insignificant waves. There came a time when the float registered a single abrupt movement, a tilt followed by a righting of the balance. Nonetheless, I kept my eyes trained up that moonlit road. Even when my friend Walter Kidman stepped up to my ear and said, Sure? and I gave it a moment's thought before answering him that I was, it wasn't as if we were keeping each other company out on that float. I had swum off that float as a boy, Walter hadn't, but as middle-of-the-night wanderers risen from our ladies' beds we both belonged, we had our right to step out onto water without getting wet. Not long later, I felt a reverse tilt and the swimming float returned to my weight, my presence, alone. I stood there a while longer. I had a memory of my aunt Ruth's husband, Uncle George, a massive man who'd survived the Pacific when his ship was torpedoed by the Japanese, cannonballing into this lake. I could see the crater he'd leave when he hit the water, and I could feel, right then, the sharp angle of the tilt in the float when he'd come down hard on both feet, followed by the float's release when he'd spring free. Man overboard! was his battle cry, and how Aunt Ruth scolded him for trying to scare us. The war was over, and as Aunt Lily kept reminding us, as though rubbing it in, We won! We won! As children we'd screamed in mock-frightened delight, and begged Uncle George for more, more thrills, more deep, near swamping tilts in the float, more men overboard, more war.

The next morning, Walter knocked at our door to announce that if I wanted to contest with him that first stack of isums, the time had come. I rolled back over, but Elaine rolled me out. Go keep your friend company, she said. Isums, she said, smothering a sleepy laugh in her pillow.

There was a larger kitchen in the new part of the house, modernly equipped, but in the original kitchen, before a small two-burner stove, Molly stood turning pancakes over in a cast iron skillet while Walter sat at a corner breakfast table, really only suitable for two, waiting to be served. Molly was not a tall woman, and she wore what in these surroundings was an elegant robe, while my grandmother might have stood before the stove that early in the morning in something as insignificant as a slip, so that as the pancakes bubbled and the batter sometimes spilled, it all got mixed up in my mind with the overflow of my grandmother's flesh, rosy in those summer mornings and brightened with a sheen. Her hair came loose from where she'd pinned it up at the back of her neck, wavy, once abundant auburn hair now unruly and mixed with gray. She'd be humming a tune, and to that tune she shifted her weight, or perhaps it was when she flipped the pancakes that her broad hips moved. I must have been panting and pleading like a dog, for she'd send me to the table, and only when I was still and attentive with my eyes full of impending wonder would she place the first golden stack before me. What did I say? I said, Thank you, Mama Grace. What else did I say? I said, What is 'ums? and she said, They're whatever you want them to be, you darling boy.

She had already poured the syrup, which ran down the clockface of the pancakes at each of the quarter hours. A stack of four, to start off. Because, depending on the day, the weather, the sunlight beyond the window, the flowers and the leaves and the birdsong out there, and depending on how sweet Mama Grace's dreams had been, how many clicks of a camera had been directed her way before her husband discovered her from his pulpit and put an end to all that, there might be more. A stack of pancakes reaching up to heaven, a veritable chain of being, known as isums to the initiated and all for me. In exchange for which I would assume the obligations of any family's firstborn once my childhood years had passed. I was being fattened up to take the weight of a family's fate onto my shoulders. My life was being sweetened, and I was being made strong.

I told Molly her isums were worthy of my grandmother's, and I commiserated with Walter since the second stack would surely pale in comparison to the one I'd just eaten. I owed him, I acknowledged, and I owed Molly, too. It was a twofold debt, which could be paid in full, Walter informed me, one combined with the other, once the fish began to jump into the boat.

And why would the fish ever want to jump into the boat? an uninformed Molly still wanted to know.

The day was clear, the wind was down, the water lay glassy and green, taking on the sun's heat there near the surface where the minnows would rise to breathe.

I owed her an explanation, if for nothing else in return for the pancakes I'd just eaten.

The tedium of fishing—did Molly have any idea? It was legendary. It was the stuff of legend. Fishing with nets was one thing, but for most of mankind fishing meant sitting on the banks of a river with a pole between your legs, or off the side of a boat. Into that vastness you dropped a tiny piece of bait, or you cast a little demitasse-sized spoon with a hook attached. There was a world down there, and what you contributed to it was such a microscopic speck in the grand scheme of things that the chances a fish would swim by and take the time to nibble seemed prohibitive. You fished on faith, you baited your hook with faith, and after so prolonged a wait, after such silence from the gods, whose faith wouldn't turn stale? A hook baited with stale faith, Molly, in a world down there full of wondrous sights, and what were your chances? You asked fish to come join you up top, and did you bait your hook with the most glittering of jewels? Did you even offer them isums? No, you offered them worms that drowned and stopped wriggling almost at once, or little minnows that swam around with a hook in their backs as though they were harnessed to a tractor-sized load. You devised little fish- or fly-like lures. You turned to artifice. You gave them a wiggle and a shine they'd never seen before and expected them to bite on the sheer novelty of the thing, as if they were teenagers larking down a shopping center mall. And it's no contest, Molly. Oh, you get bites, you get strikes, fish get bored too and the law of averages is a law that no creature is exempt from, but the tedium is vast and can seem unplumbed, and you allow yourself to become mesmerized by a bobber that can't help but move since there is not one speck of unmoving whatever in this universe of ours. Or you cast and you cast, and this time maybe that tug on your shiny lure is not a hook catching in a weed or log or bumping in a fitful skitter along the bottom, not this time, but you know better, every fisherman does, it all remains a mystery down there. We try to solve it, we even invent devices that will map out every inch of that underwater terrain, we can zoom in on all of its occupants, we can count the fish and take them one by one. But we can't. There are structures down there, houses, barns, towns we flooded, and since we once walked those streets and took our sport in those fields, we assume it's a domain that answers to us still. And it doesn't. But the lure, the mystery, the close-at-hand otherness of what once was ours can be irresistible, so we keep dropping hooks into it, subjecting ourselves to a tedium as vast as the heavens if we only knew. Which we do, Molly. But at the first tug on a hook we forget. Fishermen—and not the ones seining through the seas with their nets—are no better than boys, blinded by longing and made pigheaded by faith, who never give up, who never learn. A nibble, just a nibble, and we continue to fish . . .

The little kitchen, once the epicenter of the cabin that had become this house, was now crowded with my friends. The production of isums had ceased. Walter was going hungry, and Elaine was standing just inside the door, perhaps drawn against her better judgment by the sound of my voice. They had gathered again around me, but if I were to reach out as though over a card table to take all their hands, would they shy back, or offer one provisional hand instead of two? I had lured them all the way down here, into this very nub of a kitchen, with no Buck Coggins beside me to assure them that it wasn't all doom and gloom, that if you were part of the Whalen clan, with a dash of Pritchard blood to give you a preacher's flair, hope was at hand.

And hope had a name. It was called "the jumps."

There comes a time, Molly, I resumed my discourse, a right time and a right place, when if a fisherman's faith has not faltered, has not flickered out, it may be made whole again and robust. The gods alone decide when to send up the fish to lure a doubting fisherman back to the fold. I say there comes a time, Molly, when the fish are so ravenous to feed that, just as you have given us isums to eat, the gods will send schools of minnows up to the surface of a lake so that the fish, beautiful green-striped bass, with capacious bellies and mouths as large as infants' heads, likewise rise to the surface and put on a show. A one-price, all-you-can-eat smorgasbord, and, like most of us then, we lose sight of what our stomachs can hold and feed through our eyes. The minnows rise to the surface and the bass go back again and again, piling serving on serving, eating with sheer gluttonous delight, and in that they resemble us and in that we know them very well. Do they actually jump into the boat, Molly? Do fishermen jump into the lake? And the little minnows that aren't eaten, what happens to them? The minnows dart off in every direction, then look for another school to join. At the instant the feeding ceases and the water flashes out smooth, the fishermen might grab the sides of their boats and hold on, as if they've been brought out of a dream. True, a fisherman may fall in, but a cold sodden fisherman sobers up fast. And do fish actually jump into the boat, you ask? Fish are leaping. When fish tire of feasting on minnows, they might leap to take flies out of the air. One might very well land in your boat. Even in your lap, Molly, and look up at you and mistake you for anything but what you are. You yourself could be considered bait. You fish the jumps and you might get jumped, but that would put you among the most fortunate fishermen of all, because then you'd have a hell of a fish story to tell. Finally—I shook my head and humbly confessed—it's about the stories, Molly. It's about what you and your fish can team up to get your listeners to believe.

Walter laughed because Walter understood. With her pancake flipper in hand Molly gave a deflated little laugh, then roused herself to see if I had something sensible to add. From the doorway Elaine professed that she now understood. Man and fish team up, you could even say man and fish mate, and what do they give birth to? Why, a shaggy dog. A wet, shaggy dog. Just don't let him shake all over me!

We all laughed. We all ate pancakes, we took our time, I ate a second stack, the women, lingering over theirs, did too, and soon thereafter Walter departed and began to rummage through his tackle box. Looking over his shoulder, I observed him for a while before reaching over and deliberately closing the box. In the palm of my other hand I held out to him two of the spoons that Buck Coggins, one of the Buck Cogginses, someone in that line of descent, had loaned to me. The strictly silver one that Howie Whalen had favored and the classic daredevil spoon with the red stripe. They lay on my palm for an inordinate time while Walter studied them as though he were trying to fathom a shell game. Finally he looked up at me. I made it easy for him. I withdrew the red-striped spoon and left him the silver one. I said, You've come all this way. Be Howie Whalen for a while and you'll catch some fish. He narrowed his eyes. He smelled a trap. I shook my head. I've been being Howie Whalen practically all my life. Take your turn now, Walter.

We threaded line through the rods' eyes and tied on our lures, Walter the silver spoon, I the red-striped one. We set our drags, neither too heavy nor too light. We checked through our tackle boxes. Other spoons, plenty of spinners, and some streamlined, minnow-like plugs. Walter had his long-snouted pliers with which he'd extracted a hook from a pickerel on day one. Knives, a stringer, bobbers of diverse sizes. Hooks, line, and sinkers.

We scanned the water. That we could see, not a boat was on the lake. Was the season over and had all the summer people gone home? It had the feel of a vast abandonment, an empty stage. A misty softness on the surface of the water, to the overhanging air, had begun to lift, and the lake was gathering to a slatelike smoothness on which the activity of its inhabitants might be writ clear. I allowed Walter to observe me as from its hiding place in a crevice beside the fireplace I retrieved a key. We said goodbye to the women. They could stand on the dock and watch us, but if on the trail of the fleeing minnows we passed out of sight, they would have to take us on faith. They managed to maintain a solemn air, as though we were whalers setting out on a voyage around the world. In the boathouse I retrieved a second key, left the speedboat suspended, and flipped the switch on the hoist that allowed the fishing boat to be lowered into the water. We stowed our gear. Walter took his seat in the prow of the boat, and in the stern I used a paddle to pole us out of the boathouse and into open water. To test it I turned on the electric motor, with its middle-C hum, turned it off, and ignited the outboard motor, not as Howie had to do when he'd first taken me out, by yanking on the starter cord of a smaller and noisier motor, but by flicking a switch. The propeller churned the water with a powerful, gargling restraint. I made a single-planed gesture to Walter to indicate the flat and endless reach of the lake. It had almost nothing in common with the lake we'd first canoed out on, which a little trailing arm of a glacier had dug out, and whose water was almost that cold. This was a lake that had created itself as a dam made narrow valleys into broad bodies of water and little streamheads into coves. It smelled of the silt that had never settled, of its algae, its fish, its boathouses, and the gas films from weekend motors that had yet to dissolve. It was powerfully impure, and even as a boy you understood when you set out on it that you might not be the same boy when you got back. A thrilling prospect for a boy.

I opened the motor and directed us out toward the center of our arm of the lake, then once in open water began to choke down. With his back to me, Walter sat up in the prow of the boat, searching, I knew from his erect neck and straightened spine, for that flashing front of ripples that minnows might make as they fled for their lives. I brought the motor down to an idling gurgle, then cut it off entirely, and for an instant we could hear the smallest of waves. Walter glanced back at me only once, reluctant to take his eyes off what lay about him. I sensed he wanted to ask me a question: Tell me again, just what is it exactly I'm looking for? But then he turned to face back out, exposing to me all that curly gray hair at the back of his head. An old friend. A trusted old friend, who might not scruple to set a trap for me at the poker table, but really nowhere else. And who would expect the same of me. I stood.

It didn't happen at once. My cousin had taken me to the spot on the lake where it had seemed to happen again and again, but that was only the way memory worked. You remembered the moments that mattered, but the dailiness disappeared. Add up the truly memorable moments in your life and how long would you have lived? Twenty minutes? Half an hour? Howie Whalen, Little Howie Whalen when he'd first brought me out here, claimed a disproportionate share of my life for the actual moments we'd spent together. I looked out over the lake, and such was the greenness, such was the surface of that watery world, I might have been an infant still, first learning how to read a scribbling of foam on that cloudy green slate. Whalers in crows nests, I'd been led to believe, fell into just such suggestible trances. I gave myself a shake, started the motor, and moved us farther out into the main body of the lake, where I cut the motor again and scanned the water through a hundred-and-eighty-degree arc. Midday, and birds flew overhead, swallows, I assumed, small and split-tailed, then a landlocked gull of some sort, a potential competitor, but crossing, it seemed, from one shore of the lake to the other, and a crow taking far too much attention, making a lot of needless noise. The truth was, we were alone, entirely alone. I said what went without saying, You never know. You just never know.

We moved again. The heat of the day bore down. The body of water had broadened. We wouldn't want to go anywhere near the dam, where a current would form, then quicken, so I turned us away and up into an area of the lake where the green noticeably lightened, red clay banks sloped into the water, entering streams passed through marshes, and we saw wading birds that would eat the minnows before the bass could. Again I cut the motor. The valley here was broad, the lake somewhat more shallow, and the heat hotter still. Walter turned back to me, mostly mouthing the words. Don't tell me we forgot water! Don't tell me that! And the beer and the Beam brothers, I answered him, and for a moment we looked at each other like children, too excitable by half, and shook our heads. When Walter resumed his lookout and, standing, I resumed mine, we both saw, where we hadn't before, a slanting wing of ripples racing across the lake, and the effect was such that a whale, if we had been whalers, might have breached not a hundred feet in front of us. Walter made an urgent, revving sound down in his throat, and still standing, I took his cue, started the motor, and speeded us into what before we got there had already become an area of turbulence that any pleasure-boater would steer a wide berth around. I remembered in that instant what my cousin had told me. I could hear his voice, his quiet but authoritative drawl, as if he was used to people hanging on his words. Bass are territorial. You horn in on what they consider theirs, and they'll fight you that much harder. You can catch them then if they don't take the rod right out of your hands.

The jumps, I said, but under my voice, a word of recognition, as though welcoming an old friend. Walter held his spinning rod at the ready, from the end of which dangled Buck Coggins's silver spoon. I could pull up short of the feeding area and, from that margin, we could cast into the melee of jumping minnows and bass lashing their tails, as any sensible fishermen would have done, but I found myself taking my cousin at his word. When Walter sensed what I was about to do, he jerked around, anxious disapproval mixing with a thrill-seeking excitement on his face, as if

I were about to drive us off a cliff. What was I doing?! Stop short and cast in! We'd spend the rest of this sweltering day with nothing to drink looking for another chance like this! We were close enough now to see the dorsal fins, the lashing tails, and that glistening forest-green stripe as the bass rolled. The minnows were jumping like fleas, but they were little fish themselves, acrobatic and graceful for the instant they were airborne. It was worth stopping short just to take in the show, but I cut the motor only when we'd gone off Walter's cliff, entered the melee, and were part of that hunting ground. The feeding was so unbridled, so furious, that I sensed it might not appear again in our lifetimes. Comets passed, went back to the heavens, then generations later passed again. Otherworldly combustion— it felt like that. I cut the motor and picked up my rod, I didn't bother to direct my cast. I'd barely begun to reel in when a bass struck. I heard my cousin's voice, Little Howie Whalen's, going on. Get a bass angry and it'll fight you to the end. With a whirring of gears the fish began to strip out line, and I'd be damned! For every foot of line it took out and for every second I wasted winding it back in I missed catching that many more. I was not a diehard fisherman, not the way my cousin had been, but here was a chance to even a score I hadn't been aware existed, and I reeled in furiously so that I could cast again. Walter gave a shout when he had one on too. I got mine in first, fighting like hell as it came alongside the boat, mad, really mad, not just to be caught but to be caught in the midst of a feast, because there were so many more minnows out there asking to be eaten in large-mouthed gulps, and when I unhooked it and threw it into the bottom of the boat, I discovered I was as mad as the fish was for having slowed me down. By then Walter had unhooked his and, following my example, thrown it down with the other, and for an instant, as the bass thrashed, we looked at each other, too eager to get back to the fishing to even register disbelief. We cast into the boiling water and hooked our seconds. Hold on! I heard Walter say as he tossed his, no smaller than his first, in with the others, while I was still struggling to reel mine in. Then I called out to him, Will you look at this! Look at this! Look, Walter, dammit! I demanded as I raised my second up over the edge of the boat. Only it wasn't a second, it was a second *and* a third. Two fish caught on the same small treble hook. It's crazy, isn't it? I told you! Who's gonna believe this? You'll have to testify, you know! We'll have to get a Coggins to believe it! But Walter had already turned back to what showed no

203

sign of slowing down. He cast and then I did. A silver spoon and a red-striped one. The danger, the disaster, would be to cross each other's lines and watch the feeding finish as we struggled to get untangled. Somehow we managed to avoid that. The water continued to boil, the bass struck, turned over, dove and came up again. A strike became a second strike and then a third until a fish was hard on the hook, followed by that mulish tug in reverse, then the darting and the ratcheting out of line. And the anger in it all was palpable, the outrage, to be rudely removed like this from a feast in progress, and if either Walter or I had fallen overboard, the bass might indeed have become piranhas and shown their teeth. I flashed on that pickerel and the little saw-blade teeth that Walter had kept out of my hand. It might have gone no further than that. Look the other way and not in that pickerel's eye and I might have left Howie Whalen and his tragic kin and mine to their fates. But it was all coming to a head here, and I knew just as certainly as I knew that the isums in that first stack were mine alone to consume that it would never happen like this again. If I had Walter to thank, I thanked him, but when a fish struck that almost did pull the rod out of my hands, Walter was entirely offstage, and I got set to pit myself against all the wild dartings and furious soundings and bitter opposition I'd encountered in my life up to then, but now for the thrill of the thing, here for the taking, for the sport.

It was a beautiful fish, and it did everything a beautiful fish engaged in a life-and-death struggle could be expected to do. It pulled line out toward the horizon and then raced straight back at me just to see how fast I could reel in. It swam under the boat to see if I could keep it from tangling the line in the motor's blades. It took a sounding to the bottom of the lake and then rose to the surface in one powerful, glistening leap, flexing and shaking to dislodge the hook. When it finally came alongside the boat, it cut the water in a pattern of rapid zigs and zags as though it were spelling out for me some code. At the last moment, as it rose within reach, it opened its enormous mouth, and I gripped it by the lower lip and held it just above the surface, shielded by the side of the boat, so that not even Walter could see it. I looked down into its gullet, as pink-edged as the day it was born, thought about releasing it, thought about why we even bothered to fish, thought about making for all my skeptical friends a last meal of this last fish, thought about what it signaled, an end to fishing surely since I wouldn't catch a bigger or finer one than this, thought about how long I could maintain this paralyzing grip, a man my age, with a fish this big just waiting to make one more violent lash, thought about how many things could fit into a mouth that large, how many minnows, how many red daredevil spoons, thought about that spoon I would need to return to Buck Coggins, one of the Buck Cogginses, even if I planned never to come back here again, but then thought about why I would want to come back with Leland Oldham now gone, a toad, perhaps, in the transmogrifying way of things, become food for the fish, perhaps even become a fish, a lunker of a bass himself, one this big. I never forgot that, from my boyhood on, this had been a lake of transformations. And that was when I held up my trophy catch and showed it to Walter Kidman, whose eyes widened as though I'd turned over a hidden royal flush, a poker hand for the ages, worthy of photographs and applause. Then I unhooked my fish and threw it as unceremoniously as a man my age could into the bottom of the boat, where it made a violent thud and flopped with its smaller kin whose fate it would share. They were all the same, those fish. Big or small, they came to the same end. I shook out my line, reset my drag, and examined my daredevil spoon, the classic kind, with a red stripe down the middle to distinguish it from the silver one that my legendary and long dead cousin Howie Whalen had preferred. I felt extraordinarily alive, so much so that I didn't even register the fact that my mouth had fallen open in a classic case of a hunter coming to resemble his prey. I gulped at the air, cast out, reeled in, and cast out again, even though I could see that the jumps had ended, the surviving minnows had escaped, and what was left of the bass had gone off to regroup. But I kept casting into that now becalmed water. It was what we'd come for, after all, eight hundred miles, WPA site after WPA site, and like any great battle it had been some show. The enemy, the newly dying and the near dead, who were also our allies, our co-performers in the staging of this production, lay flopping in the bottom of the boat.

Walter must have stepped around those fish as he moved back toward me, and he must have stepped lightly, for the boat barely moved. But he'd have to wait, a last cast, which as every fisherman knew was never the last but, ad infinitum, the one before that. I cast, the red daredevil began to sink, and before I could retrieve it and cast again, Walter seized his chance. Tell me the truth, Jim, he said, firmly, yes, but sadly and wisely, too, as if he knew better than to expect an answer. Do you need a lawyer or not?